C0-BHC-584

The Best Of
Cold Blood

The Best Of
Cold Blood

Edited by Peter Sellers & John North

Mosaic Press
Oakville, ON - Buffalo, N.Y.

Canadian Cataloguing in Publication Data

Main entry under title:

The best of Cold blood

ISBN 0-88962-628-6
1. Detective and mystery stories, Canadian (English).* I. Sellers, Peter, 1956-
II. North, John, 1942-

PS8323 D4C646 1998   C813'.087208   C98-930577-5
PR9197.35 D48C6 1998

No part of this book may be reproduced or transmitted in any form, by any means, electronic or mechanical, including photocopying and recording information storage and retrieval systems, without permission in writing from the publisher, except by a reviewer who may quote brief passages in a review.

Published by MOSAIC PRESS, P.O. Box 1032, Oakville, Ontario, L6J 5E9, Canada. Offices and warehouse at 1252 Speers Road, Units #1&2, Oakville, Ontario, L6L 5N9, Canada and Mosaic Press, 85 River Rock Drive, Suite 202, Buffalo, N.Y., 14207, USA.

MOSAIC PRESS, in the USA:
85 River Rock Drive, Suite 202,
Buffalo, N.Y., 14207
Phone / Fax: 1-800-387-8992
E-mail:
cp507@freenet.toronto.on.ca

MOSAIC PRESS, in Canada:
1252 Speers Road, Units #1&2,
Oakville, Ontario, L6L 5N9
Phone / Fax: (905) 825-2130
E-mail:
cp507@freenet.toronto.on.ca

MOSAIC PRESS in the UK and Europe:
DRAKE INTERNATIONAL SERVICES
Market House, Market Place,
Deddington, Oxford. OX15 OSF

Mosaic Press acknowledges the assistance of the Canada Council, the Ontario Arts Council and the Dept. of Canadian Heritage, Government of Canada, for their support of our publishing programme.

Copyright © Peter Sellers, 1998
ISBN 0-88962-628-6

Cover design by: Richard Ponsonby
Text design by Ardello Newhouse
Printed and bound in Canada

Contents

Introduction

Back in 1987, after a year of flogging a proposal for an anthology of short Canadian crime fiction to most of the big Canadian publishers, I'd just about given up. Nobody was interested.

Finally, I reached the point where I didn't bother sending out a proposal until I'd phoned first. Nobody wanted to see it.

Then I called Mosaic Press. I shared my idea with Howard Aster who listed quietly then said, "That sounds great. Let's do it. In fact let's do a series."

Eight months later the book was out. Ten years after that, here is the final volume.

And what a decade it's been.

Authors who might never have been published without Cold Blood have won major literary awards and gone on to sign major book deals. Some of the publishers who first rejected Cold Blood have issued copycat collections. Many of our stories have been reprinted in major magazines and other anthologies, recorded as audio books, and optioned for film and television. The series has garnered a raft of laudatory reviews and more than its share of awards. Stories in the series have pulled in thirteen Arthur Ellis Best Short Story Award nominations from the Crime Writers of Canada. And three of those stories won the coveted Arthur.

It's gratifying to see that Cold Blood has accomplished all the goals I imagined for it. But, after ten years, it's time to move on to other projects. I'd like to thank Howard Aster at Mosaic Press for undertaking to publish the series and for his ongoing support. Thanks also to John North, who helped me finish Cold Blood V and make the selections for this volume.

Most of all I'd like to thank the authors who provided so many great stories over the years. Here are thirteen of the best.

Savour them.

Peter Sellers
Toronto, Ontario
August, 1997

The Best of Birtles
WILLIAM BANKIER

Along with James Powell, William Bankier was writing crime fiction set in Canada long before it became fashionable. A former ad man in Montreal, Bill grew up in Belleville, Ontario. He has also lived on a houseboat moored on the Thames in London, England and currently makes his home in Los Angeles. Bill's stories are often about the destructive power of personal relationships and the failure of communication. He looks at the down side of love with frightening clarity. Since 1962, his stories have appeared in a wide variety of publications - including every volume of Cold Blood. *He was an Edgar Award nominee in 1980, has been nominated for the Arthur Ellis Award several times, and shared the Derrick Murdoch Award in 1992. A collection of some of his finest stories,* Fear Is A Killer, *was published by Mosaic Press in 1995.*

Darius Dolan climbed the iron stairs with another beer for his wife's lover. They were sitting on pillows in the loft with the big windows propped open, watching the afternoon light fade across Old Montreal. "Your drink all right, Lucy?" he asked as he handed the pilsner glass to Raymond Saulnier.

"Don't need another thing." She looked like a doll, red-haired, green-eyed, propped against the needlepoint with her cigarettes and lighter at the ready on the rush matting beside her.

"Play us a tune," Saulnier requested, wiping foam from the black Zapata moustache. "Something in keeping with the mood."

Dolan went to the piano and lifted the cover, leaving dusty fingerprints. While they waited, he pulled his knuckles one at a time and thought about his father. The old man would have asked to hear Chopin. Dolan began to play one of the mazurkas, bending the tempo, extending a trill, putting a lot of emphasis on the left hand. The interpretation was perverse.

When he was finished, Lucy said, "I'm glad I don't feel as bad as you do."

"He's all right," Saulnier said. Before the low-key affair with Lucy Harmon Dolan began, Darius and Raymond had been close. They still worked well together, Dolan organizing the studio sessions, Saulnier coming in as part of the group to play tenor saxophone, and sometimes to vocalize on a jingle.

But it was all changing. Dolan the Anglo could still get work because he had been around such a long time. And he spoke some French and had friends and always paid the musicians on time. Still, the Francophones were moving inward and upward. Raymond Saulnier himself was branching out to front the occasional gig.

The telephone rang. Dolan found the instrument on the floor. He answered and heard Claire's voice. "Daddy, can I speak to Raymond?"

"He isn't here."

"He said he would be. Cut it out."

"Have you rented the safety-deposit box?"

"I said I will and I will. Do you want your precious coin collection back?"

"I want you to have it. I'd like it to be in a safe place."

"Let me speak to Raymond."

Saulnier took the telephone and said, after listening, "That's all right. No problem. Do you want to speak to your parents? *Ce n'est pas vrai.*"

"What's not true?" Lucy asked as Saulnier put down the telephone.

"Claire says you don't love her."

"She's wrong. I resent her self-centered behaviour. And some of her friends are fools. But I do so love her."

"I don't. She just cancelled her lesson." Saulnier was teaching Claire to play the flute. He got up and began assembling a portable screen. "It's dark enough, I think." He plugged in a carousel projector and switched it on.

"Heaven help us, the slides," Lucy said.

One by one, colourful images filled the screen. Saulnier said, "Paris. April." They were looking at a sidewalk cafe. More of the same - a *bateau mouche*, the Tour Eiffel. Lucy made him hold on child with balloon. Then the scene changed to gulls over water. "The ferry on the way to Dover."

"How many slides do you have, Raymond?"

"More than enough, Darius."

They saw views from the train window on the ride up to London. Charing Cross Station was crowded with tourists. Trafalgar Square. Admiralty Arch. Then, a sad young man with a granite wall behind him and a cap on the pavement at his feet. He was playing a guitar. "I got to know this bloke," Saulnier said. "His name is Stan Kyle. He gave me his card. If you need a guitar player, I can provide his number."

"What we need in Montreal. Another guitar player."

Lucy said. "He looks so mournful."

"He can really play," Saulnier enthused. "Classical stuff. I remember what he told me. He said, 'This used to be a good guitar and I used to be able to play it.' He said he wanted to be Julian Bream. His dream was to play some day in the Albert Hall."

"You tell me your dream," Dolan said. "I'll tell you mine."

The next slide depicted a group of young men crowded around a table in a pub. They were posing, mock-serious, like a Victorian board meeting. Saulnier continued, "This was where we got to know each other. I gave Kyle five quid and he said it paid him up for the day. This pub is around the corner. All these guys showed up later, as I was leaving." He changed slides to one of a double-decker bus.

"Go back," Lucy said.

"Pardon?"

"Can we see that one again?" Click, whirr, and there they were again on the screen, the brave young men in their seedy jackets. "The one on the end. Isn't that Jeremy Birtles?"

"He's dead," Dolan said. But he concentrated.

"We heard a rumour. Look at that face."

The man in question was head and shoulders taller than the others. A snub nose set off innocent eyes. The ginger hair was longer than when Birtles was working as a commercial artist in Montreal and hanging around with Claire Dolan. But it was the disarming smile that confirmed his identity, lips parted slightly to reveal a familiar gap between the front teeth.

"You're right, it's him," Dolan murmured. "The slippery bastard. He got somebody to spread the story so I'd forget about him."

"What happened?" Saulnier asked.

"I kept it quiet for Claire's sake. That man right there," Dolan said, approaching the screen as if he was in charge of briefing a squad of detectives, "stole my silver medallion. It was irreplaceable. I won it when I was 16, first prize at the Manitoba Piano Festival, 1959. A big thing, size of a saucer. Chopin's bust on one side, my name engraved on the other. My father must have turned in his grave when it went missing."

"Took it from your home?"

"And skipped town. At the art studio, they thought he'd gone to Toronto. The police followed up but it seemed he went back to England. Nothing further came of the investigation. Later that year, word went around that Birtles had died of kidney failure." Dolan sat down. "We believed it. I wrote off the loss."

Dolan asked the cab driver to wait while he ran inside the building on Mountain Street and pressed the buzzer for Claire's apartment. As he bounded up the stairs, she was standing in the doorway with a mug of coffee in one hand and a sticky bun in the other. She put a cheek out for a kiss and made room for him to enter.

"I can't come in. The taxi's waiting."

"That's as good an excuse as any."

"Can we not argue? I'm going on airplanes." He followed her into the vestibule. Over the shoulder of his paisley gown, he could see a proliferation of bamboo and mirrors with advertising on them.

"You'll never find Jeremy," Claire said. "But mother is right, you can use the holiday."

"I've got Stan Kyle's card. I'll telephone him and he'll put me in touch with Birtles."

"Who will immediately go underground."

"Anyway, my absence will give Lucy and Raymond a chance to sort themselves out."

"Ray never loved her," Claire said. "You're worried about nothing.

Dolan had not been in London for ten years. They had extended the Piccadilly Line to Heathrow since his last visit. He rode the train above and under ground to Earl's Court. Outside the station, he dragged his suitcase on tiny wheels around a couple of corners, stopping at a bed-and-breakfast in a converted Edwardian mansion with white pillars needing paint. Derbyshire House. His room was large with a sloping floor. The bed was small with a soft mattress. The bathroom was around the corner and down three stairs.

There was a pub in sight from his window. Dolan went out into a gentle rain, ran to the pub and had a meal of meat pie, sprouts and mashed potatoes. He drank two pints of lager. The food, the smokey room, the people - it was all so perfect that the absence of Lucy stabbed him in the heart. On earlier trips to London, they had talked about emigrating. Maybe they should have done it. That was mistake number one. The second was when he took the easy way out after the ad agencies began complaining. They started saying Lucy Harmon Dolan was the female voice in too many of the commercials he produced. He should have said he used her because she was the best. For seven years on CBC-TV, she had been the face and voice of The Hit Parade.

But Dolan had not defended her. He backed off because he was insecure over the French/English thing. Then Lucy took him off the hook. Claire was three years old at the time. She said it would be best if she stayed home and looked after the child. So she did. And she never sang professionally again.

Now Claire Dolan was 19 years old, a defiant young woman out on her own. And Lucy was seeking joy with Ray Saulnier. He wanted her to be happy. His absence over the next few days would give them all a chance to assess the situation. It was time for their lives to proceed to the next stage. What would be would be. Maybe Saulnier's accidental discovery of Birtles had been prompted by the hand of Fate.

Sensing the onset of terminal philosophical wisdom, Darius Dolan left the pub and took a long, slow walk in the rain.

Next morning, he telephoned Stan Kyle, dialing the number from the card Raymond had given him. A female voice answered, old enough to be Kyle's mother. From the way she screamed his name, she thought it was time for her son to be out of bed. Kyle came on the line like a disappointed guitar player, dragged from his dream of playing in the Albert Hall.

"Whozis?"

"My name is Dolan. I'm from Montreal." He decided not to unfold the saga of the face in the photograph. "I'm an old friend of Jeremy Birtles. I'm hoping you can tell me where to find him."

"How'd you get this number?"

"You gave your card to my friend Saulnier. He was here last month. Saw you playing in Trafalgar Square."

The voice softened. "I remember. French-Canadian geezer. Looks like a Mexican bandit." Kyle spoke away from the telephone. "Leave it. I don't want breakfast." Then to Dolan, "Why do you want Birtles?"

Dolan used his invented story. "He left some things at a girl's place. She asked me to bring them to him."

"Last we spoke, he was in a room at 23 Inverness Terrace. That's in Bayswater. He's not on the phone."

Dolan hailed a taxi for the short ride around the Park to the Bayswater Road. He found Inverness Terrace and walked along uneven paving stones past a succession of residences converted to hotels and rooming houses. Number 23 was a corner house. A man in a turban was pruning roses by the front door. Dolan said to him, "Good morning. I'm looking for Jeremy

Birtles. He's my friend and I've come all the way from Montreal to see him."

"Montreal is a fine city. My sister lives there. She teaches political science at McGill University."

"My daughter lives not far from the University. Is Mr. Birtles at home?"

"Mr. Birtles is in number 4. He came in very late last night."

The number was no longer on the door but the outline of ancient paint said 4. Dolan knocked and waited. The familiar voice called, "Who is it?"

Dolan decided to play it as if they were still in Montreal. As if he and the English artist had been all night in the jazz clubs on St. Antoine Street. Lucy had made up the bed in the spare room. Just like old times. "It's me, Jeremy. Open up."

"Darius?"

"Larger than life."

Hasty movements behind the door, then it was flung wide open and Jeremy Birtles was revealed like sunlight from behind clouds. The ginger hair was tousled and the gap-toothed grin was ready for anything. "What a surprise. Do come in!"

The room smelled of linseed oil and alcohol. Dolan saw a mattress on the floor, stretched canvasses stacked against a wall, an open case of bottled beer, a hot-plate with a muddy pot resting on it. "I'm so glad you're not dead, Jeremy."

"So am I. Does that mean something?"

"The rumour in Montreal was that you'd snuffed it."

"I was quite ill last year. Perhaps somebody got that wrong. Find a place to sit. I wish I could offer you something. We'll have to go out for breakfast. Look at you, all plump and prosperous."

There was a stool the size of a goblin mushroom. Dolan lowered himself onto it. "I traced you through Stan Kyle."

Birtles faked a shudder. "Sounds like Interpol. I've been meaning to write you a letter." He turned one of the canvasses and propped it in the light. It looked good to Dolan - a portrait of a broad-faced woman with mahogany hair. "Remember when we were out boozing and I talked about getting out of commercial art? And starting to paint what I want? Well, they got me out of the studios by firing me."

"That's just fine, Jeremy. But you and I have to get something straightened out."

"The medallion. Of course."

Dolan should not have been surprised. He knew there was something of the sociopath in Birtles' make-up. The Englishman had a way of always being on top of whatever was happening to him. Never at a loss. Anticipating the confrontation and defusing it with straightforward charm. "You admit you took it."

"And I was wrong. I remember you showing me your trophies that night. We'd both had a lot to drink. You left the room and I just slipped Chopin into my pocket. It was the wine, I suppose."

"How could you do that? You knew how much that medal meant to me."

"That was the reason. I've thought about it often." Birtles went to the window and raised the blind. He went and sat cross-legged on the mattress. He tugged at the Guinness T-shirt he was wearing to make the fabric cover his knees. "I was leaving town the next day."

"As we discovered."

"I can only explain it this way, Darius. I wanted a keepsake. Something of yours I could take with me. It had to be something of value."

There were birds chirping outside the window. After half a minute, Dolan said, "Is it okay if I reject that phony explanation?"

"You can think what you like."

"I believe you took the medallion because it's big and made of silver and you needed money."

"I would never sell your medallion."

"You've still got it?"

"Of course. But not here. I can't keep anything that valuable in this rubbish tip."

"Where is it?"

"With the few other useful things I possess. At Serena's place." Birtles inclined his head towards the canvas in sunlight. For a moment, both men regarded the painted lady who stared back with an expression of tolerant amusement. Then the artist struggled to his feet. "Let me get some clothes on and we'll go outside and make a telephone call. Serena has this lovely flat in Kensington. You'll like Serena."

She wanted to see them, but not today. Tomorrow morning, at eleven, they could come for tea or something stronger. "Serena Tennant," Birtles said when he left the telephone booth. "Her parents are rich. They sent her to Roedean. Now they keep her supplied with money and Serena fulfills her end of the bargain by not coming home."

A dozen young men in long red scarves were milling about the entrance to Lancaster Gate underground station. Their aggressive movements caused Dolan to feel apprehensive. He remembered reading about football hooligans on earlier visits to England. "Looks like the riot is about to begin," he said.

"They're Manchester United supporters. Here for the game against Wimbledon this afternoon." Birtles tried to pry open Dolan's face with a bright-edged smile. "We could travel down to Plough Lane and see the match."

"Is it far?"

"Half an hour on the District Line." The artist glanced at his watch. "We can nip in here to the 'King's Head' and throw down a couple of pints to ease the journey."

It was all coming back. In Montreal, the arrival of Jeremy Birtles had always been a breath of fresh air. He had seemed a risky person, even before the theft of the medallion. But there was something irresistible in his enthusiasm. We know guns are lethal, Dolan told himself. But what man has never lusted after the thrill of hefting one?

"Let's go for it," he said, leading Birtles into the pub.

They came out of the station in Wimbledon and began walking to the football grounds. They were part of a straggling army, most of them supporters of MUFC. Hoarse chanting erupted ahead and behind. At the corner of the Broadway, a youth raced past them, shirt-tail flying, and broke speed records veering down the slope of Hartfield Road. Twenty yards behind him, a uniformed officer, hatless, ran in pursuit. They were passing 'The Prince of Wales'. "The clever thing to do," Birtles said from the pub entrance, "is to give this crowd time to get inside the park."

"You're on," Dolan agreed.

He carried overflowing pints to a corner table. Birtles said, "Ta!" and "Cheers!" Then, "Tell me all the gossip from Montreal."

"It's changing. Still beats Toronto as a place to live. But I've done my work in English for a lot of years. Could I start working in French? Probably not. I'm history in that sweet town."

"Come and work in London."

"I could never make that big a move. I'm too old."

"Think about it. Lots of Canadians work here." Birtles winked. "And tomorrow you'll know Serena." When he came back from the bar with two more, he asked, "How's the family?"

"Claire moved out last year. She's in that old building at Mountain and Maisonneuve. Across from the sidewalk cafe."

"I remember."

"She and Lucy could no longer get along. Two strong-minded women in the same house."

"Is Lucy still singing?"

"She should. It might calm her down. Raymond Saulnier wants to use her in commercials." The beer was beginning to talk. "Raymond Saulnier wants to use her every way he can."

"Uh-oh."

"No big deal. Lucy and I had a lot of good years. Now she's getting ready to go on to something else."

"As should you."

Dolan made a face. "This old horse is out to pasture." But looking around the crowded pub at the women with their eyes and smiles, he felt as if he could start over.

They arrived at Plough Lane after half-time. They found room on the terraces at the Wimbledon end and stood pressed in closely with a crowd of several hundred. All swayed in a slow, sensuous wave from side to side, hardly aware of the game on the field. And as the throaty singing arose and drove all other thoughts from his mind, Dolan linked arms with Birtles and a stranger and they sang with surpassing joy like the devout in a great cathedral - "Walk on, walk on, with hope in your heart. . ."

Serena let him in. Dolan moved past her into a cool vestibule. He saw mahogany and oak and mirrors and silver. A vast, unframed painting nearly filled a wall between casement windows flung open with white curtains sucked out across painted sills.

"Is Jeremy here?"

"Jeremy can't make it." She was older than he expected, and more attractive. Her hair had been cut short since the Birtles portrait. Dressed in beige slacks and a loose white blouse, she presented a long curved neck and shoulder that had Dolan looking for a spot to sink his teeth. The green eyes were calm as twilight, and they flooded him with understanding. "I'm drinking gin. Would you rather have coffee?"

After the late carousal with Birtles, he was feeling seedy. But he heard himself say, "Gin is fine. What happened to Jeremy? I was with him last night."

"Vintage Birtles. He showed up here at eight o'clock this morning. Which went down badly with your hostess, I can assure you. Jeremy has decided to fly to America. Just like that, whim of the day. Stopping off first in Montreal." She brought Dolan his drink in a heavy crystal beaker. "He has friends there who can help him out with some money. I started him off with air fare. Then it's on to the West Coast."

Through one of the windows, Dolan could see Kensington Gardens with people in deck chairs scattered across the grass and rainbow-coloured ice-cream vans parked on the High Street. He said, "Then it looks like he's left me high and dry."

"Can you bear it?"

"No pain so far." He decided to get business out of the way. "Did Jeremy tell you? I'll want to pick up my medallion."

"Sorry?"

"The silver medallion you're keeping for him. It belongs to me. I won it in a piano competition." As he spoke, Dolan realised yesterday's suspicions were now confirmed. Birtles had made up a story on the spur of the moment. So he was not surprised when Serena said, "I have nothing of his. Has Jeremy been a naughty boy again?"

Dolan told the story. Because she was so simpatico, he found himself dwelling on the early days in Winnipeg when he was spending all his time practicing, attempting to please an unpleasable father. "This makes me seem like a damn fool," he concluded.

"You're not the only person he's taken advantage of."

She sat beside him on the chaise lounge. He was feeling comfortable in the elegant room. "I think if I ever saw him again, I'd want to kill him. He tells you what you want to hear. He diverts you."

"Please don't be angry. It's a waste."

"It's been so many years. Then by this fluke, I get back in touch with him. And he says no problem. I've got your medallion. But he was jerking me around. And he's gone again."

"You must be a good pianist."

"Used to be. I'm more of an arranger now. A composer. Of sixty-second commercials." He finished his drink. "You should hear the theme from Jiffo Cleanser."

"I'd like to hear you play."

There was a piano on the other side of the room. He was surprised at how eager he was to perform for her. He concentrated on walking slowly to the instrument. It's tone was the best he had encountered since the competition when he was sixteen. The late-night partying, the topping up of alcohol this morning - Dolan's inhibitions vanished. He did not even try to decide what to play. Powerful bass chords thundered from his left hand as one arpeggio after another took him through a series of key changes. Then he was playing 'Stella By Starlight' as if it had been written by Franz Liszt.

He was cocktail pianist in the classiest bar in the universe, entertaining an audience of royalty from monarchies past and present. The pyrotechnics were shameless. His arms ached when he finished.

"Bravo! Darius, that was brilliant. Play some more." She brought them both another drink and sat on the bench beside him. "You are my Chopin and I am your Georges Sand."

He drank and played again, shocked by the fleeting brush of her lips across his cheek.

They went out for lunch at two o'clock. He was stiff with gin but in control. She took him to a small restaurant on a side street within sight of the Albert Hall. "I heard of a guitar player who dreamed of playing there," he said. "He's a busker now. In Trafalgar Square."

She had the knack of keeping him talking. It was like a three-hour session with a sensuous therapist. "My father never came to visit me in Montreal. After mother died, I offered to fly him east from Winnipeg and install him in his own apartment."

"He was set in his ways."

"He despised my work. He refused to recognize that I've been a success in the music business." They were drinking red wine. He refilled their glasses from the second bottle. "There was never any guarantee I would have made it as a concert pianist. We have to go where life leads us." He remembered standing in the doorway of the old house, expecting his father to come and say goodbye. The taxi was waiting to take him to the airport. The driver sounded the horn. "Dad?" The wingback chair framed that stubborn head with its halo of white hair.

Serena said, "I'm glad life led you here, Darius."

It was on his second night sleeping at Serena's place that Dolan sat bolt upright in bed, recalling something he had told Birtles.

Serena whispered, "Are you all right?" She was grey shadow. Dawn's light hesitated between half-closed drapes.

"I know what he's up to. I told him my daughter is living alone. They used to date. I reminded him where her apartment is located."

"Why would he go there?"

"Because she's vulnerable. And he's an opportunist."

"Jeremy is a thief. Does she have anything worth stealing?"

In his mind's eye, Dolan saw the collection of gold coins in their leather and velvet case. Twenty-five of them worth close to $350 each. Case and contents would bring nine grand, easily. He told Serena about it.

"When she moved out last year, I turned them over to her. She's been talk-ing about a safe deposit box. But she hasn't done it."

At breakfast, he said, "I'm going to have to leave." To telephone Claire and try to warn her would be a waste of time. Whether Birtles had arrived or not, she would hear nothing against him. The only course was to head the man off.

"I never thought this was forever, Darius."

"When I get it sorted out, maybe I can come back."

She hid behind the teacup she was holding. "I hope you're worrying over nothing."

He rode a taxi from the airport all the way in to Centre-Ville. The late lunch people were having one more drink at the sidewalk cafe as he went inside Claire's building across the street. She had not answered the telephone when he dialed her number from Mirabel. His ring held a key to the apartment. He let himself in.

"Claire?" The place was airless. He went to the tall window be-tween the bookcases and raised it shoulder high.

Her bedroom was far neater than she had ever maintained her room at home. The sofa-bed in the living room was unfolded and made up. A suitcase on the floor overflowed male clothing. Birtles! If confirmation were needed, a book of matches on the end table bore the identification, 'The Prince of Wales, Hartfield Road, London SW19'.

Dolan felt his anger rising. The guy was unbelievable. He had taken that day of comradeship and turned it immediately to his advantage.

The coin collection! Dolan knew where Claire kept it. There was a small cabinet at the bottom of the oak bookcase near the window. In it, she stored a number of precious artifacts she did not want to leave lying around the room. He knelt by the window, pressed the door and felt it spring open. Inside he saw a stack of letters bound in ribbon and a toy plastic doll in a heart-covered dress. But the leather case was not there.

Dolan's eyes were at window level. Below, on Maisonneuve Boule-vard, he saw a familiar figure crossing from the cafe. It was Jeremy Birtles, hands in pockets, jacket flapping behind him. Since he was staying here, Claire must have dispensed another key. Dolan got to his feet and drifted inside the bedroom. He was not sure how to handle the situation. Birtles was a lot younger and probably stronger than he was. It was too late to call the police.

Footsteps on the stairs. Key in the lock. Door opening and closing. Birtles moved through the room, snuffling, clearing his throat. The telephone clicked off the cradle. Dolan ventured a glance into the room. Over the back of an upholstered chair, he saw the Englishman's shoulders and curly head. The dialing went beyond seven digits. He was taking the opportunity to run up some long-distance charges.

"Hello, Keith? It's Jeremy! How are things in glorious San Francisco? No, I'm not. I'm in Montreal. I'm settled in with the daughter of an old geezer I ran into in London. You bastard, we're just friends. The old geezer won't soon be back because I set him up with Serena. I did! That should be good for a fortnight. Don't worry about money, I'll be bringing some with me."

Dolan looked around for a weapon. He was having trouble seeing. He was blinking flashes of light. There was a bronzed horseshoe on the window ledge, a souvenir of some playground competition. He grasped it in his right hand and hearing Birtles put down the telephone, took quick steps through the doorway.

He came out of the bedroom as the Londoner got to his feet. The reaction was spontaneous. Birtles stepped back when Dolan rushed at him, the horseshoe raised. He lifted his arm to shield his head. Dolan was screaming, "You thieving son-of-a-bitch. . .!"

The window ledge caught Birtles behind the knees. He fell backwards, striking his head against the raised sash, doubling over and sliding through the aperture to fall three floors to the sidewalk.

As Dolan stood away from the window and out of sight, people holding glasses were beginning to leave the cafe and move tentatively into the street.

Not wanting to surprise Lucy with Raymond Saulnier, Dolan telephoned the house. "Hi, it's me."

"Where are you?"

"Claire's place." Quickly, he described what had happened - the pursuit of Birtles from London, the confirmation of his theft of the gold coins, then his accidental tumble through the open window. "Maybe I'd better call the police."

"Wait a minute. Did you touch him? Was there a fight?"

"No. He was taken by surprise."

"Then just come home. We'll talk about what you have to do."

Dolan left the building by the back door. He walked down to Ste. Catherine Street and hailed a cab. He was home in twenty minutes. Lucy had coffee ready, he could smell the fresh brew as he came inside. She held her arms open to him, their first embrace in quite a while. When he was seated at the kitchen table, she said, "You don't have to do anything. Claire didn't even tell me Birtles was in town. We've been having zero contact. The guy is notoriously erratic. He flies in here from London, who knows what personal problems are troubling him? He's not the first depressive to jump from a high place."

"But that isn't what happened. He was getting set to go to San Francisco."

"Having stolen your coins."

"I should have searched his suitcase. But he probably disposed of them already. He told his friend he'd be arriving with money."

"Forget him, Darius. Don't even tell Claire you were there."

It would save a lot of hassle if he could live with it. "How's Raymond?"

Her eyes flickered. "He's been working a lot. Rehearsing an album." She sipped coffee. "How was London?"

"I did what English people do. I got drunk at a soccer match."

"It was brilliant of me not to go."

"I missed you quite a bit."

The Dolan's began to have quiet pleasure. They divided the morning paper, discovered new outrages in the community and shared them, reading aloud. Darius got hungry. He opened a tin of refrigerated biscuits, put them in the oven and, eight minutes later, served them with butter and jam. There was not much wrong with the moment. The argument for keeping quiet about Birtles took on weight.

Claire arrived within the hour. She let herself in at the side door and entered the kitchen with a closed-up face. "Daddy, you're here. I thought you were in London."

"I came back."

"Well, I have an announcement to make. Raymond and I are getting married."

"I knew it," Lucy said. Her face was drained of blood. "I could tell."

"He's twenty years older than you are," Dolan said.

"So?"

"I think you'd better wait."

"You can't give me orders."

"Something has happened."

"Darius, what's the difference?" Lucy said.

It seemed now that he was always going to confess. It was happening sooner rather than later. "I saw Jeremy at your place."

"When?"

"An hour ago. I went there from the airport. It was exactly what I was afraid of. The bastard has stolen my gold coins."

"No he didn't."

"And when I confronted him, he tried to get away. Claire, he fell out the open window. He's dead."

Claire sat down at the table. She had her mother's jaw, the determined mouth turned down. "Is this some trick to break me up with Ray?"

"It's what happened."

"Did you two have a fight?"

"I never touched him. All right, I was going to. He stole my medallion years ago. And how he's done me again."

"The coin collection?" Claire reached forward and put a hand on her father's arm. "I gave it to Ray. He's using it for short-term collateral on a loan. He had to give cash to the studio where he's making his album. I'll have the coins back, end of next month."

While Dolan said nothing, Claire listened to her mother. They could not bring back Jeremy, whatever was told to the police. Involving her father in an inquest which might lead to a trial would not help anybody. She agreed to go home now, discover the sad accident, and let events take their course.

She had been gone from the house for less than a minute. Darius and Lucy were still looking at the floor when Claire came back inside, took a gift-wrapped package from her handbag and gave it to her father. "I forgot. Jeremy gave me this to give to you. He thought he'd be gone before you got back from London."

Dolan broke tape. He unfolded gold foil wrapping. The weight told him what it was before he took the lid off the box. There, in a nest of tissue, lay the medallion. He saw the bust of Chopin. He turned it over while the women watched in silence, and read his name and the inscription on the other side.

There was a piece of note-paper folded square under the medallion. He broke it open and saw the flowing script of a trained artist. Dolan read the message aloud.

"Dear Darius: I hope this comes not too late to make things right. I could have told you the truth in London, but it would have come out sounding shabby. Isn't the truth often like that? I did sell the medallion to a man in Montreal. My idea was to come here and steal it back from him, if he still had it. Which he did, and I did. But it was all so indefinite, how could I have told you what I had in mind?

"Anyway, here you are with your beautiful prize. And I've had a great few days with your charming daughter, my old friend Claire. And now San Francisco calls. I must be sure to wear a flower in my hair.

"Isn't it fine, the way things work out in the end? All the best, Birtles."

A Tale of a Tub

CHARLOTTE MACLEOD

Part of the success of the Cold Blood *series was due to the generosity of the established writers who provided many of the best original stories. Charlotte was one such supporter. Her whimsical yet elegantly plotted stories appeared in volumes II through IV, each one concerning the Reverend Strongitharm Goodheart of Pitcherville, New Brunswick. A prolific writer of highly entertaining and highly regarded cozies, Charlotte's various series include the adventures of Professor Peter Shandy – which began with her first crime novel, the delightful* Rest You Merry *in 1978 – as well as those of Max Bittersohn and Sarah Kelling. Under the name Alisa Craig, Charlotte has also written both the Inspector Madoc Rhys novels and the tales of the Grub and Stakers Gardening Society.*

"Oh, cripes! There he goes again. I wonder who's dyin' this time."

Well might Jedediah Olson ask. Ever since they'd hired the new minister of the Deliverance Church, a deathbed baptism in Pitcherville meant another thank-you job for Jed. He was not the sexton nor yet the gravedigger, he was the town blacksmith, as his father had been before him. But Jed moved with the times. He was also the town plumber, when he had anything to plumb.

This didn't happen often, since the revolutionary concept of running water inside the house had not yet really taken hold in some of New Brunswick's smaller communities. In Pitcherville there were to be sure, several sinks with faucets and drains and no fewer than three flush closets standing as testaments to Jed's more recently acquired skills. However, it was the Reverend Strongitharm Goodheart's self-filling and self-emptying bathtub that Jed had considered his chef d'oeuvre when he'd installed it in the Deliverance parsonage some eighteen months previously. Since that time Jed had developed a personal grudge against the minister's bathtub.

Strongitharm Goodheart, be it said, had heard the call to the ministry at the age of seventeen and a half, while he was in the midst of plowing a furrow on his father's farm out back of Little Pitcher. Once having put his hand to a different plow, he turned not back but finished his furrow, unhitched the horses, and headed straight for the Deliverance seminary with his mother's kiss on his brow and her willingly bestowed egg money in his pocket.

His father's blessing had been given with some secret unwillingness, for Strongitharm had always more than lived up to his name around the farm. He did express the generous opinion that his son would be a credit to the family, and was right. Strongitharm flung himself into his new studies with the same zeal he'd shown in cultivating the lower forty. Once ordained, he'd wearied not in welldoing. All things considered, the Pitcherville deacons agreed, they might have gone farther and fared worse, even though Mr. Goodheart, as he must now be respectfully known, did seem to have picked up some awfully advanced notions along with his higher education.

That a Deliverance minister should be ready, able and even delighted to go any distance in any weather at any hour to snatch a dying brand from the burning didn't surprise them any; this was just one more duty that went with the job. That he should insist on baptizing by immersion excited no remark, he wouldn't have lasted long at Pitcherville Deliverance if he didn't.

What was different about Strongitharm Goodheart was the way he chose to cope with the frequent logistical difficulties presented by iced-over ponds, frozen rivers, and (depending on the season) dried-up streams.

His method was to unhook his bathtub from its pipes, carry it downstairs on his back, lash it across the back of his Model T Ford, and drive to the house of the afflicted with the tub clattering and banging behind him. He would then lug it to the bedside and personally pump enough buckets to fill it. He'd add a few kettlefuls of boiling water to temper the chill, for Strongitharm was a kindly man, and get on with what he'd been called to do.

Strongitharm Goodheart was probably the only minister in the Maritimes who'd have had the ingenuity to think of taking the bathtub along, the zeal to attempt it, and the physical strength to carry it; but he was a humble man withal and knew his limitations. He couldn't plumb worth a hoot. Therefore, once the petitioner had been duly immersed, prayed over, dried off, and sent rejoicing on his or her way to recovery or the Pearly Gates as the case might be, Strongitharm would chauffeur his bathtub back home, carry it up to the bathroom, and send for Jed Olson to hook it up again.

The minister always offered to pay, but Jed would never take a cent. He knew Mr. Goodheart made barely enough to live on and if by a miracle there was anything left over from feeding and clothing the minister's wife and child, it went to succour the needy or buy small comforts for the aged and infirm. Jed knew his own wife would skin him if he exacted payment for helping out with the Lord's work, and Jed knew that doing a favour would give him a perfect excuse to worm the details out of the minister before anybody else did. Naturally the hangers-on around the smithy looked to Jed as their oracle and naturally they expected him to come through with the goods now.

"I heard old Mrs. Saltmarsh was slipping fast," one ventured to get the ball rolling.

Jed shrugged off Mrs. Saltmarsh. "She wouldn't need baptizin'. She's been saved ever since right after she buried 'er second husband. Ought seven I think it was. Old Hosea Doright, that travelin' evangelist who used to come around, baptized 'er after one of 'is revival meetin's. I remember my father tellin' about it. It was in April an' cold as a stepmother's kiss. The river was runnin' awful high an' when Hosea shoved 'er under the current swept 'er out of 'is hands an' carried 'er downstream till she fetched up on a snag. An' Hosea just stood there yellin', 'The Lord giveth an' the Lord taketh away. Pass me another.' Hosea was a good man, my father said, but he had an awful one-track mind. By gorry, look at that, he's stoppin' right in front of Wilt's Drygoods Store."

"You don't s'pose Miser Wilt's finally goin' to get a bath?"

That was indeed a point for speculation. James Wilt, who lived in the flat over his store and in fact owned the entire building, had a phobia against catching cold. He didn't bathe more than once or twice a year. It was whispered among the cognoscenti that he sewed himself into his Stanfield's double knits on the first day of September every year and didn't take out the stitches till the last day of June. Wilt was not a person to get close to and not many tried, for his disposition was no more ingratiating than his personal habits.

The only two people who had to suffer Wilt's presence at close quarters were his downtrodden housekeeper, a worthy widow lady named Mary Higbed, and his equally if not more downtrodden nephew. Perce Wilt had come to his uncle as an orphan at the age of twelve and been put straight to work learning the drygoods business at a wage of five cents a week plus his room and board. Perce was now thirty-two years old and had been upped, rumour had it, to five dollars a month.

Perce would no doubt fall heir one day to the Wilt fortune. The old man did well out of the store. He let Perce wait on the customers, which was probably an excellent idea, considering, while he himself ran a successful wholesale business in notions and yard goods out of the basement. James never sold on credit and never spent a cent he didn't have to. He'd skin a flea for its hide and tallow. He was generally supposed to keep his money, all in gold pieces, in an asbestos lined sack under his bed so he'd have it handy to take with him when his time came to go where he was surely headed. Only now that Mr. Goodheart was on the scene, perdition might not be quite so certain.

"Has to be either Wilt or Mrs. Higbed," said one of the boys. "Perce is too young to die."

"I dunno," said another. "Perce's been lookin' awful peaked lately."

"He's stuck on the new schoolteacher," Jed Olson spoke with the voice of authority as usual, "an' his uncle won't give 'im time off to go courtin', much less enough of a raise to set up housekeepin' on. They'd have to live up there with the old man an' what good-lookin' young woman in 'er right mind would settle for Wilt an' his underwear?"

"All right then," said the first speaker, "maybe Perce pined away or hung himself or somethin'. It's got to be one of 'em. Nobody else ever goes there 'cept a traveler now an' then."

Traveling drygoods salesmen did endure the mephitic presence of James Wilt more bravely than most because, whiffy though he might be and hard bargainer though he assuredly was, Wilt bought big and he paid cash on the button. Occasionally of them even stayed overnight in the flat, there being no commercial lodging available in Pitcherville and trains being few and far between.

To a salesman with an insensitive nose, a night with Wilt was probably no hardship. Mrs. Higbed was reputed to keep the flat neat as a pin and set a reasonably good table considering the meagreness of her housekeeping allowance. Wilt had, as Jed was able to inform the know-it-all who insisted on keeping the number of possibles down to three, a traveler staying with him right now; that good-looking fellow with the big, blond mustache who traveled in knitting needles and had stayed a few times before. He'd attended the church social last night and been observed giving the new schoolteacher a glad eye, to Perce Wilt's obvious discomfiture.

This was all very interesting, but Jed had a wagon tire to straighten. Once they'd all watched Mr. Goodheart carry in the bathtub, he put the bellows to the forge and reached for his hammer. The spectators went about their affairs. Up over the shop, the minister was attending to his.

He'd found Mrs. Higbed in a terrible taking. Mr. Wilt, she'd informed him, had an awful pain in his chest and could not get his breath. He was dying and he knew it, therefore he wasn't about to waste good money on the doctor. He hadn't even wanted the minister until Mrs. Higbed had quoted a few passages she remembered from Hosea Doright's revival meeting and taken it upon herself to see that he had a fighting chance to escape The Bad Place.

"Mr. Wilt's not a bad man, Mr. Goodheart," she all but sobbed. "Truly he isn't. People just have a spite against him because he's a little bit near with his money and doesn't always smell very nice. You'll do what you can for him, won't you?"

"I'm only the instrument, Mrs. Higbed," Strongitharm reminded her gently. "Come along, let's get some water heating. Where's Perce?"

"Downstairs in the store, as usual. Perce had to be there by half-past six to sweep out, clean the stove, lug out the ashes and all that. His uncle has always been strict about opening on time, with everything in order. But I mustn't stand here gossiping when the poor soul may be drawing his last breath, for all we know. You take the bathtub straight in there, Mr. Goodheart, and I'll see to the water."

Strongitharm was glad to put down the tub, backpacking it up a long flight of stairs hadn't been easy. He set it down as gently as he could and bent over the old man, trying to remember not to breathe.

"How are you feeling, Mr. Wilt?"

The drygoods magnate had several quilts tucked over him, all of them spotlessly clean. Only his arms were outside, covered by a dark gray flannel nightshirt. As the minister spoke, Wilt raised his right hand and clutched feebly at that portion of the quilt under which his chest presumably lay.

"Heart," he gasped. "Pain. Awful. Can't --get -- breath. Going -- to -- die."

"Going to glory, Mr. Wilt." Strongitharm took the cold, palsied hand in his own warm one and began to recite the Twenty-Third Psalm. He continued speaking words of hope and comfort until he judged the water was warm, then went to help Mrs. Higbed with the kettles.

"Perhaps you'd better ask Perce to come up," he told her gently. "Someone mentioned last night at the social that you also have an overnight visitor?"

"Mr. Ham,," she replied. "He's just finishing his breakfast. He slept in this morning because the down train's not due for another half hour."

"Is Mr. Ham a close friend of Mr. Wilt?"

"Close as any, I suppose."

"Then you may as well get him, too."

Mrs. Higbed had left off trying to hide her tears. "I'll break it to them gently."

By the time the bathtub was filled, the three were assembled around it, Mrs. Higbed sniffling into her apron in a subdued and ladylike way, Perce looking sombre and worried, Mr. Ham putting on a decent show of grief for an old and valued customer. Strongitharm bent over the bed, laid back the covers, and raised up the feeble body.

As he did so, his hand encountered a patch of dampness on the left breast of the nightshirt. That struck him as being rather odd. Mr. Wilt must have spilled something on himself quite recently though Mrs. Higbed had mentioned while they were dealing with the kettles that her employer had taken neither bite nor sip since last night's supper. He hadn't been out of bed, he would hardly have asked for a wash basin to be brought to him.

The dampness was puzzling, but hardly important at such a time as this. Murmuring appropriate words, Strongitharm eased his current penitent into the baptismal font. Knowing Mr. Wilt's personal habits, he expected the warm water to turn colour a bit. What he had not anticipated was the reddish stain that began to spread out from the region of James Wilt's chest. "Merciful Heaven!" he exclaimed, "He's bleeding!"

"But how can he be?" gasped Mrs. Higbed.

"I don't know, but we've got to find out. Let's put him back on the bed. Here, Perce, help me get this nightshirt off."

"You won't want us." Mr. Ham was backing toward the door. "Come on, Mrs. Higbed."

"No, stay," ordered Strongitharm in a tone that brooked no disobedience. "One of you hand me a jackknife or something."

Perce had a penknife with a cork stuck on the tip. Strongitharm took the cork off and began to rip stitches out of the old man's underwear, ignoring the nephew's startled cry, "But it's only March!"

Soon the bare chest lay exposed, dingy and greasy and showing a few unlovely wisps of wet gray hair. Below and slightly to the left of the nipple a hardly discernible puncture wound oozed a tiny trickle of fresh blood. Strongitharm inspected it closely, then straightened up.

"Mr. Wilt, you've been tabbed, with a long, thin, pointed weapon. Mrs. Higbed, please get the doctor, and the constable."

"Too late," gasped the victim. "My heart --"

"Your heart's working fine." Strongitharm had his hand on Wilt's wrist now, counting the pulse. "Your would-be murderer made the customary layman's mistake of thinking your heart was on your left side. Actually it's in the middle. What you have, Mr. Wilt, is a punctured lung. It's causing you a lot of pain and making it hard to breathe, but it's not likely to kill you if you're properly taken care of. Even if the wound doesn't heal right, you do have another lung, you know."

"I do?"

"Oh yes, everybody does, one on each side. Now, Mrs. Higbed, if you'll take this union suit away and bring in a washrag, some soap, and a clean towel, we'll give Mr. Wilt a nice, warm bath so he'll be ready when the doctor gets here. I'll finish the baptism at the same time. The Lord won't mind if we kill two birds with one stone."

"Never -- mind -- the -- birds," wheezed James Wilt. "Who -- killed -- me?"

"First things first, Mr. Wilt. I want you to stay perfectly still and not talk any more till the doctor comes."

The constable was first on the scene. He panted into the room shouting, "Where's the jeezledybugger that murdered Mr. Wilt?"

By now the patient was back in bed, clean as a whistle and with a hint of colour in his cheeks.

"He's not dead," the nephew stammered. "See."

"Don't make a particle o' difference. I got to take you in anyways, Perce, it's my duty. I know why you done it. You wanted your uncle's money so's you could marry the schoolteacher. You didn't dare wait any longer 'cause Mr. Ham here was fixin' to cut you out. What did you stab 'im with? One o' them spike files like they use down to the drugstore to poke the prescriptions onto, eh?"

"We don't have a spike file in the store. Uncle James thinks they're a waste of money. We just put a rock on top of the papers and keep the windows shut."

"Huh, a likely story! All right, then, what did you use? You'll have to tell the high sheriff anyway, so you might as well tell me."

"Ingrate," muttered Miser Wilt, carefully so as not to strain his punctured lung and run up the doctor's bill.

"Judge not, Mr. Wilt," said Strongitharm Goodheart, who had been doing some prayerful cogitating since Mrs. Higbed's departure. "Remember you'll still have to answer to your Maker some day, like the rest of us. I don't believe it's going to be your nephew who'll show up before the Throne with blood on his hands."

"Sorry, Mr. Goodheart, but I think you're kind o' squeezin' out a little too much milk of human kindness here," said the constable, not liking to contradict the minister but still trying to do his duty as he saw it. "If it ain't Perce, who else could it be?"

"Yes, who?" demanded Mrs. Higbed and the doctor, who had by now arrived on the scene.

"The explanation is quite obvious, I should think," Strongitharm replied. "Mr. Wilt, where do you keep your money? If you want to keep your nephew out of jail, you'd better tell me now."

James Wilt gasped a few times to indicate that he either could not or would not tell. With that, the indomitable though modest Mrs. Higbed stepped forward.

"If Mr. Wilt won't tell and it's a matter of saving the good name of an innocent young man who won't even swat a fly without apologizing to it first and has been a good and faithful nephew ever since he entered this house as an orphan boy of twelve, then I'll tell you myself, not that I'm one to snoop but I couldn't have mopped this floor twice a week faithful for the past twenty-seven years and four months without knowing about the loose board right under your bathtub, Mr. Goodheart, which if you'll move it I'll show you where the money's hidden as is my Christian duty and Mr. Wilt will forgive me because he's a good man at heart no matter what anybody says."

"I'll get a bailing bucket," said the constable, no longer a flaming angel of vengeance. "No sense straining our guts lifting all that water."

The water was dumped, the tub was moved, the hiding place revealed. And it was empty! James Wilt was all set to have a relapse and the doctor to snatch him back from the jaws of death for a tidy fee when Strongitharm intervened.

"Just what I expected. Constable, consider the facts. Perce Wilt is no dumbbell or he wouldn't be able to run the drygoods store the way he does. If he'd been guilty of attacking his uncle, he'd have had sense enough to leave the money where it was and make a sham of discovering it after Mr. Wilt died, when he'd have inherited it anyway."

"The minister's right," said the doctor. "He's right about the punctured lung, too, Mr. Wilt. We'll have you back inside that union suit in a few weeks, provided whoever stabbed you the first time doesn't take another whack. Who did it, Mr. Goodheart?"

"Well, doctor, when I lifted Mr. Wilt out of bed, I felt a wet spot on his nightshirt. Rightabout here." The minister demonstrated. "Look, here's a round hole just about the size of the wound in his chest. That proves he was stabbed through his nightshirt and all. The would-be murderer then sponged the nightshirt to get rid of the small bloodstain left when the weapon was pulled out, evidently hoping the puncture would never be noticed and the death would be put down to natural causes. But underneath his nightshirt, Mr. Wilt was also wearing his heavy winter underwear, which naturally got more blood on it than the nightshirt did."

"That's why the water turned pink when you put him in the tub," said Mrs. Higbed in awe and wonderment. "But who would wash away a small stain on top and leave a big one underneath?"

"Only someone who didn't know Mr. Wilt always sewed himself into his winter underwear and never took if off till spring. That means it had to be somebody from out of town, but also somebody who'd stayed here often enough to have found out where Mr. Wilt hid his money. Somebody who not only carried a piece of luggage big enough to hide the gold in, but also dealt in long, thin, pointed objects. If you search Mr. Ham's sample case, constable, I expect you'll find both Mr. Wilt's missing money and a large-sized steel knitting needle that's been sharpened to a dagger point.,"

"Well, I'll be --" the constable caught Strongitharm Goodheart's stern eye upon him, gulped, and added "blessed. Mr. Ham, you're under --"

From over by the depot came a long, dismal hoot. It was the morning train. With a mighty thrust of his arm, Mr. Ham hurtled the constable into the now empty tub, fled from the house, and, as they soon learned, leaped on the train in the nick of time. He had perforce left his sample case behind. It contained, as Strongitharm had predicted, a Number Six knitting needle that had been sharpened to a deadly weapon and all Mr. Wilt's hidden hoard except for thirty sliver dollars that the scoundrel must have put straight in his pocket. Ham had in fact jangled a good deal as he'd run away, Mrs. Higbed recalled.

James Wilt took his loss in surprisingly good part. He followed the doctor's orders, tenderly nursed by the ever-loyal Mrs. Higbed. He made a fine recovery and paid his bill to the doctor without even trying to deduct two per cent for cash on the button. On the first Saturday night after the doctor had pronounced him fit to be out and about, he showed up at the parsonage with a fresh cake of soap in his hand and a clean suit of underwear over his arm and requested permission to use the minister's bathtub. When he departed after scrupulously washing out the ring, he was discovered to have left a five-dollar gold piece in the soap dish. On Sunday morning he appeared in church with Mrs. Higbed, freshly barbered and smelling only of bay rum. To the wonder of all beholders, he put a dollar in the plate.

These weekly ablutions continued. So did the gold pieces, not to mention the dollars in the plate. With these important additions to his formerly pitiful income, Strongitharm Goodheart was able not only to step up his charitable works among the aged, the ailing, and the indigent, but also to keep his growing brood of happy, well-behaved little Goodhearts in shoes, porridge, and slate pencils, and to buy his beloved wife her first new hat in fourteen years.

Mrs. Goodheart soon had occasion to show off her hat at a fashionable society wedding, as she watched her beaming husband unite in holy wedlock Perce Wilt and the beautiful schoolteacher. For a wedding present, Perce and his bride received the avuncular blessing and full partnership in both the retail and the wholesale ends of the drygoods business. Shortly thereafter, James himself visited the parsonage with a blushing Mrs. Higbed on his arm to request a similar though quieter service for himself and the woman who alone of all in Pitcherville had seen the real man under the overworked union suit.

James Wilt was never heard to repine his stolen thirty pieces of silver. He never tried to find out what had happened to the treacherous Mr. Ham. Vengeance was the Lord's, Strongitharm Goodheart had assured him, and James was content to leave the job to the One best equipped to handle it.

Naked Truths

MARY JANE MAFFINI

Mary Jane is another author whose first published crime fiction appeared in the Cold Blood *series. "Naked Truths," from* Cold Blood V, *combines daft humour with deft plotting – and, in classic whodunit fashion, nothing is hidden from the reader's eyes. In 1995, Mary Jane's story "Cotton Armour" appeared in the anthology* The Ladies Killing Circle *and won the Arthur Ellis Award for Best Short Story. The previous year, her "Death Before Donuts" won the 1994 Ottawa Citizen's Write Now Short Story Contest. In addition to writing, Mary Jane is co-owner of Prime Crime Mystery Bookstore in Ottawa.*

Myself, I like to be the observer. I mostly hang back and watch what's going on and note the details and the reactions of people. That's what I'm best at. As a rule, Verona does all the talking.

This works pretty well when everyone keeps their clothes on but the minute they come off, the observer encounters a bit more trouble. And trouble's exactly the sort of thing that comes of following Verona. I should know. I've been following her since we were girls in St. Malachi's Home.

Prospecting, Verona calls these excursions of ours. Mining for gold in the hills of the unsuspecting. And it was prospecting that brought us to Whispering Pines in the first place.

"This time," she said, "opportunity's knocked, walked through the door and dropped its drawers."

"I can't believe I'm doing this," I said, as we lined up for the registration desk in what they call the Main House. Even though the four-colour brochures left no doubt in our minds about the theme of Whispering Pines, the naked, chattering people surrounding us took a bit of getting used to.

Already, I needed a smoke, but Whispering Pines was a non-smoking environment according to the brochure. Verona made sure my Players Light were safely back in Toronto.

"Stop whining," Verona said, "do you want to make a living or not?"

I wasn't so sure.

Eye contact, I told myself as we waited to sign in. And not much of that. It was too late to turn around and leave. The shuttle was already parked and Carlyle, our driver, was busy carrying stacks of small suitcases into the reception area.

We stood there with our fellow passengers from the shuttle, and gave new meaning to overdressed. Of course, Verona didn't seem to mind at all.

In the brochure they call the foyer the Grand Hall. They go in for capital letters a lot at Whispering Pines. I admired the acres of hardwood floor, the lush terra cotta and turquoise area rugs, the jade leather sofas and the ten-foot wide stone fireplace running from the floor to the vaulted ceiling. Mind you, it wasn't easy to concentrate with the number of bare backsides and frontsides that crossed my vision.

I turned my attention back to the line of people checking in and still wearing clothes.

The couple in front of us were tall, slender and thirtyish, the kind who might look all right in the altogether. In front of them stood two people who just might have been retired nuns. I tried to imagine their motivation for being at Whispering Pines. Verona said people come to Whispering Pines to experience freedom, wildness and risk in a comfortable facility without the slightest bit of real danger. Fat chance with Verona around.

A big guy about forty-five in Reeboks and nothing else zeroed in on the people waiting to register, his hand outstretched. Verona reached out to shake it.

"I'm Bob. Welcome to Whispering Pines." Bob didn't need to be dressed for success to let you know he was in charge. "I know you ladies are going to like it here just fine."

Bob had more teeth than a piano and I figured it took him a good half-hour to get his hair styled in the morning. My hand crunched when he shook it.

"We're glad to have you," Bob said.

"And we'll be glad to have you too," Verona said under her breath.

I admire that in Verona, her ability to say something behind your back right to your face without letting her smile slip. She reminds me of a cat, always looking like she knows all the answers and she's not planning to let you in on any of them.

"Go ahead and look around. Get acquainted. You'll find folks real friendly here," Bob said, sliding his hand on Verona's shoulder as he oozed toward the next lump of newcomers, shuffling self-consciously in their clothes.

"Make sure you get settled in time for the barbecue," Bob said, loudly enough to be heard all the way up and down the line.

The scent of hickory smoke drifted around the Grand Hall. Through a long line of french doors you could see pink bodies holding plates and laughing as they clustered around the row of massive black barbecues set up on the brick patio.

Behind us in the line, a bulky woman and her much smaller husband chattered.

"I already find folks friendly, don't you?" she said. "I just love to get out and meet people, don't you?"

I didn't. I just loved to curl up at home in front of a Jays' game with a brew in my hand and not one single other person within shouting distance. That's what I love. I was only there because Verona kept carping about cash flow. She gets kind of twitchy whenever her personal reserves start to dip. That's when we have to go prospecting. I guess it's just natural insecurity when you think about her background. Me, though, I don't want too much and I'm content to sit on that sofa until the bank balance drops near four figures. I suppose it's a good thing that Verona is the brains in our business and I'm the operations side.

"My name's Marg," said the woman behind us. "And this is Hedley. Say hi, honey." She pointed to a man who looked remarkably like a balding ferret.

Marg was into the size twenty plus range with a new- smelling perm and a shy smile. Her peach jogging suit probably cost her three hundred bucks but it only accentuated her bulk.

"Honey?"

Hedley didn't answer. He gawked at every woman in the room. I was pretty sure Hedley wasn't what the Whispering Pines brochure meant by mature, sophisticated people.

Hedley's eyes tracked a willowy blonde in red spike heels. She was headed towards us, smiling, when she caught her heel in the fringe of the area rug in front of the fire place. You could hear the ripping sound from where we stood. Hedley grinned as she bent over to yank her heel from the fringe.

"Hello everybody and welcome," the blonde inhaled as she reached us. "I'm Sherise, your recreational director. We're so glad you're all here."

Hedley pivoted on his small feet and stared at her breasts, conveniently at his eye level. I wondered how Marg could resist bopping Hedley a good one.

The willowy blonde's smile dimmed for a second as she observed Hedley. It's hard to know what Miss Manners would recommend in dealing with a ferret-man who has his pointed nose one inch away from your nipples. The subtleties of modern etiquette may be even further obscured when you're the recreational director in a nudist colony. But Sherise was a trooper and a resourceful one at that. I'm sure that Hedley never realized that the elbow he got in his ribs when Sherise turned to Verona was anything but an accident.

I flicked a glance at Verona to see how she reacted to Hedley. But she wasn't paying any attention to the little creep. She was watching Sherise. From Verona's narrowed eyes and pursed lips, I figured she hadn't taken a shine to Sherise. Verona's used to being the most attractive woman in any room and this Sherise gave her a real run for her money.

Sherise's curvy coral smile stayed bright. Sherise's outstretched hand hung in the air. Verona just looked at her. I broke the stand-off by reaching out to shake Sherise's hand.

"Welcome," she said, "we'll do everything we can to make your stay a real adventure."

"It already is," I said.

Sherise laughed. "You'll get used to Whispering Pines and then you'll really start to enjoy yourself."

"Really?" I said.

"Really. Well, we'll see you at the dance tonight."

"Dance?" The expression on my face was probably the same as if she'd said "We hope you'll join us for the public flogging."

"Don't miss it," she said, "buffet dinner, a great Irish band, good dance floor, the works. Now you two should hurry up and put those suitcases away and get back out here. People are dying to meet you."

She glided off to the next group of newcomers, clumsy in their clothes.

Before she got far, Bob grabbed her arm and jabbered on about her tearing the carpet that was now going to cost a frigging fortune to get fixed. It's my job to observe, so I observed. That means listening in too. Sherise yanked herself out of Bob's grip and stomped over to Carlyle. Carlyle appeared to be stuck with the carpet problem because Bob and Sherise swanned off to meet and greet.

I took the opportunity to stroll over and say hi to Carlyle as he rolled up the carpet. I wondered how it felt to work at a place like Whispering Pines and I thought I'd ask him while I still had my clothes on.

"No way," said Carlyle, as he rolled up the carpet, "this ol' uniform's ever coming off. I make that a condition. They didn't like it much at first but they don't got a lot a choice. I'm the one who knows everything goddam thing that goes on here and does everything that needs to be done. I'm the one who handles all the driving and maintenance here. Like this here carpet, eh, nothing to fixin' it, and here's that tightwad Bob carrying on like it's gonna break the bank."

He slung the carpet over his shoulder and started for the back door. "See ya," he said.

"I'll save you a burger," I said. I figured Carlyle would be a good friend to have at Whispering Pines.

"For Christ's sake, unbend a little," Verona said to me, as we headed towards our cottage. "You'd think nobody'd ever been to a nudist camp before. Everyone else feels perfectly at home."

It seemed that way. There must have been a hundred people seeming perfectly at home in the altogether and considering their general appearance I don't know why they weren't all beet red with embarrassment.

"Eye contact," I muttered. "Eye contact." I repeated it like a mantra as we strolled through the open air recreation area.

"Great location," Verona said, pointing toward the lake shimmering beyond the black pines. Miles of unspoiled, evergreen forest surrounded the water.

And acres of flesh, I thought, keeping my eyes on the cottages ahead instead of on the residents of Whispering Pines.

"Hi there," Verona said, with a frisky little wave, every time we passed another person.

Don't look down, I said to myself.

Whispering Pines was not in the least what I'd expected. For one thing, the bodies I tried not to stare at were not the kind that would ever find their way into a centrefold. Still they strolled and smiled and waved as though they felt pretty good about themselves. Go figure.

"This will be good for you," Verona said, as we passed a group of energetic folks playing tennis.

"Don't stare at any bouncing bits," I told myself.

We stopped momentarily to observe what looked like a croquet game when Marg and Hedley puffed up behind us.

"Looks like we're in the next cottage to you," Marg said. "Isn't that great? That's great, isn't it, hon?"

"I guess we'll be seeing a lot of each other." Hedley smirked.

The cottages were log with small shutters and clay pots of flowers flanking each front door. The flowers in the pots were the same as the name of each cottage.

Marg and Hedley had Marigold Cottage. We had Geranium.

The moment of truth came as we unpacked inside the pine-lined cottage with the red and green accents.

"Don't put it off," Verona said, referring to the shedding of my clothes.

"I'm not putting it off."

She smiled as she snapped open her suitcase.

"What do you have in that case?" I asked. "Why do you have a big case like that if all we need is our deodorant?"

"Nail polish," she said, pointing to what must have been twenty bottles of the stuff laid out in a nice little tray.

"Nail polish?"

"Exactly."

"What for?"

"Did you notice anything on our walk?"

I flashed her a look. I had noticed plenty and we both knew it. Even though I'd spent my walk from the main house to the cottages looking at the trees, the grass and the pathways, it's my business to pick up on everything.

"What did you notice?" she asked.

"That people here are extremely well groomed. Perfect make-up, tans, and nails. That everyone is wearing scent." I'd sniffed Stetson and Obsession and Red so far.

"That's right. It's important when you don't have clothes to help you out," Verona said. "Every little bit counts. Did you notice everybody's hair was perfect?"

Of course I noticed. Everyone's hair was flawlessly casually airy and sprayed to keep it that way. I let the comment slide. My hair would never be perfect and I couldn't have cared less. I have other strengths.

"I thought people came to these places to be perfectly natural, away from the status of clothes and away from all the crappy artifice like nail polish. This is the real me, without my thousand dollar suit. What you sees is what you gets, that kind of thing."

Verona shook her head. "You're being silly," she said, lining up her collection of lipsticks next to the nail polish on the little pine vanity.

"Well," I said, "I hope you know what you're doing, dragging us here."

"Are you kidding. This is quite a little money-making operation." Verona said, as she put on her lipstick. "Figure the amount of money we invested in our one-week stay in this cottage, and this is the cheapest of Whispering Pines' accommodations. Now multiply that by the number of guests who were there for the week. And then multiply that by 52 weeks per year."

"Fifty two ...?"

"That's right, they keep the Main House open all winter. This place is like a license to print money for that Bob guy," she said, checking her face carefully in the mirror. "Let's make that pay off for us."

Twenty minutes later I stood clothesless in the cottage. I rejected Verona's offer of eyeliner, lipstick and a quick squirt of Miss Dior. As ready as I ever could be to leave Geranium Cottage and meet our new friends. I didn't mention to Verona that I was still estimating my chances of slipping away from her, hopping into my clothes and thumbing a ride back to Toronto.

"A bit of red polish on those toes would help," she said.

"Forget it," I said, striding out the door, au naturel from one end to the other.

"Would you reconsider wearing a bit of blush?" she asked, slipping up behind me.

But I'd already forced myself outside.

A youngish, blondish man carrying a large purple towel over his arm and smelling of Drakkar emerged from Petunia, the cabin on the left. He looked a lot more like the people in the brochures than Marg and Hedley did. I would have ducked back in but Verona cut off my escape route.

I could hear her chuckling.

"You're new here, I guess," the youngish, blondish man said, extending his hand. "I'm Kevin."

Although he extended his hand in my direction, Verona shook it. I stood rooted to the ground. I didn't need Verona's offer of blush. I had my own.

"Yes," Verona said, "we just got in."

"You'll really like it here. There's a lot to do. Great people. Hope to see you at the dance tonight."

I began to develop a crop of excuses for missing the dance. Dysentery, halitosis, osteoporosis, quadriplegia.

"Hi there, neighbours," Marg boomed behind me. "Isn't this great?" She beamed at Kevin. "I'm Marg and this is Hedley."

But Hedley stared with admiration at Verona's backside.

"Nice to meet you," Kevin said fragrantly as he backed away faster than most people can move when they're going frontwards. "Sorry, got to head off now. Meeting someone for a swim. See you all later."

Marg was much improved by removing her clothes. Her three- hundred dollar jogging suit made her look dumpy, matronly and as far as you can get from stylish. But once liberated from it she billowed about, a complex blend of pink curves topping slender ankles and connecting to tiny hands with long perfectly manicured pearl-pink nails. She smelled quite nicely of White Linen and she wore make-up which I hadn't noticed before. Even her corkscrew perm had loosened up. A makeover from lumpy to lavish. Marg was exactly the kind of girl who would have turned Rubens' head.

Hedley on the other hand managed to look smaller, meaner and more on the make without the civilizing restraints of his wardrobe. Hedley led the charge back toward where the crowd was chowing down.

Verona took to the less is more situation like she'd spent her life in public without clothes. She strolled along, trim and perky from hours spent in the health club, the hair stylist and the esthetician. As we trotted across the grass common area toward the action at the barbecue, the croquet players waved to her.

"Stop shivering," she said to me. "It's not cold."

"There's a wind."

"There's no wind, it's just a warm little breeze."

Maybe so, but I was unaccustomed to having warm little breezes tickle my bum.

"You look like you have a steel rod instead of a spine. Relax. Nobody's going to talk to you if you look so tense."

Of course, that's precisely what I hoped.

The barbecue was worth the wait. The crop of new arrivals milled around with plates and frosty beer steins and hungry expressions.

"Isn't this great?" Marg said, nudging up to us at the condiment table with two hamburgers on her plate. "I love seeing all these new faces, don't you, hon?"

But hon was not focusing on faces. His head jerked this way and that as each new set of breasts bobbed by.

"...isn't it, hon?" Marg repeated. Expecting a reply.

"Oh yeah," Hedley chuckled, taking a bite of his hamburger. "And not just new ones."

"What does that mean?" Marg said, with a small furrow between her perfectly plucked brows.

"It means," Hedley said, with his mouth full, "that I saw someone I met before when the someone was someone else. That's all." His mean little eyes flickered with amusement, making me think of a rat in an alleyway.

"Oh Hedley," Marg said, giving a vicious squirt with the ketchup dispenser, "talk sense."

Verona and I exchanged looks. She shook her curls. Emphatically. No way Hedley could have ever met us when we were someone else.

Hedley slid toward Verona like a kid heading for a dessert table. She edged passed him, leaving the same distance between them. I had to admire the way she managed to get a mustard smear across his belly as she passed him. Verona bit into her hamburger like she tasted success.

Around us Bob and Sherise worked the crowd, shaking hands, smiling, nudging shoulders, patting arms, throwing back their heads and laughing at the same tired little jokes. They looked good together, perfectly maintained, flawless skin and teeth, hair sprayed to casual perfection.

"So what did you get so far?" Verona whispered when I caught up to her later.

"A few good prospects. I think I have a line on at least one man of the cloth, although it's not on him now. Excellent representation from the banks too, unless I'm losing my touch, but I don't see anyone political so far. I think Carlyle will prove quite useful."

"Yummy," she said, "keep at it. I smell money already."

The wind picked up and giggling guests held onto the paper napkins on the table. I brushed my hair out of my eyes. "I told you to use a little hairspray," Verona hissed. None of the other women had to brush their hair out of their eyes. Bob's locks stayed put even when the wind began to seem more like a gale. Trust that oversized phoney to wear a toupee even in a nudist colony. Probably glued on too. Only Hedley's sparse strands fluttered in the wind as he stood back and watched the crowd, his eyes glistening.

As I sashayed off to deliver Carlyle his burger, all I could hope was that Verona was right and this little gold mine would top up the coffers for the next six months.

The August air had a fall nip in it as we walked through the dusk to the Main House for the dance. Kevin joined us as we left Geranium Cottage. We wore the all-weather coats the brochure recommended you have on hand at Whispering Pines for the occasional cool weather challenge. I found the coat distracting, the feel of silky lining unfamiliar against my skin. The outdoor recreation area was full of giggling, chatting people heading towards the dance, every hair in place. I could smell their fresh deodorant and toothpaste and hairspray, not to mention the perfume and aftershave.

I much preferred the scent of wood smoke from the large stone fireplace in the Main House. It promised warmth although I was hoping I could keep my raincoat on. But I didn't get away with that. A naked girl in a little cap collected all the coats and jackets at the door.

We shared a table with Marg and Hedley and Verona pressured Kevin into joining us. Carlyle had converted the Grand Hall to a festive dance theme. There were round tables with green cloths and flickering candles, a raised stage for the band, coloured ceiling lights and even one of those suspended glittering glass balls. The room was full of noise and laughter but I was busy trying to get used to the feel of the vinyl seats. The band provided an excellent distraction. I would have bet the week's revenue at Whispering Pines that this was their first gig in the altogether.

They shared self-conscious grins although most of the guys had guitars or drums or a keyboard to hide behind. Except for the fiddle player. The fiddle player's blush still hadn't died down half an hour after the guys started to set up on the stage.

I nursed my Blue and watched them. Misery loves company. The red-headed fiddle player's sharp-boned face and lean body complemented an endearing lack of muscle development. His brown eyes said I'm only doing this because I need the money. You could tell by the blush. And he wasn't a talker. In the entire half an hour, he didn't say one word to the other guys in the band. Just a nod or a half-grin when necessary. He struck me as the kind of guy you could sit on the sofa with, each with your own beer, watching the game and not yammering at each other. He looked like he needed a smoke too.

So when I accidentally bumped into him at the bar during intermission, I was surprised when he looked into my eyes and grinned. By the time I got back I had an extra stein of Blue, a smile on my face and a telephone number written on my hand, just like a teenager.

All around our table people were restless, waiting to clap and dance and hop around without their clothes, impatient for the band to play again. Not me. As the band started to play You've Lost that Loving Feeling the crowd surged to the front, laughing and swaying in time. Marg and Hedley were there. Verona too dragging Kevin behind her. I could see Bob and Sherise encouraging the foolishness, calling out to stragglers at the tables.

I clutched my Blue and stayed in my chair. Ahead of me a sea of bums moved to the music. I was having dirty thoughts about the fiddle player when all hell broke loose.

It started with Marg's scream, high, bubbling, drifting above the gyrating crowd. The first reaction was confusion. The gang on the dance floor took nearly a full minute to spot Hedley writhing on the floor. From my spot at the table I could see Verona's face. I pushed my way up through the crowd. Easier said than done since people started to panic. Some pushed to get closer, most pushed to get away. In the tangle of bodies, chairs were knocked over, people tripped and shrieked.

By the time I reached the centre of the floor, Hedley's eyes stared without blinking at the glittering glass ball in the ceiling. A festive ribbon of red trickled from the puncture in his chest down his rib cage and onto a widening puddle on the parquetry. What kind of weapon would inflict such a tiny wound and still lead to death?

Marg's wail still rose high and steady over the crowd.

With the speed the Ontario Provincial Police got there, I figured they'd been just waiting for the opportunity to drop in on the folks at Whispering Pines.

And as if the stress of checking out a murder scene wasn't bad enough, there was the awkwardness of where to look. I caught the cute young constable's eye a couple of times. I thought he was probably telling himself to maintain eye contact and to not look down. I understood.

"I think he likes you," Verona said. "Better be careful. Don't want to get too close."

I knew what she meant and there was no danger. I was very, very correct in my discussions with Constable Duffy, never mind if he was as tempting as a triple fudge sundae.

During the investigation, Verona was the only cheerful person left at Whispering Pines.

"Murder," she whispered in my ear, "who would have thought that would happen? What a stroke of luck."

Fine for Verona to feel so chipper, but I didn't care for the riskiness in a situation where one naked person could skewer another naked person in front of a hundred other naked people and hide the evidence right under every other naked person's nose. Also I'm never all that comfortable around the police.

The rest of the people hung around in dejected pink lumps. Some were clutching the styrofoam cups of hot coffee that Sherise and Carlyle handed out. Others, like Marg, had blankets slung over them to fight off shock. Marg was in bad shape. I didn't think a blanket would do the trick.

"I don't know what she's howling about," Verona said. "She's better off without the slimy little creep."

I was inclined to agree but I could still see Marg's point of view. Sure he'd been a slimy little creep but he'd been her slimy little creep.

The wicked, fun-filled atmosphere in the Grand Hall got bleaker and colder as the night stretched on. The scent of blood and death goes badly with sweat, spilt beer and stale perfume, perhaps that's why my stomach was heaving. We huddled as far as we could get from the yellow tape that surrounded the scene. The conversations were furtive and low, the people deflated, the freedom and laughter doused. People exchanged shifty, embarrassed glances whenever someone's bare bum squeaked on the vinyl chairs.

"This has certainly taken the fun out of the Whispering Pines experience for me," a red-haired woman wearing an acre of cubic zirconium said as her husband covered her bony shoulders with a Hudson's Bay blanket.

"No kidding," the guy next to her said. He sounded cool but he kept rubbing the side of his bald head until it was red.

Conversations buzzed and fizzled as the OPP IDENT team bagged and vacuumed every scrap of fuzz and dust in area surrounding Hedley. Plain clothes investigators came for the men, one at a time.

"What do they want?" the cubic zirconium woman asked.

"They just need to sort out what happened," her husband said. "Nothing to worry about."

"They're looking for the murder weapon," I said.

The bald guy stood up, shook his body and giggled. "Well, I got nowhere to hide it."

Everyone looked at him, ugly thoughts written on their faces.

"No way," squeaked the bald guy, interpreting the looks, "whatever killed that guy was sharp, sharp, sharp."

He had a point. Something portable yes, small and easy to slide into Hedley and then back out again without being seen. And the police didn't seem to have found it on the dance floor.

I looked off to the farthest corner of the room where the band was. Nervous and naked, trapped after the gig from hell, they were lighting up under one of the No Smoking signs. It was all I could do not to join them.

Instead, I sidled up to Kevin by the stone fireplace.

"I hope this doesn't make the papers," he said.

His forehead was rumpled and the goose bumps on his arm were visible from where I stood. I didn't have the heart to tell him that this sort of thing is what newspapers exist for.

Together we watched as a woman officer joined the team. Acid burning in my throat replaced the heaving in my stomach.

It was time for us girls to go through our paces.

"You'd think the police'd never seen a murder before," Verona said as she sat on the red and green checked quilt in Geranium Cottage and touched up the silver polish on her toe nails.

"It could be a first for them, murder in this setting."

"Don't be provincial," Verona said, leaning back to admire her work.

"Well, that body search was a first for me. And I can't say I ever want another one."

Verona grinned.

"I wish you wouldn't keep grinning," I snapped. "This murder is not amusing, it's very inconvenient. How are we going to top up our revenues with the law crawling all over the place?"

Verona looked up and grinned. "You know, I've seen Sherise somewhere before too. I think you better follow up on it. And you're the one who notices everything and since we want to get out of here quick and with a bit of income, let's put those two things together and give the law a hand."

In the morning, I dropped in for a little chat with Carlyle. After all, he was the man who knew everything and did everything at Whispering Pines. Sure enough, he was able to confirm my idea about what was long and sharp and extremely portable and where it would be. That took care of the how of Hedley's death. The why seemed straightforward. Hedley had spotted someone who didn't want to be spotted. Someone who apparently had a powerful reason for not being spotted. High stakes of some kind. But Hedley had arrived when we did and walked over to the barbecue with us. He hadn't had a chance to meet many of the other guests. Just the staff, ourselves and Kevin.

Which was bringing us to the who. A handful of people interested me too. Kevin, for instance. Why did he back away from Hedley so fast when they met? Why was Kevin so worried about the papers? Was he somebody? Was he somebody's son? Was he the person Hedley said he'd seen somewhere else as someone else?

On the other hand, could the murder have been provoked by Hedley, himself? He seemed to bring out the worst in people. What about some jealous husband? Maybe Sherise after Hedley came one inch too close once too often? And what about Marg? If ever a woman had a husband worth killing, it was Marg.

Well, whoever it was, the killer had planned it, brought the weapon to the dance and used the music and action as a cover.

But the police had not turned up the weapon in the room or in any of the body searches. I thought about that as I shlepped back to Geranium Cottage, nodding to the tennis players bravely swinging despite the murder. The smiles were dampened a tad, the waves less carefree, but every perfect hair was still in place. Halfway to the cottage, I jerked to a stop. The final piece popped into the puzzle.

"Did you get it taken care of?" Verona asked, after Carlyle drove me into the nearest village and back. Carlyle and I reeked of Players Light and I was enjoying wearing my clothes again, even if I picked up few disappointed looks walking back to Geranium Cottage. It was one positive thing I'd take away with me from Whispering Pines, a true pleasure in the feel of my jeans.

"It's gone," I said, "Special Delivery."

"Did you make your calls?"

"Yep."

"And?"

"Jackpot. It was her all right. Him too. A lot of people were able to confirm the connection."

Verona, of course, wore only a grin. She gave one of her catlike stretches. "I almost hate to leave this place," she said, "there's something about going around naked that frees you up emotionally." She glanced at her watch. "Good. I checked the office and he should be there now. Slip out of your duds and we're ready to roll."

"Let me tell you how you did it." Verona sat across the desk from Bob, her eyes glittering, looking like she owned the knotty pine office. But then she always enjoys the part where you trap the guilty party and toy with him. That's the cat in her, I guess.

"I don't know what you ..."

But Verona didn't give Bob the satisfaction of listening.

"Hedley recognized you, didn't he?"

Bob shook his head. Deep red blotches surfaced on his chest and neck. "He certainly didn't ...."

"I think he did, Bob." Verona's little cat smile spread over her face. "I think he recognized you from a different place when you were using a different name."

She looked at me. "Don't you agree?"

I rearranged my facial expression so that Bob and Verona could interpret it in any way they wanted. I hate the part where she toys with the guilty party.

"I think he recognized you in your former occupation as a small time porno flick maker and distributor. That really wouldn't have gone down well with your clients, would it, Bob? Might have made them a bit skittish. They might have been a bit reluctant to socialize with Sherise if they fully understood her career path. And they might have wondered if you have cameras scattered around here recording things that could come back to haunt them. They might even have slipped into their clothes and headed home, wanting their piles of money back. Word would get around pretty quickly. That would definitely cause a nasty blip in your cash flow."

No answer from Bob on this one.

"And, of course, the police might have been interested in talking to you. Something tacky about an outstanding warrant related to the age of some of the girls in your films."

Behind the gleam in Verona's eye, you could see the chill.

"What did he ask for his silence, Bob? Money? Women? Or did he want to torment you?"

"I don't know what you're talking about," Bob said. The muscle twitching on his upper lip said otherwise.

"I think you do," Verona said. "I think you do and I think it worried you. I think it worried you enough to get rid of Hedley."

Bob crossed his arms over his chest and stared out the window. Two OPP cruisers were idling in the parking spaces in front of the Whispering Pines office. Constable Duffy and his colleagues were winding down their on-site investigation.

"It was the carpet needle, wasn't it, Bob? Long and sharp and available. You gave him a quick jab in the heart and that was it. Easy to do with the crowd around dancing. Nobody would see you do it and nobody would even figure out what happened to Hedley until he was actually on the floor for a while. Simple and elegant. Allow me to compliment you."

The look on Bob's face, I was glad he didn't have that carpet needle with him.

"And then," Verona said, "slipping the needle under your hairpiece while you were bent over Hedley. I gotta hand it to you, Bob. Unfortunately for you, my colleague, unlike the rest of the gang at the dance, makes her living from being a good observer. And she noticed your hair was too good to be true."

Bob flashed me a look. He puffed out his chest, which probably worked well for him in the world of business. It was less effective without a suit and useless with two women who had him by the short and curlies, so to speak.

"This is a ridiculous allegation," he said. "You couldn't possibly have any proof of such nonsense. Where's the weapon then?"

Constable Duffy climbed out of the car and started toward us.

Verona chuckled. "We know exactly where the weapon is. Back with Carlyle's repair kit."

Bob shot a look through the window where Officer Duffy was strolling toward the office. Bob turned the colour of natural yogurt. He opened his mouth but no sound came out.

"I'm sure Officer Duffy would find it amusing," Verona smiled. "It would save him a lot of work. Especially since my colleague managed to retrieve the hairpiece you disposed of. Hardly singed. I imagine it has traces of Hedley's blood on it. Doesn't take much I hear with the magic of DNA analysis. And it won't be hard to trace the hairpiece to you." She smiled at me, fondly. "My colleague doesn't miss much."

I nodded my head at Bob. After all, I take a certain professional pride in my work.

Constable Duffy's footsteps crunched on the steps outside.

I could hear Bob's quick intake of air. There was no way out of the office without knocking over Constable Duffy.

"I think this Duffy likes you," Verona said to me, "he probably sits around imagining you with your clothes on."

"Not my type," I snapped as the door opened.

Bob squirmed in his chair. Sweat trickled down the sides of his face.

"Well," Constable Duffy said to Bob, "we'll be leaving now. But the investigation will continue. Afternoon, ladies. You'll all be available if we have other inquiries?"

Bob nodded without a sound.

"Of course," Verona said.

I smiled.

"Okay, Bob," Verona said as the pine door closed behind Constable Duffy, "let's get down to business."

Bob sat there, his back rigid, his skin grey as putty. His mouth opened twice without sound. On the third try he managed to ask, "What business are you in?"

I watched Constable Duffy's blue uniform as he ambled to the cruiser. He opened the driver's door and climbed in. He must have seen me watching because he raised his hand in a little wave.

I waved back.

"We're in the discretion business, Bob, and we see you as a major client." Her lips curved like a shiny pink scimitar. "I guess you can look on it as a sort of insurance against being arrested. We don't come cheap, but I think you'll be pleased with our service."

Bob watched the cruisers pull slowly out of the parking spot. His confidence seeped back in from some offsite storage. As the second cruiser pulled out of sight, his old smile slid back into place.

Verona chuckled.

"Don't get that look in your eye," she said, "there's no use at all trying to use that carpet needle on us. My colleague has already sent the evidence to our legal advisors. Just in case, you understand. A bit of a cliche, I realize, but what can you do? So you can see it's in your interest to have nothing happen to us at all."

She smiled compassionately at Bob.

"We only deal in cash," she added. "One time payment only. Absolutely no gouging."

I smiled myself. The price would be a bit higher than usual because Carlyle would be getting an appropriately hefty tip. I like it when things turn out well for everyone. And once again, they had. Our little cash flow problem was taken care of, we were on our way out of Whispering Pines and I still had the fiddle player's number written on my hand.

Out of Bounds
JOHN NORTH

Longtime crime fiction reviewer for the Toronto Star, John became a pub-lished author himself in Cold Blood II. *This powerful story, from volume III, was nominated for an Arthur Ellis Award in 1991. A passionate golfer, John has now used that background for several stories – but "Out of Bounds" was the first and arguably the most gripping. In addition to appearing in four editions of* Cold Blood, *John assisted with the completion of* Cold Blood V *and with the selection of stories for this volume.*

The weather forecast provided the last necessary element of the plan. Con-tinuing cold and windy with the probability of rain later in the afternoon. As long as the rain really held off until the late afternoon, conditions would be ideal.

Daniel never tired of the view from the back kitchen window. He watched the northeasterly wind tug at the few remaining leaves on the big oak tree in an attempt to add them to those that rippled and swirled across the wide stretch of lawn. Everything had been dried out by the gusts of the last few days and the last traces of green had disappeared from the field of corn at the back of the property. On the hill slopes across the valley the black earth of the ploughed fields stood out from the tawny colour of the countryside.

His ears registered the sounds of Edna assembling bags, keys and coat for the visit to her sister, while his eyes watched a black Jeep Cherokee shoot backwards out of its garage two hundred yards away. His neighbour Arthur was off on another of those interminable errands and projects that kept him busier in retirement than he had been when he worked as a civil engineer. The Huggetts were their only close neighbours and lived just down the hill on the other side of the now bare expanse of apple trees. The ideal distance, far enough to ensure privacy, but close enough to prevent a feeling of isolation.

The Huggetts were an interesting couple both as individuals and as a pair. Arthur had spent most of his career overseas building huge projects funded by the oil money in the Arabian Gulf. When his wife died he had taken an early retirement and returned to Canada. After years of building huge docks, dams and roads he had become fascinated by electronic gadgets and computers and spent most of his time in his workshop tinkering with things that Daniel barely recognized. He and Phyllis had met at a computer show where she was looking for a personal computer. She was a sociology professor at the university forty miles away, divorced five years earlier, and fifteen years younger than Arthur. This year she had a time-table that scheduled the end of her last class of the week by eleven o'clock Thursday morning. Until recently the pair had been a source of great comfort, but now they were central to Daniel's current dilemma.

"I'm finally off now, dear," Edna said as she came into the kitchen. "I had hoped to be away by nine, but with one thing and another ..." Her voice trailed away as she slid the newly-baked box of cookies from the counter into an already bulging shopping bag.

"You'll be there in plenty of time, you always are." Daniel pecked absently at her proffered cheek. "It's only ten past nine now and there was nothing on the radio about problems on the highway. There's rain forecast, but not until late in the afternoon. With any luck you'll have an easy drive and I'll get in one last game before they close the course."

"You and your golf," she grumbled good-naturedly with the tolerance of the occasional player for the true addict. "This will be about the fifth last game you've managed. Still, it never seems to stop you writing and it does give you some exercise. I've made a stew for tonight and there's some of the cold lamb in the fridge if you want lunch."

"I'll probably have a sandwich at the golf club."

"It would be a big help if you could put the stew in the oven at about five-thirty," Edna said as she crossed towards the garage door. "I'll phone if I'm going to be later than seven."

As Daniel watched her back down the driveway he realized that his last excuse had literally gone. Edna's day-long absence was another key item necessary for the perfect murder. If he could get it out of the way today he would be able to concentrate on planning their winter trip south.

It took only a few minutes to take care of the last few details. His ten-speed bike was leaning up against the wall at the back of the garage. He checked that the tires were still hard and put it in the car trunk along with the new pair of gardening gloves and tweed cap he had bought in two different chain stores last week. Inside the cap was an unused plastic supermarket bag he had only touched with gloves. The brown corduroy pants, dark socks and a heavy yellow sweater should protect him from the weather and blend in with the scenery. He was impatient to get started but knew that if he left before ten o'clock the timing would not work. He walked back to the kitchen to drink a cup of unwanted coffee and to review the situation for the umpteenth time. A huge gust of wind buffeted the house and the kitchen light flickered briefly.

Three years ago when he and Edna had cashed in on their twenty-five years of hard work and careful investment their assets had turned out to be considerable. The modest bungalow had been snapped up for cash within a week of being put on the market and they learned that while they had lived there the city's expansion had transformed their neighbourhood from "suburb" to "convenient to downtown". While the sale of the house had provided enough cash to buy this house outright and still leave a considerable sum in hand it paled in comparison to the money realized by the sale of the plastics moulding company. Edna's quarter century of teaching grade four students had provided a secure enough base for Daniel to transform a one person operation in a rented space to a thriving concern with a freehold factory and thirty employees. Altogether the sales of the business, the house and various stocks and bonds guaranteed them both lifetime security.

The move had been a good one for both of them and to their surprise neither of them missed the city. They spent considerable time tinkering with various aspects of the house and garden and took trips abroad at least twice a year. Once they were settled, and after they learned not to feel anxious at not having to work each day, each gradually did the things they had always wanted to do. Edna spent a lot of time doing volunteer work at the hospital and Daniel had some success writing technical articles for trade magazines.

When he took stock of his life Daniel was ambivalent. His life with Edna was comfortable if not exciting. He was healthy, reasonably well-off and lived in a pleasant community close to a golf course he enjoyed. Although he sometimes felt confined by his cosy environment he did not want it disturbed and was prepared to go to considerable trouble to preserve the status quo. He realized that his present problem was the result of his curiosity and a constant desire to be a participant rather than a spectator. It was these factors that had led to the brief, intense affair with Phyllis. When she had made her availability clear three months earlier he had been flattered by the attention of the attractive and intelligent younger woman and had assumed that marriage to a man fifteen years her elder was the reason she started the affair.

After several weeks the novelty had worn off and Daniel realized the risks he was running. He had tried to withdraw from the liaison, but Phyllis had not been at all co-operative and had threatened to tell Edna and Arthur about the affair unless he continued it. In the course of several bitter arguments he had been unable to dissuade her from this course of action and she had imposed a deadline of Saturday evening when the two couples were to have supper together. After a lot of thought Daniel decided he was unwilling to spoil his own and two other lives to enhance one so he decided to end Phyllis's.

When he'd arrived at the conclusion that her murder was necessary his analytical mind considered, and rejected, many possible methods. In the final analysis he needed to create a plausible setting for her death and, just in case anything went wrong, provide himself with a cast iron alibi. Once he had a plan formulated, it was just a case of waiting for the right combination of circumstances - and today was the day.

The plan would only work on a Thursday before the golf course closed for the season. The weather had to be cold enough to keep all but the hardiest golfers at home, while not being bad enough for the course to be closed for the day, stop Edna making her weekly visit to her sister, or delay Phyllis's return from the university. Last, but by no means least, neither he, Edna, Arthur nor Phyllis could be ill.

When the numbers on the stove clock clicked around to 10:00 Daniel took a deep breath and walked through to the garage. He backed the car out and paused briefly at the end of the driveway to use the electronic door closer. City habits died hard. It was a quarter of a mile to the highway and the stop sign opposite the enormous beech tree dominating the Morgan's entire yard. He tooted to Mrs. Morgan who shifted her attention from the pile of burning beech leaves. She waved and then turned back to her bonfire as his car turned north on the two-lane highway.

A mile north he turned off the deserted highway onto the dead-end farm road that ran along the back of the golf course. After half a mile he stopped under the trees. He wound down the window and listened for a few seconds. Hearing nothing but the wind he released the trunk catch, got out, removed the bike, gloves and cap from the car and carried them along the faint path into the woods. He dropped the bike into the deep leaves, tucked the gloves inside the cap which he then wedged between the brake cable and handlebars and quickly brushed leaves over it. When he reached the edge of the trees he glanced back and saw nothing out of place. He turned the car around on the still-deserted road and drove back to the highway.

At 10:20 Daniel drove into the almost empty parking lot of the Seneca Hills Golf Club and took a spot where the car was clearly visible from the door of the pro shop. He locked the car and headed for the clubhouse. Leaves had blown into the short stairwell down to the changing rooms, and several followed him into the deserted locker room. He changed into his brown spikeless golf shoes and left his street shoes on the steward's counter to be cleaned. Five minutes later he was in the pro shop looking at the tee-off sheet. The only other players on the course was a foursome of Japanese names that had started out at 9:30.

"Really going out there, are you?" said Bob as he added Daniel's name to the sheet. As he said it the windows shook from the force of the wind. "You'll be lucky to stay upright."

"Might as well. It could be the last game of the year and it's going to be at least five months until you reopen."

"You'll get no sympathy from me," said Bob. "You've said that at least five times in the last two weeks. It might have more effect if you and Edna didn't manage to get several weeks down south every winter."

"It's my pleasant and self-imposed duty to see that the courses of the Georgia coast are properly maintained," Daniel replied with a straight face. "If I didn't the golf magazines would have nowhere for their east coast staff to spend their winter expense accounts."

"It's good to know we can rely on you," Bob said. "Here's Mike with your bag now. Have a good game."

On the first hole Daniel teed up his ball before stepping away and taking a few practice swings. He felt surprisingly relaxed. He had expected to be nervous and to play poorly, but to his surprise he hit the ball straight down the right-hand side of the wide fairway and followed it with another long straight shot. For the next six holes all parts of his game were sharp and by the time he completed the seventh hole he was only four over par.

When he walked through the trees to the eighth tee and looked down the short fairway he saw he had caught up to the group of players that started almost an hour before him. He hit his shot and walked to where the ball stopped - seventy yards short of the green and sixty yards from the front of the small pond that guarded it. He watched the four players ahead of him. Each wore bright padded cold weather clothing and the distinctive green and white toques sold in the Seneca Hills pro shop. They played with silent deliberation and each member of the group marked, cleaned and stalked his ball as if a major championship was at stake. When the last of them putted out and replaced the flag, they trotted over to the right side of the green where they had left their golf carts. They stood in a ragged line and looked expectantly down the fairway at Daniel.

He hit a high wedge shot over the left side of the pond, and was gratified to see the wind pull it back towards the pin. When the ball stopped fifteen feet from the hole the line clapped in polite applause. One of the four went to take out the pin and the other three made gestures that made it quite clear they were expecting him to putt out and play through. He took a brief look at the line of the putt, decided it was straight and hit it firmly. The ball dropped into the centre of the cup and the four applauded again. Daniel retrieved the ball, replaced the pin and bowed to the group. As he walked away he hoped they hadn't thought he was mocking them. The action had been automatic and had seemed a perfectly natural and appropriate response at the time. He wasn't really sure what made him do it.

After a brief stop at the snack bar, he sipped a take-out coffee from the styrofoam cup as he walked down the slope to the tee of the long tenth hole. He waved to Bob who was hunched over a cigarette outside the pro shop door probably thinking very nasty thoughts about those who imposed no smoking policies in workplaces.

By 1:15 he had played eighteen holes and was back in the snack bar. Anna, the pleasant woman who was a fixture behind the counter, served him a club sandwich and coffee. She cleared up the counter space and appeared to listen while he replayed the highlights of his round. She nodded occasionally, always at appropriate times, as she wondered if there was any possible golf shot she had not heard described in immense detail during her time there. Still it was slow at this time of year and even Daniel was a welcome break in an otherwise boring day.

It was almost 2:05 when he returned to the pro shop via the locker room. He looked at the sheet to make sure no one else was likely to be out on the course. "No one else daft enough to go out after me, Bob?"

"Not yet. A couple of the members phoned to see if we're open. They thought they might try to get out for a quick nine holes later. Fat chance, the weather will stop them."

Daniel knew that this would not be popular with Bob since it would prevent him closing early. "I couldn't do anything right with my fairway woods. Since there's nobody else out there I'll play the back nine again and hit some practice balls."

"Go ahead," Bob laughed. "You won't be in anybody's way. I warn you, though, Murphy's Law will be in effect. If you do find out what you're doing wrong, and even more unlikely, manage to correct it, the weather will worsen and the course will close tomorrow."

When the clock in the pro shop reached 2:10 Daniel checked that his watch showed the same time and headed for the door. "Tell Anna to keep the coffee warm, Bob. I'm going to need one when I get in."

Daniel teed off on the dog-leg tenth hole and once again managed a respectable drive to the bend of the fairway. When he reached it he hit his second shot towards the green and was surprised to see his three wood shot bounce and roll way down the fairway. In case Bob was watching he dropped three other balls and hit them towards the green. None was as good as his first ball, but any would have been an acceptable shot on a normal day.

He had decided to try to do everything as close to normal as possible, so he collected his practice balls from the fairway, pitched up onto the green and putted out. Despite the increasing tension he forced himself to play the short par three eleventh hole.

His watch read 2:27 as he walked through the trees and onto the twelfth tee. He took a long look around, saw nobody, pushed his bag through a gap in the fence and scrambled through after it. On the other side of the fence the leaves were deep where the blowers used to keep the golf course clear had added to the not inconsiderable efforts of the maples and beeches. He dropped the golf bag at the base of the largest maple and removed the top of a navy blue rain suit from its large side pocket. When he put it on and closed the zipper the dark fabric of the jacket completely concealed the yellow sweater. He brushed leaves over the golf bag and headed through the woods towards the concealed bicycle.

Looking back towards the golf course he could see no trace of his progress through the yellow and orange leaves. It took him about a minute to reach the spot where the bike was concealed. With his left hand, still in its golf glove, he pulled the bike upright, leaned it against his body and pulled out the tweed cap. He removed his golf glove, stowed it carefully in his back pocket and put on the cotton gloves. The plastic bag went into the pocket of the blue jacket and the cap onto his head. Rather than take any chance of leaving a trail he lifted the bike and shuffled towards the road. Still no traffic. He mounted the bike and headed away from the highway.

This was the section with the highest risk of being seen and he pedalled as fast as he could along the road. In the sheltered roadway between the woods and the corn field the wind was not a problem. After a couple of hundred yards he reached the steel gate which marked the end of the track to the back section of Murtaugh's farm. He jumped off, lifted the bike over the gate, and scrambled after it. In front of him the dark rutted clay of the farm track went straight up the gentle slope between the two fields of high corn.

As he rode up the rise he realized that while the corn had sheltered him on the road it was now acting as a funnel to drive the wind straight towards him. The higher he climbed, the stronger the wind seemed to get. From the top of the rise the flat track stretched straight away into the distance. He changed gear, put his head down and pedalled doggedly. The wind, even if it slowed him now, would give him a boost on the way back.

The rutted track was interrupted only by a cross track separating the corn fields before it reached the smaller track skirting the orchard and the back yards of the two houses. His house on the right still appeared deserted, while a sporty green Mazda now sat on the Huggett's driveway. Phyllis was back as usual from her Thursday class. He turned left to the gap in the ledge then through it onto the narrow bare path to the back door of the house.

He leaned the bike against the back of the garage where it was invisible from the road and realized that he was panting slightly and that his hands were trembling. Whether this was due to anticipatory fear or the jarring of the frozen ruts, he was not sure. He glanced quickly at his watch, 2:40. Still on schedule. He pushed open the rear door of the garage and took a long wooden-headed screwdriver from the open toolbox under the workbench.

The side door of the house was, as usual, unlocked and as he pushed it open Daniel dropped the screwdriver onto the hard earth of the flowerbed. He listened carefully, heard nothing and then called out. "Phyllis, are you there? It's Daniel."

"In the living room," she called out. "Come on through."

He walked silently down the short hall being careful to walk only on the carpet and avoiding the polished wood floor. The room was bright with the afternoon sunlight and Phyllis sat in a blackleather armchair pulled up close to the fire burning in the large fireplace. She put down the book she had been reading and looked at him curiously. "Oh dear, you're clearly not here for a stolen afternoon of lust," she sighed theatrically. "You look as if you're dressed for golf."

"Absolutely right on both counts. I came to make one last try to make you see sense. I suppose there's no chance you've come to your senses and abandoned your lunatic plan?"

Phyllis uncoiled from the chair and walked to where he stood near the door. "It's no use standing there looking stern, Daniel. You know I'm not going to change my mind. Deep down you don't really want to stop. Let me get you a drink and we'll sit down and talk about it."

As she moved towards the table to his right where the ice bucket and the various glasses and bottles were displayed Daniel took two steps towards the fireplace and closed his gloved hand around one of the oak logs stacked beside it. The heavy log hung from his right arm as he moved back behind her.

"Phyllis, please don't do it. It's really not worth ruining our four lives."

She looked back over her shoulder, her face flushed. "Yours, you mean, you pathetic little bastard. You couldn't scramble into bed fast enough to have your fun and now you've had enough you just want to return to comfortable Edna and pretend it never happened."

"Yes," said Daniel as she turned away again. "That's exactly what I do want." He swung the log back behind his shoulder, paused briefly, and brought it down hard on the back of her head.

Her body slumped sideways across the arm of the sofa and she slid face down onto the floor. He stood over her for a moment and watched a trickle of blood emerge from the hairline at her neck and disappear beneath the neckline of her sweater. He was sure she was dead. He dropped the log and backed away. He had thought about this moment many times during the last few weeks and had tried to anticipate his reactions. It was, however, far easier than he had imagined.

He crossed to the patio doors, lifted away the broom handle from the bottom track and made sure the lock was fastened. He hurried back outside through the kitchen, picked up the screwdriver and circled the kitchen extension to the flagstone patio. He leaned hard against the doors, inserted the screwdriver into the track between the door and the frame and leaned on it with all his weight. The aluminum bent slightly but the door still remained locked. He moved the screwdriver to the top of the frame and leaned again on it with all his weight. The aluminum bent slightly but the door remained locked. He moved the screwdriver to the top of the door. Once again he inserted the screwdriver into the widening gap by the lock and pushed hard. The buckled frame gave up suddenly and he was able to push the door and screen smoothly back long their tracks.

Four steps took him to the massive oak dresser in the corner of the room where he removed the plastic bag from his jacket pocket and placed it open on the ledge. He then put several of the smaller silver items from the display shelves into the bag and shifted the positions of several of the larger items. Stepping over Phyllis's crumpled figure he crossed to the fireplace, took another log and smashed the lock on the cupboard section at the base of the dresser. He pulled away the shattered door and put three of the small jade figures on the shelves into the bag.

He looked carefully around the room and was pleased to see that he created just the effect he had wanted - Phyllis as the victim in an interrupted burglary. He picked up both logs from the floor, tossed them into the flames and hurried out through the broken door to the back of the garage.

His watch showed 2:55 when he mounted the bike and started the ride back. After a brief pause at the hedge to make sure that nobody was about he turned left along the edge of the orchard. Once on the track with the wind at his back he made good time back to the gate. Seconds later he was over it and on his way back along the farm road. Just as he dismounted at the edge of the woods the sun disappeared behind a solid bank of clouds that covered the western horizon.

This time he carried the bike further into the woods before concealing it behind the stump of a large beech tree. He kicked leaves over it and looked back towards the road. His passage had left no noticeable tracks in the leaves and in any case the brisk winds would soon eradicate any traces. He planned to recover the bike later in the week, and if anyone found it or noticed its absence in the meantime he would claim it had been stolen. The garage was always open when someone was at home and the bike was often not used for several days at a time. After another glance at the hiding place he set off towards the golf course.

At the big tree, he retrieved the golf bag and brushed the leaves off it. He leaned over the fence and looked up the twelfth fairway and back through the trees to the eleventh green. Nobody in sight. Before climbing back through the fence he made the quick transformation from burglar to golfer. The blue rain jacket was brushed off, folded and returned to the golf bag along with the tweed cap. The gardening gloves were removed and his golf glove put back on his left hand. He brushed a few remaining leaves off the golf bag and checked his watch. It was exactly 3:05 - thirty-eight minutes since he had left the course and about forty-two since he had last been in sight from the clubhouse. Unless he had been really unlucky his alibi was firmly in place.

Halfway up the twelfth fairway he paused at the bunker to fill both gardening gloves with sand. After raking the sand trap he crossed to the pond on the opposite side where he threw them into the deepest part. He watched anxiously for a few moments to make sure they stayed there but could see nothing in the black ruffled water.

He ducked into the bushes beyond the pond, stooped to pick a ball half buried in the leaves and emerged halfway down the long curving fairway of the fifteenth hole. He still seemed to be alone on the course as he cut across the fairway and moved into the trees on the far side. His target was the pond guarding the green on the sixteenth hole which he could see through the bare trees. He skirted the left edge of the pond, weaved through a stand of pine trees and emerged onto the seventeenth tee. He teed off in case anyone watching from the distant clubhouse and played the last two holes in normal fashion. As he walked up the last fairway the wind strengthened again and the skies grew even darker.

He put his golf bag down inside the club storage room, took out the tweed cap and shoved it deep into the lost and found box behind the door. He noted with satisfaction that the time was 3:30 - about right for a practice round on the back nine. By the time he had changed his shoes and got back to the pro shop fifteen minutes later there were only two cars in the parking lot, his and Bob's. As the door opened Bob glanced up from the golf magazine he was reading at the counter and looked at the clock.

"That was quick," he said. "I hadn't expected to see you until about four o'clock. Good game?"

"I always seem to play better when it's not important. I was really starting to hit the ball well but it got too cold to hang about out there. What I need is a quick coffee and a brandy to restore my body temperature to normal."

"I'm afraid you're out of luck. There was some problem earlier with the power going on and off so Anna closed up and went home."

"Not to worry, I can wait until I get home." Daniel laughed and glanced at his watch. "It's only a quarter to four so you'll be able to get away early too."

"I'd almost rather stay here," Bob replied. "I'll have to rake the leaves at home. No excuses permitted."

Daniel waited while Bob locked the cash register, picked up his jacket, and set the alarms. The first fat drops of rain fell as he locked the door. The two men hastily wished each other all the best and dashed for their separate cars.

The rain suited Daniel perfectly since it would obliterate any faint tracks left by the bike. He whistled the overture from The Gondoliers as he drove slowly on the wet road. He slowed to make the turn from the highway opposite the Morgan's now tidy yard. Just as he was about the turn into his driveway flashing lights and a blaring horm erupted behind him. He stopped, wound down his window and peered out into the cold rain. Arthur stopped alongside, leaned over the passenger seat of the jeep and lowered his window.

"Come and have a drink on the way home, Daniel. Edna won't be back yet and I want to show you my latest toy. I wired most of it up yesterday as a surprise for Phyllis. It's a combination video/alarm system to monitor key areas of the house. When it's activated motion detectors start the recorder going. State of the art, of course, compact colour camera, battery backup, the whole lot. I installed the mini-camera in the living room before I left this morning, but didn't connect the alarms so she could get back into the house without problems. I can hardly wait to see her face when I show her what she's been up to since she got back at lunchtime."

Not realizing the impact of what he'd just said Arthur wound up his window and drove away. Daniel sat very still, his mind racing. After all that - the whole thing on videotape. Death in living colour.

"Don't panic, there may still be a way out. Think."

Arthur would find the body as soon as he went in. First, stop him from phoning the police. Second, destroy the videotape. Third, get the hell away from there. There was no time to waste.

He rammed the car into gear and accelerated after the Cherokee. As it pulled up beside Phyllis's Mazda Daniel skidded in behind it. By the time Arthur had collected the various packages and magazines from his front seat Daniel was on the driveway waiting for him. The rain had stopped, and the wet asphalt of the driveway shone in the late afternoon light.

"Tell me about this new toy of yours, Arthur."

"Are you feeling all right? You usually avoid my technical explanations like the plague. After about thirty seconds your eyes glaze over and you start to stifle yawns."

"Sorry, I didn't realize I was that transparent. Since we moved here the only thing that has bothered Edna is security. She's read too many stories about isolated houses in the country and worries about a possible burglary."

"Phyllis is worse. The main drawback of being married to a sociologist specializing in crime is her tendency to note and remember incidents of crime and violence. With the silver and jade we've collected on our trips I thought I'd take a few precautions to keep her happy. Bit of self-indulgence really, designing and building it. The hardest bit, though, was installing it without clashing with all the antiques. Come and see."

Arthur started off round the side of the garage. Daniel followed, thinking furiously. The tape was the basic problem. He had to get it and erase it. He tried to figure out the probable sequence of events. Arthur would find the body and immediately phone the police. There was a phone in the living room, so he needn't leave the room. Daniel had no chance to be alone and recover the tape. Unless he got really lucky he'd have to kill Arthur as well.

"I still can't imagine where you hid the camera and recorder."

Arthur slowed down and turned to his friend. "These new cameras are awfully small you know. The one in the living room is mounted behind a small hole on top of that hideous old dresser. Behind that carved facade there's loads of room up there for the VCR as well."

"Great," thought Daniel. "The whole murder centre stage."

As soon as they rounded the corner of the garage Arthur saw the open screen door and the damaged frame. They both ran towards the door. Arthur dropped his packages and magazines and rushed to his wife's body. "What the hell's going on?"

Daniel crossed to the box of logs and picked one up. While Arthur searched frantically and futilely for a pulse Daniel brought the log down hard on the back of his skull. Arthur slumped forward over his wife's body and rolled sideways. Daniel thought perhaps he hadn't killed him so he hit him twice more.

Using the same log he poked at the dying embers of the fire into a glowing red heap. Withhis other hand he grabbed some kindling from the box and threw it onto the embers where it instantly caught alight. He placed the log on the flames. He picked up one of Arthur's dropped magazines and put it on the seat of the wooden side chair. Using a tissue from his pocket he lifted the chair over to the dresser and climbed on it being careful to keep his foot on the magazine.

Once you knew where to look it was easy to see the camera hole. He smiled directly into the lens as he climbed on the chair and looked over the top front of the dresser. Reaching over with the tissue he pressed the stop, eject and power buttons of the VCR in that order. With the cassette in his left hand he climbed down and used the tissue to move the chair back to its original position. He took the magazine and threw it and the tissue into the flames which were now busily consuming the log.

Two minutes later he was peering cautiously around the corner of the garage at the three vehicles. There appeared to be nobody on the road so he ran to the car, backed quickly down the driveway and onto the road. The rain had started again.

When he sat in his garage trying to calm down he realized that, provided no one had seen his car at the Huggett's, all he had to do to be back in the clear was to erase the evidence. He could see no quick way to destroy the tape without leaving traces and dared not chance hiding it. The easiest solution would be to tape over it. Maybe one of the channels would be showing a golf tournament or something he could reasonably be expected to tape.

In the den he made yet another mental note to reset the VCR timer. It had gone off earlier in the week when the power had been interrupted and they hadn't used it since. He pushed the videocassette into the slot on the VCR and pressed the rewind button. While he looked in the TV Guide for a suitable program the machine rewound the tape and then stopped with a loud click.

He found a golf tournament and set the channel selector then paused before pressing the record button. It was still only just before five o'clock and he could not pass up a chance to see what Phyllis's murder had looked like. He stabbed at the play button. On the screen two men entered the Huggett's living room, one crossed to the body lying on the middle of the floor and the other to the fireplace. He continued to stare in horror and, as his smiling face filled the screen, he managed to press the stop button.

He shook his head in disgust. Arthur had died for nothing. The only thing on the tape was the second, unnecessary killing. He rewound the tape, started the recording of the golf and walked through to the kitchen.

The figures on the stove clock clicked over to 2:30 as he switched on the radio. The five o'clock local news started with an item about the power cuts. The storm had toppled a tree onto the power lines near the river and had caused local blackouts for most of the afternoon. What a pity he hadn't caught the four o'clock news on the car radio, Arthur would still be alive.

Ah well, one way or another it was probably going to be a long night. He didn't need the extra aggravation of Edna complaining so he might as well put the stew in the oven.

Man on the Roof
JAS R. PETRIN

A native of Winnipeg, Manitoba, Jim has built a solid reputation as a writer of finely crafted crime stories over the past dozen years. His work appears regularly in Alfred Hitchcock's Mystery Magazine *and he is featured in every volume of* Cold Blood *but the first. Although his work is often marked by an off kilter humour, this Arthur Ellis nominated story from* Cold Blood III *is a powerful exercise in pure suspense. Jim has garnered several other Arthur nominations, winning the award in 1989 for his story "Killer in the House". His work has been extensively reprinted, recorded on audio tape and adapted for film.*

Climbing was no different than any other risky job. You had to be alert. You had to keep your nerve. It had nothing to do with bravado. It was simply a matter of skill. Gorman had climbed hundreds of buildings in his time; this one was no different, and that was what he wanted to keep firmly fixed in his mind - the idea that this was routine work.

The fog was good. It would be his friend. It would hide him as he climbed. And more importantly since his vertigo attack of three years ago at the Hotel George, its blanketing haze would preserve him from any chance glimpse of the drop below.

The abyss.

The void.

He had scaled the first security fence almost as if it had not been there at all. Up and over. Eighteen feet of barb-topped chain link and it hadn't even slowed him down. He allowed himself to draw a small pride from that; it was always best in the face of doubt to dwell on one's successes.

He didn't know why the vertigo attack had hit him when it did. Perhaps because he had stayed at the work too long. All he knew was that in a single moment he had gone from a confident, practised professional climbing smoothly up the wall of the Hotel George, one hundred feet above the street, to a man stricken with a terror so paralyzing it had reduced him to a trembling coward in a single instant. The vertigo seized him like a taloned hawk. It was as if the city, one moment spread out below him in lethargic neon majesty, had lurched suddenly into motion, proceeding grandly in a huge, slow revolution around him as his blood clotted in his veins, his mouth dried, his heart hammered at his ribs like a captive wanting out. His fingers imbedded themselves like hooks into the fissures of the mortar and brick. Mind and body in mutiny against him.

Dawn came. Morning passed. Still he clung there. Pigeons fluttered and cooed curiously around him. It was ten a.m. before he was spotted and the police and fire department crawled in like Matchbox toys to fetch him down; he rode to the police station in the back of a patrol car in handcuffs, trembling uncontrollably, like a man with fever.

It was not being in custody that caused him to shake; it was dealing with the fact that he had lost his nerve. He had never once even considered the possibility that it could happen to him, and he had lost his nerve.

He had sworn he would never climb again. More importantly, three years later he had sworn he would never climb for LaCoste.

But here he was.

Gorman crossed the grassy strip of ground that separated the fence from the outer wall, moving quickly but carefully in the fog. He kept his eyes open for trip wires. This was no fat and sleepy hotel where room guests sprawled half drunk in their beds with their jewellery lying out on their bedside tables next to their pocket change. He was dealing with professionals here; the best in the business. It would pay to remember that.

At the wall of the building he stopped, stood inches away from it for a moment, hands spread wide and pressed up flat against the stone. He was like an artisan measuring his work. The wall was gritty and chill; damp with the mist that had stolen down along the river from the marshes in the north.

There was almost no wind. That was good too. He took the light aluminum grapnel from his belt, hefted it on its thin rope, whirled it until it whickered, and then let it fly. It tinkled over the parapet high above and held, first time. An omen. A sign that there was nothing to fear, that he had not lost his touch. His hands gripped the thin dacron line, snapped it taut, then took up its elasticity gently with the weight of his body as he began to walk the wall.

He could do this one last job. He knew he could. Even though it should never have come to this, an old man back at a young man's game. He had assets put by; he could have retired after doing his time. That was one reason why he had turned down the work offered to him by LaCoste in the first place.

He had not liked his new cell mate, LaCoste, who was a quick little man, defiant and shrewd. He looked like a snitch, smelled of dried sweat, and he spent too much time in lockdown to be completely trusted: a younger man letting on he was oh-so-well-schooled in crime but who was too untried, too laughably inexperienced to be convincing. And he'd been wheedling. He wanted Gorman's help.

"Lori's smart," he had said. "She never steers me wrong about the take. There was a fortune in that place, in spite of what happened. Believe it." His girl was a cleaner with a maid service. She was also very good at opening locks. It was a fine scam she and LaCoste had got going. Being bonded and a obvious suspect, she never took anything herself, but simply spotted for LaCoste, took inventory, sketched maps, prepared the way for him. It was simple enough to leave a door or a casement latch ajar - he had heard LaCoste joke that she was one of the few cleaning ladies who still did windows.

Gorman was annoyed. "So why are you telling me?"

LaCoste sat on the edge of his lower bunk blinking up at him, nose twitching. He look startlingly like an oversized rodent, sharp-featured and supple. His hair was pulled back from his brow and was as slick as an oiled pelt. Even his skin glistened. He looked as though, with a minimum of effort, he could press himself through the bars, oil his way through the many doors and gates and escape back into the sewer from which he had come.

"Why am I telling you?" he repeated. "Why am I telling you? Because you're the best, that's why. Everybody knows that." Had LaCoste not heard of Gorman's vertigo attack at the top of the Hotel George? Apparently not. Except for a few policemen, Gorman was sure that nobody knew - only his own soul-mate Mila. "You climb like a cat," LaCoste said. "That's the work. You could break into the top floor offices of the Trizec without passing through the lobby or cracking a window - you'd run up the outside walls and get in down the chimney. I need a man like that for high-wire jobs. Eagle's nests. I need an expert. There's nobody else comes close. And you're available."

Gorman lay on his top bunk, hands behind his head, wishing the little rat would shut up. "You're sure of that, are you?"

"Oh course I'm sure. Why shouldn't I be? I heard the guards talking. You're out of here, back on the street at the end of the month, What is it -- two, three weeks?"

Gorman had spent the better part of three years on the inside; LaCoste had arrived to begin his stay only a few weeks ago, after his last job had gone wrong.

"In seventeen days, eleven hours and ..." Gorman consulted his watch. "... twenty-three minutes - I'm out of here."

The rodent leered. He had yellowish, wide, sloping teeth that could have gnawed through a leg-iron. "You sound anxious."

"Everybody in here is anxious. But I can wait. If I wanted to I could walk out of here tonight." It was a childish boast, and he regretted making it before the words were out of his mouth. But it was true. He had the route worked out, and the method. In three years of confinement he had learned which guards could be bribed to look the other way, to leave a latch undone. The rest would be easy for a high-wire man. A quick climb to the roof through the air conditioning ducts, and from there across the tiles, away from the main block to a less secure, less well-lighted wing, and then down. Piece of cake for a high-wire man.

Only for this high-wire man, the thought of those heights made his head reel.

"So why don't you go then? What are you waiting for?"

Because I'm afraid I might fall, he almost said. Instead he replied, "I'm almost a free man. Why take the risk?"

The rodent studied him. "You'll be wanting work when you get out. You'll be wanting some cash." LaCoste didn't know about Gorman's retirement fund either; there was a lot LaCoste didn't know. He was an abysmally ignorant little man. "You'll be wanting something to sharpen your claws on, some quick jobs where you can pick yourself up a little operating capital. I got those jobs, and all the background information you need to bring them off. I'm a climber. I'd do them all myself if I could, but I'm locked in here. Lori would work with you if I told her to." He laughed. "It might be a great set-up for me. I'd be safe in here, wouldn't I? But I need you, Gorman. We can cut a deal. Something more than fair, seeing as I'd do all the prep work."

"But I'd do all the climbing, wouldn't I?"

The rodent shrugged; his shoulders were so narrow they hardly seemed to go up and down. "What can I tell you? You're the high-wire man, aren't you? You're the expert - like a plumber. When a pipe needs fixing you don't go at it with Scotch tape and string, you call in a plumber. I trust experts to do their thing."

"I'm going to retire."

"You got lots of years left. We'd be partners."

"You screwed up on your last job."

The rodent's lip curled. "You read about it?"

"I don't read the papers. They depress me."

"Well, I don't mind telling you, Gorman, I get rattled when I climb. My nerves ... And then, if something goes wrong inside ..." He let out a long whistling breath. "If something goes wrong inside, like there's some-body at home, or something, I tend to get excited, know what I mean? I tend to get rough. Now, in that last job ..."

Gorman was curious. He rolled on his side and looked down over the edge of the bunk.

"What about that last job?

Pleased at Gorman's interest, LaCoste sat up. His little eyes jerked about as he recalled the scene. His speech grew more animated.

"A mistake. Just a mistake. Lori did her best, but ... It's why I'm here. I knew the schedule of the place. There wasn't supposed to be anyone home. It was supposed to be empty, the woman out visiting, the old man away like he'd been for ages, God knows where. Only, there she was any-way."

"There was who?"

"The woman. Who else? It's funny. I was so sure I was alone in that place, I was standing in the den taking a cosy look around, then in she walks straight out of the kitchen at me. I must've jumped as high as she did. Then ... I guess maybe I panicked."

Gorman looked at his cell mate, at the furtive, leaping eyes, the nar-row, shiny face, and he saw lurking there the violence that the woman must have seen, the explosive ferocity of a small cornered animal. Disgusted, he lay back down on this bunk and looked at the ceiling again. He despised amateurs.

"So you assaulted her," he said.

"Well, what was I supposed to do? Sit down and watch while she phoned the cops on me? What would you have done?"

"I sure as hell wouldn't have done that."

"Well," said LaCoste, "that's the whole point, isn't it? I said I needed you, didn't I?"

LaCoste was talking fast as he always did, but there was an ill-concealed resentment beginning to smoulder behind his little liquid eyes; pique at Gorman's reluctance, at Gorman's obvious contempt. His pupils moved in quick short leaps tracking Gorman's own: left, right, then back again. "So Lori screwed up. Everybody's allowed one screw-up, ain't they?" He reached up from his lower bunk to grip Gorman's knee; a gesture of solidarity, but Gorman's skin crawled. "Come in with me. Hell of a deal, pal. You can't say no."

Gorman peered down into the clever little eyes with distaste and wondered what LaCoste would do if he were to reach down and yank out those ridiculous scraggly little hairs that the silly ass called a beard.

Gorman gained the parapet easily. He stooped to haul in the rope, but did not disturb the grapnel. Force of habit; normally he would need that on his way back. He left the rope coiled neatly beside it and turned to assess the next stage of the climb. There had been less of an effort made here to deny a hand- or foothold; the builders had placed their faith in the featureless face of the lower wall, in the security fence, and in the door and gate alarms; they had not given the top forty feet of the building the attention it deserved. A mistake on their part. A vertical four-inch conduit was clamped securely to the brick here, the sort that contained electrical cables. To Gorman it was as good as a ladder. No doubt it had been installed years after the wall was built, a breach in security unforeseen by the original planners.

He gave the pipe a tug, found it solid and began to climb. The mist drifted around him, comforting and soft. In a moment he could no longer see the ground. He felt no fear. What was it LaCoste had said he needed? Something to sharpen his claws on? Perhaps the little rat had been right.

Still, he ought not to be here. Retirement: after his attack, that had been his plan - his and Mila's. There had been more than enough put aside for it. And he would have retired according to plan if there'd been anything left of his life worth retiring to.

He had guarded his private life from the authorities, had not told them where he lived: no fixed address is what they had been forced to log against his name. Nor had he phoned Mila from the prison. Not even to tell her he was coming home. He did not want to take the slightest chance that his call might be traced.

That had been the worst shock of his life, coming after the long lonely bus ride from the prison, rolling away from that swine LaCoste, home to Mila through the night. The penthouse apartment dark and deserted - no Mila waiting. His first emotion upon seeing no light in the topmost windows of the highrise had been disappointment; how could he call it a home-coming without Mila?

A poorly secured clamp pulled suddenly loose, and with a tortured creak the conduit swayed a few inches out from the wall. Gorman caught his breath, halted. He clung to the pipe at the mercy of the fates. He waited for the screech of metal that would signal the start of his plunge. But after a moment the conduit seemed to stabilize. He began slowly to climb again. A concrete nail had pulled free, that was all. Poor craftsmanship. No one took pride in their work nowadays.

"I'm retiring," Gorman had repeated.

"So come out of retirement."

Gorman had kept on thinking about LaCoste's botched break-in.

"Just who was this target you so royally screwed up, anyway?" Gorman felt a twinge of curiosity about LaCoste's operation, even though he had no intention of climbing again. "What was it? Who was it?"

"What do you mean, who and what? What difference does that make? A mark, a target. Who cares?"

"A good set-up man cares about everything. He does his homework."

LaCoste's dark face turned poisonous.

"I done my homework! I knew everything I needed to. I knew the layout - living room, bedrooms, the whole floor plan. The alarms. I knew what the stuff in there was worth! My Lori knew before I went in - she seen it!" He drew back from Gorman with an injured look. "Don't tell me I never done my homework."

They sat in silence for a while, studying one another. LaCoste would have made a lousy cardplayer. His little eyes tumbled with his thoughts. His hatred was displayed on his face like a sign in a window. Finally he said, "I think I know why you're side-slipping me, Gorman. I can see right through you. Retiring - crap! That's not it at all. You're just plain ner-vous, aren't you? You don't want no more high work. You can't face it. You've lost your nerve. You're scared."

Hearing LaCoste put into words the fears that had hung wraithlike for so long in the dark at the back of his mind, had seemed to lend substance to them, make them more real. They crept out into reality to slip into the corners of the cell, behind the toilet, under the bunks, ready to come at him with their knives and hooks when the lights went out. He shuddered. Last night he'd dreamt he had fallen from the top of the CN Tower onto a wrought iron fence; there had been no sensation of falling, only the whistle of the air in his ears, long minutes of the ground rushing up at him with its row of sharpened spears.

LaCoste took a cigarette from his shirt, lit it with a practised snap of a Zippo lighter, blew smoke out of his nose and tipped his head to one side. All the time he didn't take his eyes off Gorman, watched him like a man who has just witnessed a metamorphosis. Busy eyes. Eyes that never kept still in their sockets.

LaCoste said, "Yeah. I pegged you wrong. I see that now. I'll have to get me somebody else. A younger guy. Somebody with guts."

Gorman's backhand seemed to lash out of its own volition. It caught the smaller man on the side of his oily face, snapped his head back and sent him spinning sideways off his bunk. But LaCoste was quick. Before he even hit the floor he had a shank in his hand. He seemed to have snatched the wicked blade from nowhere, like a conjuror producing a card.

His breath was ragged in his throat. "Do that once more, Gorman, and I'll kill you, so help me, God. Bulldog me again and I'll rip your throat out." He dragged himself like a wounded cur into his bunk. "You're making a big mistake," he said. "We got a good thing going, me and Lori. I'll retire one day with millions, and where'll you be?" He had lain hidden for a moment breathing heavily; then he had said, "I'll get you up on a building again. You'll climb for me yet, Gorman."

As it turned out, LaCoste had been right.

Gorman reached the top of the pipe. There was a wide rain trough here, flimsily attached. He eased himself over it gingerly, not wanting to cause the slightest sound. And then he was on the roof.

It was a roof of slate tile, with a slope of some thirty degrees. He would have to watch his footing here. A single slip and... But he wasn't going to think about that. He began to move forward, his Nikes finding marginal purchase on the tiles as he put each foot down, rubber soles sliding toward the eaves on the fog-slicked tile. One foot ahead of the other; that was how it was done. A huge bulk loomed out of the mist on his left; a cowling, something to do with the air conditioning; below it would be the network of ducts that he sought; they ran everywhere throughout the old building, a virtual freeway to a man who could climb and gain access. At the peak of the roof a wind-torn bit of flashing projected upwards and he had to step over it carefully.

As he straddled the building, one foot on either side of the peak, the fog lifted in the distance and he saw the city like a ten-mile dance of electric light at the foot of the sky, and just for a moment he felt the old thrill of satisfaction that climbing had given him once. A sense of power, of being on top of it all while the rest of the world crawled ant-like below.

Then the fog settled in again, snuffing out the sight. He moved on, angling down the perch of the roof this time, and in a few more minutes he came in sight of his objective - the dome that crowned the top of the main building. All access doors to the roof were routinely and carefully checked, but the dome - perhaps because it was thought to be impregnable - was ignored. Just one more tricky bit of climbing would bring Gorman up to it.

Where the two uneven wings of the main building came together there was a flat wall facing him, perhaps twenty feet high. It was featureless, without a handhold. But there was, he knew, a cornice that followed the older wall and adjoined a matching bit of stonework on the new wing; an effort by the builders of the newer extension to preserve architectural purity. It was as good as a sidewalk to Gorman, a causeway round the periphery of the blank gable-end.

He padded down the slope to the edge of the roof and without hesitation stepped over the eaves and onto the cornice. It wasn't much of a sidewalk, only eighteen inches wide. A trick of the wind tugged the fog away at that moment, and for an instant the ground was visible - a thread of highway far-off in the distance where tiny cars followed their lights. Without warning vertigo seized him. It took him in the gut, in the big tendons of his legs, making his body so weak and his knees jerk so violently he had to sit down fast on the brink of the eaves. He tried to swallow, found he had no spit in his mouth, tried to swallow again and trembled.

He heard LaCoste's needling voice echoing in his head: "You can't face it. You've lost your nerve. You're scared."

The wall of the main building dropped away vertically between his knees; he caught a glimpse a stone courtyard far below, a spidery black iron fence or railing which was so much like the one in his dream it made his head go around. Then the fog pushed back in, and he couldn't see the ground anymore, only a swelling of the mist a hundred feet below where it was given body by the sodium glow of the security lights in the forecourt. A shudder pierced him, a violent quaking that shook his entire frame. Perhaps it was worse not being able to see the ground. Too easy to believe the drop was even greater than it really was - more than a hundred feet, perhaps five hundred, a thousand feet, a mile ...

With his heart pounding fiercely, he drove these ideas off. Gradually he steadied himself. But still his body was slick with sweat - the night wind blowing cold upon his body freshened him. He got up, took a first step, and with the fingertips of his left hand trailing along the wall, slowly walked the cornice past the gable-end that had blocked him. Another fifteen steps brought him face on with a tall dormer window that cut upwards through the eaves and peaked high above the roof. Its limestone facing stood out eight inches from the facade, broken where the mortar had slipped from between the stones, an easy step ladder to the roof for a strong and limber man with a steady nerve, a man such as he had once been. His pulse still thumped harshly in his breast, but he went up the facing without missing a step.

Next he climbed the seam at which the dormer met the steep slope of the roof - much steeper than the roof of the lower wing, but he made it to the top. Once there he straddled the dormer like a boy on a fence row and paused to catch his breath.

He did not intend to fall if he could help it. He had done his home-work well on this one. He knew the dome was just above him; he had only to climb the steep gradient of roof tile to reach its base. Still, he did not trust himself to look up at it, even though he knew he must in order to orient himself with the unlocked trap. And if he did not look up at it, he would not see how the final stage of the climb should be done.

Slowly he tilted back his head, gripped the spine of the dormer more firmly, and opened his eyes. The sight that immediately filled his eyes took him instantly back to the Hotel George. The same panic squirmed again in his guts, clawing up into the back of this throat. Lit dimly by some scattered lights that shone below and behind him, the dome was a bulbous black mass. The mist had torn open to show him through one long rent the sky, and he saw quick grey clouds scudding above and behind the dome, their direction of motion oblique to the lights he had seen moving on the highway below. The two motions combined seemed to lend the entire rooftop a giddy twisting movement, and just as before he felt that the building had come alive beneath him.

He grit his teeth.

He must not give way to panic. Not this time. He must think about Mila. What poor Mila had endured was far worse than this. A fall to the courtyard below would be a merciful end by comparison. He forced himself to dredge up the scenes from that night...

... letting himself into their penthouse suite and finding its contents tumbled and tossed, disarranged first by the intruders and then, as he learned later, by the police. Fear had struck him as he surveyed the devastation - true fear. Fear for Mila. He had dashed into the bedroom calling for her, found it torn to pieces, a scene of violence. The wall safe behind the head of the bed hung open like a tiny gutted tomb.

Half-crazed he had dragged the building manager out of bed, a nervous little Rumanian who, alarmed at Gorman's state, had babbled almost hysterically to him about the break-in.

"It was months ago. They came from the outside, Mr. Gorman. Who would have thought it possible at such a height?"

"And Mila?" he had screamed, seizing the manager by his pyjamafront and hoisting him into the air. "What about Mila?"

The manager knew little. Only that the intruder had dealt her a heavy blow to the head. "She must have awakened and surprised him." They had wheeled her out on a gurney and down to a waiting ambulance. There had been much confusion. Policemen in uniforms and plainclothes. Questions, so many questions. But this the manager remembered: Mila had been whisked away to the hospital - perhaps the Misericordia, the one they called the Misery. Perhaps she was still there.

Gorman had driven like a madman through the city. And now, perched at the base of the dome, he recalled her as he had found her there:

Mila on the edge of a hospital bed so high her pale blue feet dangle half a foot above the floor. To her, a precipice, higher than any building. Her eyes peaceful, wide, but empty, two round limpid lakes devoid of animation. The delicate hand curling limply in his own; press it - no response. Asking questions and hearing no reply. Gorman had allowed the nursing staff the lead him trembling back to the elevator.

He had spent an hour pacing the dark streets among the tall houses around the hospital, stopping for long minutes to stare out over the river, his anguish for Mila steadily souring into a bitter rage, an emptiness in his gut that was a hunger for vengeance.

But first he must confirm his suspicions. This he could do. Three decades in the life's blood of the crime world gave him and advantage over even the most dedicated police detective. He went back to his car, drove into the core of the city and began his enquiries.

And so what now if he fell?

He opened his eyes again and stared long and hard up at the dome. He saw the thin lines of the maintenance trap etched in dark relief against its tiled skin. He pushed the thought of the abyss inches behind him from his mind, the yawning gulf, and got to his hands and knees. Then he stood. He climbed the steep slope determinedly to the foot of the dome, trod the great rings at its base like steps and started sure-footedly up the curve of the dome itself. As he rose above the protective peak of the roof, the wind suddenly quickened. It rippled his sleeves, snapped his collar at his neck, carried a trailing shirttail streaming behind him like the flag of all crimedom. He was engulfed in a misty turbulence. He crawled doggedly up the great inverted bowl of the dome like a fly. Fingers and toes; that's all you had. If they failed you, the ...

Better to think about Mila.

Think about the guilt - that was the worst.

Without warning the wind fell to nothing, as if it had been called to heel for afflicting the man who climbed like a cat. Gorman inched on up the curving surface. A moment later he was at the trap. If it was locked, if his contacts within had failed him, then his climb had been in vain.

But it was not locked.

The trap lifted easily, as had been arranged; he hoisted it open, climbed a few feet higher, took a last look out over the misted night, then stepped inside, onto the highest trestle of a steel catwalk. He lowered the trap behind him. He would be safe for a while now, able to catch his breath. This was the only place Security did not bother to check on their incessant patrols. It had the added advantage of being handy to the ducts. He needed the ducts. He slipped out the black rubber flashlight he always took with him on a job, black electrical tape encasing it in a tube of thin foam which would deaden its sound should it fall, and switched it on.

The steel catwalk he perched on was one used by maintenance workers who needed access to the roof; it was high above the floor, the uppermost of two levels below the dome. Now he moved quickly, padding down the steel rungs of the catwalk to the landing floor, then down a more substantial staircase to the attic below. There he went purposefully along a dirty corridor, bowing his head to clear the underside of the sloped roof he had scaled a moment ago. At the end, he pushed open a door and found himself in the equipment room which housed the huge metal plenums of the air conditioning ducts. Without hesitation he approached the first of these, unlatched a huge access panel which hinged outward like a door, clambered inside and shut himself in.

He knew what he must do. He knew the route. He had gone over it for months in his mind. He pressed his head and shoulders into one of the four openings which led from inside the plenum - the second from the left - and stretching full out on his belly with the flashlight flat out ahead of him, began to worm his way into the duct; the blowers would not come on for at least another hour - that too had been arranged. There was a thick smell of dust that made him want to cough. At one point a vertical shaft opened under his forearms, dropped away into the blackness like a well, and he had to bridge it with his body and drag himself across. Then a steeply falling slope led him down and down. Fifteen minutes took him to another horizontal passage. Following this, he counted the branchings in the yellow light of the torch, then finally turned sharp right. He switched off the torch, wormed his way forward again as quietly as possible, then came to a stop at a steel grating.

A feeble light glimmered beyond.

He was absolutely sure of his position now.

He took hold of the grating, hooked his fingers into its grid, shifted it gently forward, rotated it slightly, pulled it inside. The rivets which originally secured it had been filed through many months ago; when he had been thinking of escape.

The scene below him was familiar. The stairwell at the end of tier four. The door that led into the range itself was off-stop, that too had been managed. He sucked in his breath. He knew the scents. Even the sounds were old acquaintances; the low snores and grunts, the thin brittle coughs reverberating off steel and stone. The heels of the strolling guard ticking distantly somewhere like a clock, the guard who would be nowhere near the quietly unlocked cell where LaCoste now lay in Gorman's old upper bunk, flat on his back the way he always slept, mouth hanging open, eyes shut up tight.

LaCoste the mastermind.

The man who did his homework - except that he didn't even know who he was robbing.

Gorman eased himself silently out of the duct.

The Tamerlane Crutch

JAMES POWELL

A master stylist and an ingenious plot maker, James Powell is arguably Canada's most highly regarded writer of short crime fiction. He is a multi-Arthur Award nominee- including a nomination, in 1991, for this story from Cold Blood III. *In addition, Jim is a winner of the Ellery Queen Readers' Award and co-recipient of the CWC's Derrick Murdoch Award in 1992. This sly and dexterous story combines two enduring but totally different classics into something unique and unforgettable. Jim's stories appeared in the* Cold Blood *series only twice, but they raised the level of both those volumes markedly. In 1990, some of the finest examples of Powell's early work were collected in the critically acclaimed book,* A Murder Coming.

Marley was dead, to begin with. There was no doubt whatever about that. Old Marley was as dead as a doornail. And when a man's partner is killed he's supposed to do something about it. It doesn't make any difference what you thought of him. He was your partner and you're supposed to do something about it. Ebenezer Scrooge, in nightcap, dressing gown and slippers, took another swallow of lukewarm gruel before moving closer to the tiny fire in the grate. The fog creeping through the keyhole had brought the frosty night in with it. Staring down into the flames the miser reviewed the events of the calamitous day. How had it all begun?

Early that cold, bleak morning while Scrooge sat busy in his countinghouse office, door ajar to keep an eye on his clerk, Bob Cratchit, who would rather warm his fingers at the candle than copy letters, the door to the foggy courtyard had flown open. The handsome middle-aged woman who stepped inside had excited and gladsome eyes although the golden hair that peeked from under her bonnet carried a heavy burden of silver. All this Scrooge caught in one glance before returning to his banker's book. Scrooge had nothing against a pretty face. But such a visitor at this season usually meant he was about to be dunned by another charity such as this year's madcap project to provide every poor, able-bodied child in London with an orange on Christmas morning and every crippled one with a crutch. Scrooge regretted having instructed Cratchit to turn such busybodies away. He should've handled the matter himself. "Are there no prisons?" he'd have asked. "And the Union workhouses, are they still in operation? The tread-mill and the Poor Law are in full vigour then?" And what could anyone answer to that?

He was interrupted from this pleasant reverie by Bob Cratchit. "A lady to see you, sir," said his clerk, adding a hasty, "on a matter of busi-ness."

"Have I the pleasure of addressing Mr. Scrooge or Mr. Marley?" asked the woman in a musical voice.

"Marley has departed," said Scrooge, without rising from his stool.

"My name is Dirndl Wunderlich, Mr. Scrooge. I understand you are a miser, quite a tight-fisted hand at the grindstone."

Scrooge bowed modestly, at once pleased and made wary by the flat-tery.

"I have arrived in your country in search of a man, a Muscovite who has come into possession of an heirloom belonging to my family. I am prepared to pay you the sum of twenty guineas for its recovery."

Scrooge sighed. "Let us not waste our time, Madame," he said. "We misers are not in the business of recovering things belonging to others." As he spoke he searched among the papers on his desk until he found the ad-dress of Messrs. Spade and Archer, two gentlemen considerably in arrears in what they owed the countinghouse. Making a mental note never again to loan out money to a man who called him "Sweetheart" Scrooge said, "How-ever let me put you in touch with two private investigators who will handle this matter quite to your satisfaction."

"Such people do not work on Christmas Eve, Mr. Scrooge," insisted Dirndl Wunderlich. "Misers do. Indeed, I understand you are a master at the art of extracting your due by threatening people with the law. I wish to rent that skill."

"For the sum of twenty guineas," added Scrooge.

The woman gave an eager nod. "Come, I'll lead you to the man this very minute. A while ago I left my hotel in search of a restaurant selling those new what-do-you-call-'ems, the fried meat patty on a bun."

Scrooge scowled. "Bah, hamburg," he said for he did not care for London's latest eating craze.

Miss Wunderlich continued. "Anyway, by some stroke of luck who should I see hobbling along in the fog ahead of me in Piccadilly Circus but my fat Muscovite. I followed at a distance, hoping he'd lead me back to his hotel where I could set someone like yourself on him. But he just kept walking around and around Piccadilly Circus. Finally I decided to chance it and dash here. If we move quickly ..."

As she spoke the outer door flew open and there, an apparition against the palpable brown air swirling in the courtyard, stood a moaning figure with a face like a door knocker, a figure weighed down by chains, ledgers, padlocked cash boxes and heavy purses wrought in steel. Scrooge had always regretted Marley's tendency to flaunt his miserliness. "My partner," he explained to Miss Wunderlich.

"The departed Marley's ghost!" she gasped.

"Hardly," said Scrooge. "Jacob departed for home a while back to get some hot salt in a black sock for his toothache." Indeed Marley sported such a poultice in a folded kerchief bound round his head and chin. "Come in, Jacob," invited Scrooge. As he outlined Miss Wunderlich's offer, he gestured at his ledgers and added, "I've got my hands full here. But a bad toothache'll put you in just the mood to shake a Muscovite loose from ill-gotten gains."

Marley rolled his eyes and, groaning like a spectre, he followed the woman back out into the fog.

Several hours later an astonished Scrooge was following a police constable's broad back through the cold, bleak, biting weather on his way to identify a murder victim believed to be his partner. Marley murdered? Jacob Marley dead?

The lamp outside the police station was a ruddy smear upon the fog. Inside the Day Inspector stood like a maitre d' beside his reservations book. That gentleman put down his pen and, giving Scrooge a look that said, "We know your kind, Mr. Scrooge. You'll get the table you deserve from us," he escorted the miser to an outbuilding in the yard where Marley's body lay, eyes weighted down with two large pennies. "Found in an alley behind the Bristol Hotel. Do you know it, sir?"

Scrooge nodded. "A fleabag."

The Day Inspector's solemn nod confirmed this. "You will note, sir," he continued, "that the victim was shot twice. Once in the ankle and once in the heart. A peculiar thing that." Here the Day Inspector withdrew to give Scrooge a few moments to mourn his late partner.

Scrooge looked down at the dead body. Well, Jacob, he thought, you've been murdered. Tell me, what would you do about it if I was lying there and you were standing here? Nothing. There's no profit in sentiment. So why do I feel I should do something? Scrooge shrugged and, pocketing the two coins from the dead man's eyes as Marley would have done, he returned to the police station proper. The Day Inspector was waiting at the front door. As Scrooge passed the man held out his palm without speaking. Scrooge dutifully deposited the two large pennies there. Yes, they did know him around here.

Outside the fog and darkness had thickened. People ran about with flaring links, proffering their services to go before horses in carriages, and conduct them on their way. Foggier yet, and colder! The gruffy old bell in the ancient tower of the church near the countinghouse struck the hour with tremulous vibrations as if its frozen teeth were chattering in its frozen head. In the main street before the courtyard labourers repairing the gas pipes had lighted a great fire in a brazier, round which a ragged party of boys were gathered, warming their hands and winking their eyes before the blaze in rapture.

As Scrooge passed a small man who had been watching these boys with considerable interest separated himself from the holly sprigs and berries of a poulterer's window and fell in step with the miser. "Mr. Scrooge," said the man in a high pitched thin voice, "My name is Niles Truck. I am trying to recover a crutch that has been - shall we say? - mislaid. I thought, and hoped, you could assist me."

Scrooge looked Truck up and down. He was a small-boned dark man of medium height with Levantine features. He wore gloves of yellow leather, fawn half-gaiters and a tight wool coat. The miser shook his head. "A person mislays a bumbershoot or a parasol or a walking stick," he insisted. "Not a crutch."

"Nevertheless, I'm prepared to pay one hundred guineas for its recovery," said Truck, as they turned into the countinghouse courtyard. "No questions asked."

"Who says I've got your damn crutch?" snapped Scrooge.

Truck answered by ramming a blunderbuss barrel into the miser's kidneys. "Please clasp your hands together behind your neck," ordered the Levantine, prodding the miser forward through the countinghouse's chill outer room to the chill inner office. With whining complaints about the English climate, Truck tried to light the candle with a trembling match.

Scrooge chose that moment to spin around, knock the blunderbuss aside and apply the Pennypincher's Nerve Pinch, one of the finest moves in the misers' martial arts arsenal. Truck slumped where he stood, the weapon slipping from his fingers. Holding the man up with one hand Scrooge rummaged through his pockets with the other, dumping their contents on the ledger open on his sloping desk. Then he forced Truck up onto a high stool and left him to recover. Rummaging through the items on the desk he found a Greek passport that identified Truck as a currant merchant. (Scrooge wondered if the man ever dealt in a new strain called the Humboldt, having himself lost a bundle a year of two ago investing in Humboldt currant futures. "Bah, Humboldt," he scowled.) The contents of the pockets also included a paper cone of violet pastilles and an advertising broadside. Sucking on a pastille Scrooge perused the announcement for the Christmas pantomime entitled "Ali Bow-Wow and the Forty Fleas" to be performed by the resident company in the lobby of the Bristol Hotel. Here Truck groaned, stirred and might have fallen from his perch if Scrooge hadn't cuffed him awake. "All right, Mr. Truck," he snarled. "Spill everything or you'll get another taste of the pinch."

Truck licked his lower lip nervously. Then the thin high-pitched words came tumbling out. "I was taking my morning constitutional in Piccadilly Circus when I saw her, Dirndl Wunderlich, the woman who stole the Tamerlane Crutch from me."

"The what?" demanded Scrooge.

"A priceless jewel-studded crutch with a provenance lost in the mists of history," said Truck, adding in a voice turned shrill, "But it belongs to me. It's mine! I paid for it with three years of shame, humiliation and ..." Strong emotion choked off the Levantine's words. He breathed deeply several times and went on in a more subdued voice. "Keeping my distance I followed the thieving woman around and around Piccadilly Circus for a good hour hoping she'd lead me to the crutch. But our first stop was when she broke off and led me here. Then I followed her and this old guy wearing a lot of chains and cash boxes back to Piccadilly Circus. Then they headed off to a rundown part of town and a hotel called the Bristol. Well, I waited in the street but they never reappeared. They must've slipped out the back." As he spoke Truck poked two fingers under his shirt and scratched absently. "So I came back here, hoping to pick up her trail again. I ..." Truck's eyes followed Scrooge's gaze as it moved from his scratching fingers to the broadside about Ali Bow-Wow and the Forty Fleas.

"You lying Levantine ankle-shooter," snarled Scrooge, knocking the little man off the stool with a backhand slap. "You followed Marley into the hotel and out the back door. First you shot him in the ankle so he couldn't escape. Then you reloaded and shot him in the head." Scrooge advanced on the prostrate man. "Listen," he said, "when a man's partner is killed he's supposed to so something about it. It doesn't make any ..."

"But why would I shoot him in the ankle first?" whined Truck, pushing himself backwards along the floor with his heels. "Why wouldn't I just shoot him in the head and get it over with?"

Scrooge stopped. The man had a point.

Truck sat up and rubbed his cheek. "Boy, I don't know how that 'ankle-shooting Levantine' crack ever got started. We really aren't that way," he insisted. "But, you're right, Mr. Scrooge. After a bit I did go into the hotel lobby. There was a very shaggy dog dressed in a big green turban and a red vest lying in one corner of the lobby while a modest crowd stared at it through rented magnifying glasses. When I saw the place had a back door to it I hurried out into the alley. But they were long gone. Then I saw a foot sticking out of the doorway. It was your partner, dead as a doornail."

"And where does the fat Muscovite fit in?"

Truck's olive features took on a grey cast and his eyes filled with fear. He scrambled to his feet. "Gutmanov? Gutmanov here?"

Jabbing a bony finger into Truck chest Scrooge urged, "Do yourself a big favour. Tell me what's going on."

Truck thought a bit. Then he shrugged and told his story. If the man was to be believed he had spent his life tracking the whereabouts of a mysterious object called the Tamerlane Crutch, collecting and cataloguing any shred of information, each rumour and every story no matter how wild. Suddenly one day all signs pointed to the island of Malta where a reclusive multimillionaire named Constantine lived with his very extensive crutch collection - no two alike - kept from rival collectors in a well-guarded vault deep in the cellars of his impregnable home. But Truck thought he'd concocted a way to penetrate the Constantine vault. To this end he spent three years touring the Mediterranean as a receiver with a troupe of low vaudevillians. Night after night he took custard pies in his face, was beaten about the head with rubber chickens and endured having his suspenders snipped with big shears to expose his bright underdrawers. At last the troupe was booked into Malta's Valletta Opera House. Constantine had a box seat for opening night for, as Truck had calculated, any man with so large a collection of rubber crutches would be a big fan of low vaudeville and could be expected to come backstage after the performance to meet the cast. But to Truck's dismay he saw Dirndl Wunderlich in the audience. If she'd follow him to Malta then Gutmanov, the fat Muscovite, couldn't be far behind.

Truck had no time to lose. After the performance he showed enough interest in rubber crutches to earn an invitation to see Constantine's collection
that very night.

The vault resembled a curative religious shrine with crutches hanging everywhere. After putting Constantine and the heavily armed watchman in stitches by stumbling around with rubber crutches in his armpit
Truck was rewarded with a conducted tour of the collection. The object he
coveted so much was not behind glass with the finer pieces. Disguised with
black paint it stood among others in an open barrel labelled 'Assorted Novelty Items'. The crutch was tagged, 'Fifteenth Century item from Samarkand
vicinity. Black enamel over raised baguette and cabochon design.'

As he bid the millionaire good night Truck mentioned he had a crutch,
an old family heirloom, which he would like to donate to the collection.
When Constantine expressed interest Truck rushed back to his hotel and
working from memory built a reasonable facsimile of the crutch in the barrel. "Fifteenth Century Samarkand, you say?" said the doubtful collector
the next evening. "Well, I could be wrong but I think I've got one of those.
But let's take a look." Back down in the vault the millionaire quickly located the crutch in the barrel. "Thank you very much, young man," said
Constantine with a shake of his head. "But 'no two alike' is my motto."
Then while the watchman tried to doze in his chair in the corner and
Constantine demonstrated some of his finer musical crutches Truck deftly
switched his imitation for the real Tamerlane Crutch.

Back out on the narrow winding street it seemed to Truck that every
passerby's glance pierced the crutch's black enamel to the treasure beneath,
every shadow harboured a gang of thieves and each footstep behind him
spoke menace. He sought out the brighter streets and came back to his hotel
by a roundabout way. But as he stepped inside his room he was struck a
great blow on the head. When he recovered consciousness the crutch was
gone. The smell of Dirndl Wunderlich's edelweiss perfume still hung in the
air. So the Levantine set out after her and his search had brought him to
London.

At the conclusion of the story Scrooge showed Mr. Niles Truck the
door, saying, "You want your damn crutch? Be at my apartment tonight at
the stroke of twelve." Then, alone, he rubbed his stubbly chin and resolved
to discover the identity of Marley's killer. A man should certainly do what
he can to help a murdered partner find rest - provided it didn't cost him
anything. Would Truck come at the appointed hour? If he did, Scrooge
suspected that Dirndl Wunderlich and the fat Muscovite wouldn't be far
behind.

Scrooge took another sip of gruel, scowled and spat it into the fire.
The damn stuff was stone cold. How long had he been sitting there? And
why did misers have to drink gruel? Why not a whisky of the Scottish
persuasion? Scrooge had to smile at himself. No. Gruel came with the
miser territory. He'd known that from the start. Years ago whenever his
schoolmates talked about what they'd be when they grew up he'd always
said, "A miser." How they'd laughed! Yet one of them wanted to be a
surgeon and cut people up and another a soldier and blow strangers' arms
off and a third a judge who'd make men dance at the end of a rope.

Scrooge pulled still closer to the fire but found small comfort there
until among the little tongues of flame another scene from the past came to
life again. He saw himself, Scrooge the young man, sitting in a bower with
a beautiful young woman. It was Belle! Dearest Belle. No, he'd never
forget that moment. She had just broken off their engagement. She wouldn't
marry an aspiring miser. "But, Belle," he'd insisted, "you should love a
man for what he is, not how he makes his livelihood. Come marry me. Be
a miser's wife and live in a miser's house with all the miser's little children
running around inside. Oh, what fun we'll have!" But Belle didn't share
Scrooge's conviction that miserliness and laughter could go hand in hand.
Had she been right? Could Scrooge's whole life have been a mistake?

At first, after their break-up, he'd fallen in with a crowd of young
spendthrifts and prodigals. Who else would accept a man who never bought
a round of drinks or picked up a dinner check? And when Scrooge's com-
panions grew low on money he obligingly loaned them funds at as reasonable rates as they'd have found anywhere. But that man spoke true who
said there was no better way to lose friends than by lending them money.
Yes, being a miser proved a lonelier life than he'd expected. So he'd gone
into partnership with Marley, thinking two misers might get along famously.
But Dutch treat was tedious. Bah, humdrum, thought Scrooge. Yet in his
heart of hearts he still thought that misers could have fun, too.

Suddenly the chimes of a neighbouring church struck twelve and
roused Scrooge from his reverie. He'd left the apartment door unlocked for
Truck. But even before the chimes died away the miser heard a foot and an
active crutch approaching from room to room. Suddenly the door flew
open and an immensely fat man with glossy cheeks, a tall fur hat and one
foot swathed in bandages limped into the room with the help of a black
crutch. The man's face brightened when he saw Scrooge. "Allow me to
introduce myself, sir. I am Caspar Gutmanov. We begin well, sir. A man
who locks his doors reveals a suspicious nature. Suspicion breeds treach-

ery." The Muscovite looked around the room warily. "I'd hoped to find Mr. Niles Truck here. He must've given me the slip along the way."

"I thought he'd get here first, too," admitted Scrooge, gesturing the fat man into a chair. "Without him to lead you, I'm surprised you knew where to come."

"Fortunately I saw a door knocker down below that was the image of your partner Jacob Marley."

Scrooge bowed to the man's power of observation. Then he suggested, "If Truck's given you the slip maybe he's figured out the Piccadilly Circus business, too."

"Gad, dovechick, you amaze me," smiled the Muscovite with admiration. "Yes, perhaps you're right. A droll thing the Piccadilly Circus business. You see, this is the season when I most like to lug my belly out into the streets, gouty foot and all, if that curse is upon me. I really want the little people to see me as they rush about with their widow's mites and sweaty farthings trying to scrape something together for Christmas. I want them to know that every single night of the year I consume ten of their petty Christmas dinners. Yes, I like that. But today as I walked in Piccadilly Circus who should I see mincing along ahead of me but Niles Truck, the very man I outwitted to obtain this." Gutmanov banged his crutch on the floor. "To see what he was up to I trailed him around and around Piccadilly Circus and then to your countinghouse where I discovered Truck was following a disgruntled ex-employee of mine, a Miss Wunderlich. When she and your partner Jacob Marley hurried back to where we'd started with Truck on their tail I followed along behind. After we'd made two or three more swings around Piccadilly Circus, I following Truck and Truck following Miss Wunderlich, I realized to my amazement that Miss Wunderlich was following me. How could I elude her without losing Truck? I decided to lead the way to the Hotel Bristol, an establishment which had a rear entrance. By slipping out the back and hobbling around to the front I hoped to escape her while taking up position behind Truck. But Marley knew about the back door. Out in the alley he shouted to Miss Wunderlich, 'You go that way. I'll go this.' So I ducked into a doorway hoping he'd walk right by."

"But he didn't," said Scrooge. "So you shot him in the ankle with that pistol you've got hidden in your foot bandages. When he fell to the ground you reloaded and shot him in the head. But you won't get away with it. I'll see to that. Listen, when a man's partner's killed he's supposed to do something about it. It doesn't make any difference what ..."

"Dovechick," said Gutmanov, "I could've killed your partner with one shot. Nothing easier. He was a miser after all." Scrooge's incredulous laughter made the fat man shrug. Then, as if to change the subject, he said, "Ah, my dear fellow I believe you've dropped a sixpence there on the floor."

Scrooge bent over quickly. Then, with his cheek against the floor, he found himself staring down the barrel of the bandaged foot. The Russian's heels were cocked. Scrooge knew that by tapping them together the man could trigger the hidden gun.

"Yes, I could've killed Marley," smiled Gutmanov. "But I just wounded him in the ankle. I wanted to get out of there and get back on Truck's trail."

Scrooge glared at the man. "A crime like that could mean transportation to New South Wales. Sydney."

"Capital," chortled the fat man. "Very well, call the police. I am an agent of the Tsar of Russia. All they can do is deport me and my crutch back to my homeland." He smiled at the thought, stroked the black enamel and said, "Let me tell you about this crutch. Four hundred years ago a mighty warrior called Tamerlane or Timur the Lame held sway over all the lands and peoples from the Volga to the Persian Gulf and from the Hellespont to the Ganges. After each of his great military victories his subjects presented him with a ceremonial crutch decorated with precious inlay and priceless gems, but none more sumptuous than the one after his defeat of the Ottoman Sultan Bazajet whom Tamerlane afterwards carried about with him imprisoned in an iron cage for all to see." While he spoke Gutmanov took out a pocket knife and began to scrape at the black enamel as if to prove his words. "So valuable was this crutch that even Tamerlane, who was not shy about such things, wrapped it in tissue paper and put in away for special occasions. Perhaps this was why it alone survived the turmoil following Tamerlane's death.

"Oh, many like Niles Truck have pursued the crutch across the centuries just for the monetary worth of the thing. My Imperial master cares little for that. But he knows that every wild tribe from Samarkand southward would follow the man who possessed this symbol of ancient authority to hell and beyond. With the Tamerlane Crutch as our battle flag Russia will sweep down through India, conquer Burma and, avoiding the invincible defenses of the Great Wall, strike a mortal blow at China's soft underbelly."

Here the fat man brushed away the enamel scrapings to reveal a bright blue jewel. He purred approvingly and continued his story. "Well, if anyone was going to learn the whereabouts of the crutch I knew it would be Truck. So I hired people to keep a constant watch on him, not least among them Miss Wunderlich. The night he stole the crutch I was waiting for him outside Constantine's and followed him back to his hotel. But I found him unconscious on the floor of his room, the crutch at his side. I took it and fled across the rooftops, hurrying down to the harbour where I signed on as a deckhand aboard a ship bound for London under charter to the Valletta Crutch and Citrus Exporting Company."

Here Gutmanov offered the crutch for Scrooge's examination. But he stopped abruptly and frowned down at it. With a loud curse he fell to scraping wildly, his fat face trembling like an outraged pudding. Then he dropped the crutch, moaning, "They're not jewels! They're violet pastilles!"

The clatter of the crutch had scarcely died away when Truck appeared in the doorway blunderbuss drawn. "You will please clasp your hands behind your necks, gentlemen," hissed the Levantine. Keeping his eyes fixed on them he came into the room and picked up the crutch. Fondling it lovingly he told Gutmanov, "When I heard you behind me in the fog, I ducked into an alley and let you get ahead of me. But before I could kill you and take my treasure you turned in here." Truck aimed his weapon at the fat Muscovite's chest. "Well, when it comes to dying, one place is as good as ..." Suddenly Truck felt the stickiness of the pastilles in his warm fingers. He looked down. "But this isn't the Tamerlane Crutch," he whined indignantly, "It's my fake!"

High heels approached through the apartment. "Quick, you two," urged Scrooge, "into that room over there." They obeyed, Truck handing over the crutch so the gouty Muscovite could hobble quickly across the floor. The door had scarcely closed when Dirndl Wunderlich, erect and alert, swept into the room. But when she saw Scrooge was alone she faltered and, it seemed to Scrooge, her hair took on more silver. Then she got a grip on herself. "I'm sorry about what happened to Marley," she said. "I didn't know Gutmanov was armed. You lost a partner. I lost my last chance to hit it big."

"The Tamerlane Crutch, you mean?" asked Scrooge. "Was that why you killed Marley?"

Dirndl Wunderlich turned those wonderful eyes on him for a moment. Then she said, "All right, I killed him." She licked her lips anxiously. "Look, there he was writhing on the ground, one hand around his ankle, the other holding onto that damn toothache of his. And me with the priceless crutch slipping from my grasp. I shouted for him to tell me which way Gutmanov'd gone. But his own pain was all he was thinking of. In a rage I gave him one of Mother Wunderlich's Lead Toothache Pills right in the noggin." She hung her head contritely. "I guess the laugh was on me because later I realized we'd all been following each other. I didn't have to kill Marley. By sticking close to Truck I'd have been sure to pick up

Gutmanov's trail again. But now they've both given me the slip. It's all over."

"Why tell me?" asked Scrooge.

"Because I'm not as young as I used to be," said Dirndl Wunderlich. "Because I need to settle down in some cozy little business. You're short one partner. I've got a little money set by and some jewels. I could get the hang of misering. 'Scrooge and Wunderlich', doesn't that have a lilt to it? Of course, that'd just be around the office. At home it'd be Ebenezer and Dirndl, Dirndl and Ebenezer. What do you say?"

Ebenezer and Dirndl? Damn, Scrooge liked the sound of it. Could life be granting him this one last chance to grab his dream of miser happiness? Perhaps. But first he had to explain that she'd killed his partner for a piece of wood studded with violet pastilles.

Dirndl's eyes grew wide as he spoke. Now they narrowed. "Listen," she said, "that night in Malta when the Tamerlane Crutch was stolen Gutmanov had ordered me to stand watch outside Truck's hotel. I remember seeing this skulky type wearing a long cape and a slouch hat down over his eyes slip into the hotel. I even remember remarking to myself, 'Dirndl, there goes a cape big enough to hide a crutch under.' At first I thought it was Truck. But he showed up a few minutes later, crutch and all. Gutmanov arrived a bit later just in time to pass the man in the cape coming out of the hotel. Now my little plan had been to wait for the fat Muscovite to come back out and then trade him one of Mother Wunderlich's Lead Barter Tokens for the Tamerlane Crutch. But Gutmanov skipped out over the rooftops. When I finally went up to Truck's room the little man was unconscious on the floor and the crutch was gone."

"I don't get it," admitted Scrooge.

"What's to get? Constantine spotted the switch, beat Truck back to the hotel, knocked him out and switched the crutches back. But Gutmanov didn't know that. When he found Truck unconscious he stole the fake. That means Constantine's still got the real one."

There was blunderbuss play in the other room. When Dirndl and Scrooge burst through the door they found the fat Muscovite dead on the floor under the open window with the Levantine's body stretched across his. "Looks like they heard you," said Scrooge. "Gutmanov tried to get a head start for Malta. Truck stopped him dead but made the mistake of leaning over his victim to make sure. Gutmanov still had a heel tap left in his gouty foot."

"But don't you see what this means?" cried Dirndl. "That means we're the only ones left who know where the Tamerlane Crutch is."

"Except for Constantine," insisted Scrooge.

"I rather think Mr. Constantine thought he was just getting one of his crutches back from some thieving collector," said Dirndl. "No, only you and I know it's the Tamerlane Crutch. We'll work the years necessary to get another crack at it."

Suddenly Scrooge understood. "You mean custard pies and the whole bit?"

"A small price to pay," said Dirndl. "The Tamerlane Crutch'll make us the miser Emperor and miser Empress of India and China. And, oh, what fun we'll have!"

Scrooge smiled sadly. No, it was too late for that now. "Listen, Dirndl," he said, "when a man's partner's killed he's supposed to do something about it. It doesn't ..." Here there was a sound of many flat footsteps and policemen burst into the room. The clock said ten minutes to one. Scrooge muttered darkly. He'd told them to come at one on the dot. He handed Dirndl over to them, resigned that he'd never get to give his big speech.

Scrooge retired to his four-poster, snuffed out the candle flame and fell into a sound sleep. But his late partner's spirit was not quite laid to rest. Scrooge dreamed that Marley's ghost took him by the elbow and, both invisible, they flew out of night's darkness into the brightness of Christmas Day and flitted all about the city looking in at revellers' windows. They watched the Lord Mayor, aided by his fifty cooks and fifty butlers, keeping Christmas as a Lord Mayor's household should. And they visited Camden Town and Bob Cratchit's little house where they found Scrooge's clerk serving up some hot mixture compounded with gin and lemons which simmered in a jug on the hob. "A toast!" he cried. "I give you, Mr. Scrooge, the Founder of the Feast!"

"What a fool Bob Cratchit was," thought Scrooge. "Was there ever such a goose?"

Here Tiny Tim, the Cratchits' little crippled son, tottering happily about the room with the charity crutch he'd found in his Christmas stocking, cried out a joyful, "God help us everyone!"

Marley's ghost moaned agreement, squeezing Scrooge's forearm to draw attention to the crippled boy, his door knocker of a face giving his partner a meaningful look. Scrooge nodded. Yes, he understood.

Grinning eagerly, Jacob Marley's ghost rushed Scrooge away from the light of Christmas Day and back into the darkness from which they'd come.

Scrooge awoke from this crowded dream with the sunlight lying heavy on the floor of his bedroom, a smile on his face and the sure conviction that he had smuggled a very important discovery from the land of sleep. But what had it been? Ah, yes. All that flying about from window to window had inspired him. He'd design and market a contraption, a kind of magic window frame for the kingdom's poor to set in the middle of their modest living rooms and use it to peek in at the dining rooms of their betters. Yes, he, Ebenezer Scrooge, could bring about a frugal world where one goose could as good as feed ten thousand people and the nightly joys of one small prosperous jocular family could supply the domestic pleasure of an entire nation. And every few minutes tradesmen would pay Scrooge for the privilege of appearing in the window to hawk their wares. Scrooge was warming his hands at that happy thought when the whole thing evaporated as the fantasies of sleep do in the morning light. "Magic window frames for the poor? What a far-fetched idea! What humbug!" thought Scrooge.

The miser sat on the edge of the bed and shook his head, still haunted by his dream. Then he remembered old Marley's ghost pointing out Tiny Tim to him. That was it! With a whoop of joy Scrooge ran to the window, opened it and put out his head. "You there," he called to a child he recognized who was passing by sucking on an orange. "You're the talkative boy, aren't you?"

"I'll tell the world," said the boy.

"An intelligent boy," declared Scrooge. "And, do you know where my clerk, Bob Cratchit, lives?"

"I'll tell the world."

"Then run there at once. Tell him Mr. Scrooge says a crutch worth its weight in jewels was mistakenly mixed in among those distributed to the crippled poor this morning. Tell him to expect offers for Tiny Tim's crutch but not to sell it until Mr. Scrooge puts his bid in. Hurry now. There'll be sixpence in it for you if you get back here before I change my mind."

Scrooge closed the window and laughed out loud. Yes, within the hour all London would know the news and be bidding up those crutches. With one glorious lie Scrooge had accomplished more for the city's crippled poor than any charity subscription. And it hadn't cost him a penny.

"A Merry Christmas to us all!" cried the miser. Then with a gleeful laugh Ebenezer Scrooge, of Scrooge and Marley, leaped into the air and kicked his skinflint heels.

Fan Mail

PETER ROBINSON

Peter is one of the most popular and respected crime writers Canada has ever produced. His award winning, bestselling Alan Banks novels have brought him international acclaim. Peter's first published short story was this one from Cold Blood II. *It was also an honour to be able to publish the first Alan Banks short story, "Anna Said..." in* Cold Blood IV. *In 1991, Peter's story "Innocence" from* Cold Blood III, *won him his first Arthur Ellis Award. Since then, he's won twice more – for Best Novel in 1992 for* Past Reason Hated *and in 1997 for* Innocent Graves. *"Fan Mail" was unjustly overlooked in the Arthur judging in 1990. It's a brooding character study that features the gripping storytelling that has become Pete's trademark.*

The letter arrived one sunny Thursday morning in August, along with a Visa bill and a royalty statement. Dennis Quilley carried the mail out to the deck of his Beaches home, stopping by the kitchen on the way to pour himself a gin and tonic. He had already been writing for three hours straight, and he felt he deserved a drink.

First he looked at the amount of the royalty cheque, then he put aside the Visa bill and picked up the letter carefully, as if he were a forensic expert investigating it for prints. Postmarked Toronto, and dated four days earlier, it was addressed in a small, precise hand and looked as if it had been written with a fine-nibbed calligraphic pen. But the postal code was different; that had been hurriedly scrawled in with a ball-point. Whoever it was,

Quilley thought, had probably got his name from the telephone directory and had then looked up the code in the post office just before mailing.

Pleased with his deductions, Quilley opened the letter. Written in the same neat and manner hand as the address, it said:

Dear Mr. Quilley,

Please forgive me for writing to you at home like this. I know you must be very busy, and it is inexcusable of me to intrude on your valuable time. Believe me, I would not do so if I could think of any other way.

I have been a great fan of your work for many years now. As a collector of mysteries, too, I also have first editions of all your books. From what I have read, I know you are a clever man, and, I hope, just the man to help me with my problem.

For the past twenty years, my wife has been making my life a misery. I put up with her for the sake of the children, but now they have all gone to live their own lives. I have asked her for a divorce, but she just laughed in my face. I have decided, finally, that the only way out is to kill her, and that is why I am seeking your advice.

You may think this is insane of me, especially saying it in a letter, but it is just a measure of my desperation. I would quite understand it if you went straight to the police, and I am sure they would find me and punish me. Believe me, I've thought about it. Even that would be preferable to the misery I must suffer day after day.

If you can find it in your heart to help a devoted fan in his hour of need, please meet me on the roof lounge of the Park Plaza Hotel on Wednesday, August 19 at two p.m. I have taken the afternoon off work and will wait longer if for any reason you are delayed. Don't worry, I will recognize you easily from your photo on the dust-jackets of your books.

Yours, in hope,
A Fan.

The letter slipped from Quilley's hand. He couldn't believe what he'd just read. He was a mystery writer -- he specialized in devising ingenious murders -- but for someone to assume that he did the same in real life was absurd. Could it be a practical joke?

He picked up the letter and read through it again. The man's whining tone and cliched style seemed sincere enough, and the more Quilley thought about it, the more certain he became that none of his friends was sick enough to play such a joke.

Assuming that it was real then, what should he do? His impulse was to crumple up the letter and throw it away. But should he go to the police? No. That would be a waste of time. The real police were a terribly dull and literal-minded lot. They would probably think he was seeking publicity.

He found that he had screwed up the sheet of paper in his fist, and he was just about to toss it aside when he changed his mind. Wasn't there another option? Go. Go and meet the man. Find out more about him. Find out if he was genuine. Surely there would be no obligation in that? All he had to do was turn up at the Park Plaza at the appointed time and see what happened.

Quilley's life was fine -- no troublesome woman to torment him, plenty of money (mostly from American sales), a beautiful lakeside cottage near Huntsville, a modicum of fame, the esteem of his peers -- but it had been rather boring of late. Here was an opportunity for adventure of a kind. Besides, he might get a story idea out of the meeting. Whey not go and see?

He finished his drink and smoothed the letter on his knee. He had to smile at that last bit. No doubt the man would recognize him from his book-jacket photo, but it was an old one and had been retouched in the first place. His cheeks had filled out a bit since then, and his thinning hair had acquired a sprinkling of grey. Still, he thought, he was a handsome man for fifty: handsome, clever and successful.

Smiling, he picked up both letter and envelope and went back to the kitchen in search of matches. There must be no evidence.

* * * * *

Over the next few days, Quilley hardly gave a thought to the mysterious letter. As usual in summer, he divided his time between writing in Toronto, where he found the city worked as a stimulus, and weekends at the cottage. There, he walked in the woods, chatted to locals in the lodge, swam in the clear lake and idled around getting a tan. Evenings, he would open a bottle of chardonnay, reread P.G. Wodehouse and listen to Bach. It was an ideal life: quiet, solitary, independent.

When Wednesday came, though, he drove downtown, parked in the multi-story garage at Cumberland and Avenue Road, then walked to the Park Plaza. It was another hot day. The tourists were out in force across Bloor Street by the Royal Ontario Museum, many of them Americans from

Buffalo, Rochester or Detroit: the men in loud checked shirts photograph-
ing everything in sight, their wives in tight shorts looked tired and thirsty.

Quilley took the elevator up to the nineteenth floor and wandered
through the bar, an olde-worlde place with deep armchairs and framed
reproductions of old Colonial scenes on the walls. It was busier than usual,
and even though the windows were open, the smoke bothered him. He walked
out onto the roof lounge and scanned the faces. Within moments he noticed
someone looking his way. The man paused for just a split-second, perhaps
to translate the dust-jacket photo into reality, then beckoned Quilley over
with raised eyebrows and a twitch of the head.

The man rose to shake hands, then sat down again, glancing around
to make sure nobody had paid the two of them undue attention. He was
short and thin, with sandy hair and a pale grey complexion, as if he had just
come out of hospital. He wore wire-rimmed glasses and had a habit of
rolling his tongue around in his mouth when he wasn't talking.

"First of all, Mr. Quilley," the man said, raising his glass, "may I say
how honoured I am to meet you." He spoke with a pronounced English
accent.

Quilley inclined his head. "I'm flattered, Mr...er...?"

"Peplow, Frank Peplow."

"Yes...Mr. Peplow. But I must admit I'm puzzled by your letter."

A waiter in a burgundy jacket came over to take Quilley's order. He
asked for an Amstel.

Peplow paused until the waiter was out of earshot. "Puzzled?"

"What I mean is," Quilley went on, struggling for the right words,
"whether you were serious or not, whether you really do want to --"

Peplow leaned forward. Behind the lenses, his pale blue eyes looked
sane enough. "I assure you, Mr. Quilley, that I was, that I *am,* entirely
serious. That woman is ruining my life and I can't allow it to go on any
longer."

Speaking about her brought little spots of red to his cheeks. Quilley
held his hand up. "All right, I believe you. I suppose you realize I should
have gone to the police?"

"But you didn't."

"I could have. They might be here, watching us."

Peplow shook his head. "Mr. Quilley, if you won't help, I'd even
welcome prison. Don't think I haven't realized that I might get caught, that
no murder is perfect. All I want is a chance. It's worth the risk."

The waiter returned with Quilley's drink, and they both sat in silence
until he had gone. Quilley was intrigued by this drab man sitting opposite

him, a man who obviously didn't even have the imagination to dream up his own murder plot. "What do you want from me?" he asked.

"I have no right to ask anything of you, I understand that," Peplow said. "I have absolutely nothing to offer in return. I'm not rich. I have no savings. I suppose all I want really is advice, encouragement."

"If I were to help," Quilley said. "If I were to help, then I'd do nothing more than offer advice. Is that clear?"

Peplow nodded. "Does that mean you will?"

"If I can."

And so Dennis Quilley found himself helping to plot the murder of a woman he'd never met with a man he didn't even particularly like. Later, when he analyzed his reasons for playing along, he realized that that was exactly what he had been doing -- playing. It had been a game, a cerebral puzzle, just like thinking up a plot for a book, and he never, at first, gave a thought to real murder, real blood, real death.

Peplow took a handkerchief from his top pocket and wiped the thin film of sweat from his brow. "You don't know how happy this makes me, Mr. Quilley. At last, I have a chance. My life hasn't amounted to much, and I don't suppose it ever will. But at least I might find some peace and quiet in my final years. I'm not a well man." He placed one hand solemnly over his chest. "Ticker. Not fair, is it? I've never smoked, I hardly drink, and I'm only fifty-three. But the doctor has promised me a few years yet if I live right. All I want is to be left alone with my books and my garden."

"Tell me about your wife," Quilley prompted.

Peplow's expression darkened. "She's a cruel and selfish woman," he said. "And she's messy, she never does anything around the place. Too busy watching those damn soap-operas on television day and night. She cares about nothing but her own comfort, and she never overlooks an opportunity to nag me or taunt me. If I try to escape to my collection, she mocks me and calls me dull and boring. I'm not even safe from her in my garden. I realize I have no imagination, Mr. Quilley, and perhaps even less courage, but even a man like me deserves some peace in his life, don't you think?"

Quilley had to admit that the woman really did sound awful -- worse than any he had known, and he had met some shrews in his time. He had never had much use for women, except for occasional sex in his younger days. Even that had become sordid, and now he stayed away from them as much as possible. He found, as he listened, that he could summon up remarkable sympathy for Peplow's position.

"What do you have in mind?" he asked.

"I don't really know. That's why I wrote to you. I was hoping you might be able to help with some ideas. Your books...you seem to know so much."

"In my books," Quilley said, "the murderer always gets caught."

"Well, yes," said Peplow, "of course. But that's because the genre demands it, isn't it? I mean, your Inspector Baldry is much smarter than any real policeman. I'm sure if you'd made him a criminal, he would always get away."

There was no arguing with that, Quilley thought. "How do you want to do it?" he asked. "A domestic accident? Electric shock, say? Gadget in the bathtub? She must have a hair curler or a dryer?"

Peplow shook his head, eyes tightly closed. "Oh no," he whispered, "I couldn't. I couldn't do anything like that. No more than I could bear the sight of her blood."

"How's her health?"

"Unfortunately," said Peplow, "she seems obscenely robust."

"How old is she?"

"Forty-nine."

"Any bad habits?"

"Mr. Quilley, my wife has nothing *but* bad habits. The only thing she won't tolerate is drink, for some reason, and I don't think she has other men -- though that's probably because nobody will have her."

"Does she smoke?"

"Like a chimney."

"Quilley shuddered. "How long?"

"Ever since she was a teenager, I think. Before I met her."

"Does she exercise?"

"Never."

"What about her weight, her diet?"

"Well, you might not call her fat, but you'd be generous in saying she was full-figured. She eats too much junk food. I've always said that. And eggs. She loves bacon and eggs for breakfast. And she's always stuffing herself with cream-cakes and tarts."

"Hmmm," said Quilley, taking a sip of Amstel. "She sounds like a prime candidate for a heart attack."

"But it's me who --" Peplow stopped as comprehension dawned. "I see. Yes, I see. You mean one could be induced?"

"Quite. Do you think you would manage that?"

"Well, I could if I didn't have to be there to watch. But I don't know how."

"Poison."

"I don't know anything about poison."

"Never mind. Give me a few days to look into it. I'll give you advice, remember, but that's as far as it goes."

"Understood."

Quilley smiled. "Good. Another beer?"

No, I'd better not. She'll be able to smell this on my breath and I'll be in for it already. I'd better go."

Quilley looked at his watch. Two-thirty. He could have done with another Amstel, but he didn't want to stay there by himself. Besides, at half past three it would be time to meet his agent at the Windsor Arms, and there he would have the opportunity to drink as much as he wanted. To pass the time, he could browse through the magazines and imported newspapers in the Reader's Den. "Fine," he said, "I'll go down with you."

Outside on the hot, busy street, they shook hands and agreed to meet in a week's time on the back patio of the Madison Avenue Pub. It wouldn't do to be seen together twice in the same place.

Quilley stood on the corner of Bloor and Avenue Road among the camera-clicking tourists and watched Peplow walk off towards the St. George subway station. Now that their meeting was over and the spell was broken, he wondered again what the hell he was doing helping this pathetic little man. It certainly wasn't altruism. Perhaps the challenge appealed to him; after all, people climb mountains just because they're there.

And then there was Peplow's mystery collection. There was just a chance that it might contain an item of great interest to Quilley, and that Peplow might be grateful enough to part with it.

Wondering how to approach the subject at their next meeting, Quilley wiped the sweat from his brow with the back of his hand and walked towards the bookshop.

*   *   *   *   *   *

*Atropine, hyoscyamine, belladonna...*Quilley flipped through Dreisbach's Handbook of Poisoning one evening at the cottage. Poison seemed to have gone out of fashion these days, and he had only used it in one of his novels, about six years ago. That had been the old stand-by, cyanide, with its familiar smell of bitter almonds that he had so often read about but never experienced. The small black handbook had sat on his shelf gathering dust ever since.

Writing a book, of course, one could generally skip over the problems of acquiring the stuff -- give the killer a job as a pharmacist or in a hospital dispensary, for example. In real life, getting one's hands on poison might prove more difficult.

So far, he had read through the sections on agricultural poisons, household hazards and medicinal poisons. The problem was that whatever Peplow used had to be easily available. Prescription drugs were out. Even if Peplow could persuade a doctor to give him barbiturates, for example, the prescription would be on record and any death in the household would be regarded as suspicious. Barbiturates wouldn't do, anyway, and nor would such common products as paint thinner, insecticides and weed killers -- they didn't reproduce the symptoms of a heart attack.

Near the back of the book was a list of poisonous plants that shocked Quilley by its sheer length. He hadn't known just how much deadliness there was lurking in fields, gardens and woods. Rhubarb leaves contained oxalic acid, for example, and caused nausea, vomiting and diarrhea. The bark, wood, leaves or seeds of the yew had a similar effect. Boxwood leaves and twigs caused convulsions; celandine could bring about a coma; hydrangeas contained cyanide; and laburnums brought on irregular pulse, delirium twitching and unconsciousness. And so the list went on -- lupins, mistletoe, sweet peas, rhododendron -- a poisoner's delight. Even the beautiful poinsettia, which brightened up so many Toronto homes each Christmas, could cause gastroenteritis. Most of these plants were easy to get hold of, and in many cases the active ingredients could be extracted simply by soaking or boiling in water.

It wasn't long before Quilley found what he was looking for. Beside "Oleander", the note read, "See digitalis, 374." And there it was, set out in detail, Digitalis occurred in all parts of the common foxglove, which grew on waste ground and woodland slopes, and flowered from June to September. Acute poisoning would bring about death from ventricular fibrillation. No doctor would consider an autopsy if Peplow's wife appeared to die of a heart attack, given her habits, especially if Peplow fed her a few smaller doses first to establish the symptoms.

Quilley set aside the book. It was already dark outside, and the downpour that the humid, cloudy day had been promising had just begun. Rain slapped against the asphalt roof-tiles, gurgled down the drainpipe and pattered on the leaves of the overhanging trees. In the background, it hissed as it fell on the lake. Distant flashes of lightning and deep rumblings of thunder warned of the coming storm.

Happy with his solitude and his cleverness, Quilley linked his hands behind his head and leaned back in the chair. Out back, he heard the rustling of a small animal making its way through the undergrowth -- a raccoon, perhaps, or even a skunk. When he closed his eyes, he pictured all the trees, shrubs and wild flowers around the cottage and marvelled at what deadly potential so many of them contained.

* * * * *

The sun blazed down on the back patio of the Madison, a small garden protected from the wind by high fences. Quilley wore his sunglasses and nursed a pint of Conners Ale. The place was packed. Skilled and pretty waitresses came and went, trays laden with baskets of chicken wings and golden pints.

The two of them sat out of the way at a white table in a corner by the metal fire escape. A striped parasol offered some protection, but the sun was still too hot and bright. Peplow's wife must have given him hell about drinking the last time, because today he had ordered only a Coke.

"It was easy," Quilley said. "You could have done it yourself. The only setback was that foxgloves don't grow wild here like they do in England. But you're a gardener; you grow them."

Peplow shook his head and smiled. "It's the gift of clever people like yourself to make difficult things seem easy. I'm not particularly resourceful, Mr. Quilley. Believe me, I wouldn't have known where to start. I had no idea that such a book existed, but you did, because of your art. Even if I had known, I'd hardly have dared buy it or take it out of the library for fear that someone would remember. But you've had your copy for years. A simple tool of the trade. No, Mr. Quilley, please don't underestimate your contribution. I was a desperate man. Now you've given me a chance at freedom. If there's anything at all I can do for you, please don't hesitate to say. I'd consider it an honour."

"This collection of yours," Quilley said. "What does it consist of?"

"British and Canadian crime fiction, mostly. I don't like to boast, but it's a very good collection. Try me. Go on, just mention a name."

"E.C.R. Lorac."

"About twenty of the Inspector MacDonalds. First editions, mint condition."

"Anne Hocking?"

"Everything but *Night's Candles.*"

"Trotton?"

Peplow raised his eyebrows. "Good Lord, that's an obscure one. Do you know, you're the first person I've come across who's ever mentioned that."

"Do you have it?"

"Oh, yes." Peplow smiled smugly. "X.J. Trotton, *Summer's Lease*, published 1942. It turned up in a pile of junk I bought at an auction some years ago. It's rare, but not very valuable. Came out in Britain during the war and probably died an immediate death. It was his only book, as far as I can make out, and there is no biographical information. Perhaps it was a pseudonym for someone famous?"

Quilley shook his head. I'm afraid I don't know. Have you read it?"

"Good Lord, no! I don't read them. It could damage the spines. Many of them are fragile. Anything I want to read -- like your books -- I buy in paperback."

"Mr. Peplow," Quilley said slowly, "you asked if there was anything you could do for me. As a matter of fact, there *is* something you can give me for my services."

"Yes?"

"The Trotton."

Peplow frowned and pursed his thin lips. "Why on earth...?"

"For my own collection, of course. I'm especially interested in the war period."

Peplow smiled. "Ah! So that's how you knew so much about them? I'd no idea you were a collector, too."

Quilley shrugged modestly. He could see Peplow struggling, visualizing the gap in his collection. But finally the poor man decided that the murder of his wife as more important to him that an obscure mystery novel. "Very well," he said gravely. "I'll mail it to you."

"How can I be sure...?"

Peplow looked offended. "I'm a man of my word, Mr. Quilley. A bargain is a bargain." He held out his hand. "Gentleman's agreement."

"All right." Quilley believed him. "You'll be in touch, when it's done?"

"Yes. Perhaps a brief note in with the Trotton, if you can wait that long. Say two or three weeks?"

"Fine. I'm in no hurry."

Quilley hadn't examined his motives since the first meeting, but he had realized, as he passed on the information and instructions, that it was the challenge he responded to more than anything else. For years he had been writing crime novels, and in providing Peplow with the means to kill

his slatternly, overbearing wife, Quilley had derived some vicarious pleasure from the knowledge that he -- Inspector Baldry's creator -- could bring
off in real life what he had always been praised for doing in fiction.

Quilley also knew that there were no real detectives who possessed
Baldry's curious mixture of intellect and instinct. Most of them were thick
plodders, and they could never realize that dull Mr.Peplow had murdered
his wife with a bunch of foxgloves, of all things. Nor would they ever know
that the brains behind the whole affair had been none other than his, Dennis
Quilley's.

The two men drained their glasses and left together. the corner of
Bloor and Spadina was busy with tourists and students lining up for char-
coal-grilled hot-dogs from the street-vendor. Peplow turned towards the
subway and Quilley wandered among the artsy crowd and sidewalk cyclists
on Bloor Street West for a while, then he settled at an open air cafe over a
daiquiri and a slice of kiwi-fruit cheesecake to read the *Globe and Mail*.

Now, he thought as he sipped his drink and turned to the arts section,
all he had to do was wait. One day soon, a small package would arrive for
him. Peplow would be free of his wife, and Quilley would be the proud
owner of one of the few remaining copies of X.J. Trotton's one and only
mystery novel, *Summer's Lease*.

* * * * *

Three weeks passed, and no package arrived. Occasionally, Quilley thought
of Mr. Peplow and wondered what had become of him. Perhaps he had lost
his nerve after all. That wouldn't be surprising. Quilley knew that he would
have no way of finding out what had happened if Peplow chose not to contact him again. He didn't know where the man lived or where he worked.
He didn't even know if Peplow was his real name. Still, he thought, it was
best that way. No contact. Even the Trotton wasn't worth being involved in
a botched murder for.

Then, at ten o'clock one warm Tuesday morning in September, the
doorbell chimed. Quilley looked at his watch and frowned. Too early for
the postman. Sighing, he pressed the SAVE command on his PC and walked
down to answer the door. A stranger stood there, an overweight woman in a
yellow polka-dot dress with short sleeves and a low neck. She had piggy
eyes set in a round face, and dyed red hair that looked limp and lifeless after
a cheap perm. She carried an imitation crocodile-skin handbag.

Quilley must have stood there looking puzzled for too long. The woman's eyes narrowed and her rosebud mouth tightened so much that white furrows radiated from the red circle of her lips.

"May I come in?" she asked.

Stunned, Quilley stood back and let her enter. She walked straight over to a wicker armchair and sat down. The basked-work creaked under her. From there, she surveyed the room, with its waxed parquet floor, stone fireplace an antique Ontario furniture. "Nice," she said, clutching her purse on her lap. Quilley sat down opposite her. Her dress was a size too small and the material strained over her red, fleshy upper arms and pinkish bosom. The hem rode up as she crossed her legs, exposing a wedge of fat, mottled thigh. Primly, she pulled it down again over her dimpled knees.

"I'm sorry to appear rude," said Quilley, regaining his composure, "but who the hell are you?"

"My name is Peplow," the woman said. "Mrs. Gloria Peplow. I'm a widow."

Quilley felt a tingling sensation along his spine, like he always did when fear began to take hold of him.

He frowned and said, "I'm afraid I don't know you, do I?"

"We've never met," the woman replied, "but I think you knew my husband."

"I don't recall any Peplow. Perhaps you're mistaken?"

Gloria Peplow shook her head and fixed him with her piggy eyes. He noticed they were black, or as near as. "I'm not mistaken, Mr. Quilley. You didn't only know my husband, you also plotted with him to murder me."

Quilley flushed and jumped to his feet. "That's absurd! Look, if you've come here to make insane accusations like that, you'd better go." He stood like an ancient statue, one hand pointing dramatically towards the door.

Mrs. Peplow smirked. "Oh, sit down. You look very foolish standing there like that."

Quilley continued to stand. "This is *my* home, Mrs. Peplow, and I insist that you leave. Now!"

Mrs. Peplow sighed and opened the gilded plastic clasp on her purse. She took out a Shoppers Drug Mart envelope, picked out two colour photographs, and dropped them next to the Wedgwood dish on the antique wine table by her chair. Leaning forward, Quilley could see clearly what they were: one showed him standing with Peplow outside the Park Plaza, and the other caught the two of them talking outside the Scotiabank at Bloor and

Spadina. Mrs. Peplow flipped the photos over, and Quilley saw that they had been date-stamped by the processors.

"You met with my husband at least twice to help him plan my death."

"That's ridiculous. I do remember him, now I've seen the picture. I just couldn't recollect his name. He was a fan. We talked about mystery novels. I'm very sorry to hear that he's passed away."

"He had a heart attack, Mr. Quilley, and now I'm all alone in the world."

"I'm very sorry, but I don't see..."

Mrs. Peplow waved his protests aside. Quilley noticed the dark sweat stain on the tight material around her armpit. She fumbled with the catch on her purse again and brought out a pack of Export Lights and a book of matches.

"I don't allow smoking in my house," Quilley said. "It doesn't agree with me."

"Pity," she said, lighting the cigarette and dropping the spent match in the Wedgwood bowl. She blew a stream of smoke directly at Quilley, who coughed and fanned it away.

"Listen to me, Mr. Quilley," she said, "and listen good. My husband might have been stupid, but I'm not. He was not only a pathetic and boring little man, he was also an open book. Don't ask me why I married him. He wasn't even much of a man, if you know what I mean. Do you think I haven't known for some time that he was thinking of ways to get rid of me? I wouldn't give him a divorce because the one thing he did -- the only thing he did -- was provide for me, and he didn't even do that very well. I'd have got half if we divorced, but half of what he earned isn't enough to keep a bag-lady. I'd have had to go to work, and I don't like that idea. So I watched him. He got more and more desperate, more and more secretive. When he started looking smug, I knew he was up to something."

"Mrs. Peplow," Quilley interrupted, "this is all very well, but I don't see what it has to do with me. You come in here and pollute my home with smoke, then you start telling me some fairy tale about your husband, a man I met casually one or twice. I'm busy, Mrs. Peplow, and quite frankly I'd rather you left and let me get back to work."

"I'm sure you would." She flicked a column of ash into the Wedgwood bowl. "As I was saying, I knew he was up to something, so I started following him. I thought he might have another woman, unlikely as it seemed, so I took my camera along. I wasn't really surprised when he headed for the Park Plaza instead of going back to the office after lunch one day. I watched the elevator go up to the nineteenth floor, the bar, so I waited across the

street in the crowd for him to come out again. As you know, I didn't have
to wait very long. He came out with you. And It was just as easy the next
time."

"I've already told you, Mrs. Peplow," he was a mystery buff, a fellow collector, that's all --

"Yes, yes, I know he was. Him and his stupid catalogues and collection. Still," she mused,"it had its uses. That's how I found out who you
were. I'd seen your picture on the book covers, of course. If I may say so,
it does you more than justice." She looked him up and down as if he were a
side of beef hanging in a butcher's window. He cringed. "As I was saying,
my husband was obvious. I knew he must be chasing you for advice. He
spends so much time escaping to his garden or his little world of books that
it was perfectly natural he would go to a mystery novelist for advice rather
than to a real criminal. I imagine you were a bit more accessible, too. A
little flattery, and you were hooked. Just another puzzle for you to work
on."

"Look, Mrs. Peplow --"

"Let me finish." She ground out her cigarette butt in the bowl. "Foxgloves, indeed! Do you think he could manage to brew up a dose of digitalis
without leaving traces all over the place? Do you know what he did the first
time? he put just enough in my Big Mac to make me a bit nauseous and
make my pulse race, but he left the leaves and stems in the dustbin! Can
you believe that? Oh, I became very careful in my eating habits after that,
Mr. Quilley. Anyway, your little plan didn't work. I'm here and he's dead."

Quilley paled. "My God, you killed him, didn't you?"

"He was the one with the bad heart, not me." She lit another cigarette.

"You can hardly blackmail me for plotting with your husband to kill
you when *he's* the one who's dead," said Quilley. "And as for evidence,
there's nothing. No, Mrs. Peplow, I think you'd better go, and think yourself lucky I don't call the police."

Mrs. Peplow looked surprised. "What are you talking about? I have
no intention of blackmailing you for plotting to kill me."

"Then what...?"

"Mr. Quilley, my husband was blackmailing you. That's why you
killed *him*."

Quilley slumped back in his chair. "I what?"

She took a sheet of paper from her purse and passed it over to him.
On it were just two words: Trotton -- Quilley." He recognized the neat
handwriting. "That's a photocopy," Mrs. Peplow went on. "The original's

where I found it, slipped between the pages of a book called *Summer's Lease* by X.J. Trotton. Do you know that book, Mr. Quilley?"

"Vaguely. I've heard of it."

"Oh, have you? It might also interest you to know that along with that book and the slip of paper, locked away in my husband's files, is a copy of your own first novel. I put it there."

Quilley felt the room spinning around him. "I...I...." Peplow had given him the impression that Gloria was stupid, but that was turning out to be far from the truth.

"My husband's only been dead for two days. If the doctors look, they'll *know* that he's been poisoned. For a start, they'll find high levels of potassium, and then they'll discover eosinophilia. Do you know what they are, Mr. Quilley? I looked them up. They're a kind of white blood cell, and you find lots of them around if there's been any allergic reaction or inflammation. If I was to go to the police and say I'd been suspicious about my husband's behaviour over the past few weeks, that I had followed him and photographed him with you, and if they were to find the two books and the slip of paper in his filed...Well, I think you know what they'd make of it, don't you? Especially if I told them he came home feeling ill after a lunch with you."

"It's not fair," Quilley said, banging his fist on the chair arm. "It's just not bloody fair."

"Life rarely is. But the police aren't to know how stupid and unimaginative my husband was. They'll just look at the note, read the books, and assume he was blackmailing you." She laughed. "Even if Frank had read the Trotton book, I'm sure he'd have only noticed an 'influence', at the most. But you and I know what really went on, don't we? It happens more often than people think. Only recently I was reading in the newspaper about similarities between a book by Colleen McCullough and *The Blue Castle* by Lucy Maud Montgomery. I'd say that was a bit obvious, wouldn't you? It was much easier in your case, much less dangerous. You were very clever, Mr. Quilley. You found an obscure novel, and you didn't only adapt the plot for your own first book, you even stole the character of your series detective. There was some risk involved, certainly, but not much. Your book is better, without a doubt. You have some writing talent, which X.J. Trotton completely lacked. But he did have the germ of an original idea, and it wasn't lost on you, was it?"

Quilley groaned. Thirteen solid police procedurals, twelve of them all his own work, but the first, yes, a deliberate adaptation of a piece of ephemeral trash. He had seen what Trotton could have done and had done it himself. Serendipity, or so it had seemed when he found the dusty volume in a second-hand bookshop in Victoria years ago. All he had had to do was change the setting from London to Toronto, alter the names, and set about improving upon the original. And now...? The hell of it was that he would have been perfectly safe without the damn book. He had simply given in to the urge to get his hands on Peplow's copy and destroy it. It wouldn't have mattered, really. *Summer's Lease* would have remained unread on Peplow's shelf. If only the bloody fool hadn't written that note...

"Even if the police can't make a murder charge stick," Mrs. Peplow went on, "I think your reputation would suffer if this got out. Oh, the great reading public might not care. perhaps a trial would even increase your sales -- you know how ghoulish people are -- but the plagiarism would at the very least lose you the respect of your peers. I don't think your agent and publisher would be very happy, either. Am I making myself clear?"

Pale and sweating, Quilley nodded. "How much?" he whispered.

"Pardon?"

"I said how much? How much do you want to keep quiet?"

"Oh, it's not your money I'm after, Mr. Quilley, or may I can you Dennis? Well, not *only* money, anyway. I'm a widow now. I'm all alone in the world."

She looked around the room, her piggy eyes glittering, then gave Quilley one of the most disgusting looks he'd ever had in his life.

"I've always fancied living year the lake," she said, reaching for another cigarette. "Live here alone, do you?"

Somewhere They Can't Find Me
PETER SELLERS

Founding editor of the Cold Blood *series, Peter is also an accomplished writer of short crime and horror fiction. His story, "This One's Trouble" was nominated for an Arthur Ellis Award in 1991. In addition to the* Cold Blood *books, Peter has also edited the collections* A Murder Coming, *stories by James Powell and* Fear is a Killer, *stories by William Bankier. In 1992, in recognition of his work with the* Cold Blood *series, Peter was a recipient, along with both Bankier and Powell, of the CWC's Derrick Murdoch Award. A collection of his stories, called* Whistling Past the Graveyard, *will be published in 1998 by Mosaic Press.*

They came for Tully early Sunday morning. By the time the door of his cell clanged open he was already dressed and sitting on the edge of his bunk.

"Out, Tully," one of the guards said. There were two of them, both with riot sticks in their hands.

Tully got up and shuffled towards the door. His shoes without laces flopped up and down and chafed his heels but he didn't mind much. He didn't expect a long walk and in his future he saw sandals on his feet and felt sand between his toes. Tully's cellmate, a jailhouse veteran named Larue, poked his head out from under his stiff blanket. His hair stuck out like fur on a wet cat. Which was also how he smelled. "Where you goin', Tully?" he asked with a laugh. "Church?"

Tully grinned back at him. "You could say I'm gonna talk to my saviour."

The guard stepped back and to the side and Tully walked out past him. The guard slammed the cell door shut and locked it and prodded Tully forward with the end of his riot stick.

Larue shook his head and pulled it back under the blanket.

The holding area consisted of a bank of eight cells, each designed to sleep up to four men but at times filled with twice that many. Each cell was locked up separately for the night, then in the morning all the doors opened and the prisoners spilled out into a bullpen about sixteen feet across which ran the length of the eight cell fronts and had a single barred door at one end.

Tully's cell was furthest from the door. They walked the length of the bullpen past eyes which peered out at them without curiosity. The first guard opened the door in front of Tully, they all went through, and the second guard locked it behind them. Tully hoped to God it was the last time he ever heard that noise.

They took Tully to one of the private consultation rooms where prisoners and lawyers got together to work out their plea bargains. This was separate from the regular visiting area which was a big open space watched by armed guards. Visitors were searched on their way in, and prisoners on the way out. The private rooms were not much different from the cells. They were a little bigger and they had tile on the floor, cracked and stained though it was. And there were fans on the ceiling, but they spun around without doing much to improve the air. The big difference was the presence of a small scarred table and a few moulded plastic chairs. After three weeks of nothing to sit on but a board hard bunk or the concrete floor these chairs looked as inviting to Tully as wing chairs in a five star hotel lobby.

There were three men in the room waiting for him. Two of them were the kind of big, hard-eyed men the federal cops have mass produced in a factory somewhere. They stood with their backs to different walls, at right angles to one another, so they wouldn't get caught in a crossfire. They both had the haircuts which the government bought wholesale by the truckload the day after they went out of style. And beneath their jackets they had guns which Tully knew they didn't just fire weekends at the shooting gallery.

The third man was sitting down, legs crossed at the knees. There was a manilla file folder on the table beside him with Tully's name on it. He was holding a cigarette between yellowed fingers. The smoke from it drifted up above his head four or five feet and hung there like a tiny cloud. Although Tully figured it wouldn't have the guts to rain.

"You can go," the man said to the jailhouse guards and they left without a word. He looked at Tully for a long time. Tully returned the favour. "Sit down," he said finally. His voice was flat and nasal. "My name's Loncraine."

Tully smiled. "Oh yeah. Renzo told me about you."

"So you know why I'm here."

"You wanna make a deal."

Loncraine's light brown hair was fashionably longer than the other two cops and his mustache was cut precisely. Tully got the impression he measured and trimmed one hair at a time. He wore an Italian suit and a silk tie and his initials were embroidered on the French cuffs of his shirt. He dropped his cigarette to the floor and ground it out with sharp, rough motions. Then he took another from a silver case and lit it with an old-fashioned flint lighter. "Yes," he said at last. "We're going to make a deal."

"You sound pretty sure of yourself."

"Let's just say I'm pretty sure of you. For one thing, you don't have a lawyer. I know the court appointed one for you and I know he told you about us and I know you had him taken off your case."

Tully laughed. "I didn't need no Legal Aid type," he said, scratching his unshaven jaw. His beard had always come in slowly and after three weeks without a razor it was at that irritated stage that had always made him shave it off before. He thought he might leave it on this time, though. It fit, somehow, with his new image of himself. "They're fine if you got the need or you don't got the dough. These are not my problems. It ain't the money, it's the principle. Me, I'm a principled guy. Some people might think 'Who the hell is he trying to kid?' but it's true. I never cut nobody wasn't trying to cut me. I never stuck a gun in nobody's ribs that wasn't trying to stick one in mine first. And I never lied to nobody. I may have run for Luciani and Benedetto but my word is my bond, okay? And when I started with 'em they told me, 'Tully, you ever get busted all you gotta do is call and we'll take care of you.' Lawyer, bail and everything. So I get busted and the court gives me this Legal Aid asshole. I gave him the brush and I called like they said. Three weeks later I'm still sitting on my ass and I ain't heard one lousy word of Latin yet."

Loncraine listened without expression or movement. The ash grew on the motionless cigarette until it fell to the floor of its own weight. When Tully had finished he said, "That's how I know we're going to make a deal."

"Just like Renzo did?"

Loncraine nodded. "He told me the same story, Tully."

Renzo had been gathered up, like Tully, in one of the federal government's periodic sweeps of organized crime. He'd parleyed his inside knowledge and his relative unimportance into a position as a star Crown Witness and the promise of a new life under the Witness Relocation Program. Three days before he took the stand, he called Tully to say good-bye and to mention Loncraine, should Tully ever want out himself.

"Right now, Tully, Luciani and everybody else we picked up, all of whom have posted extremely large bonds for themselves by the way, are only thinking about their own necks. They don't give a damn about you. Never did. You're going to take a fall for them and they're going to rely on your loyalty and fear to keep you quiet. And yes, we could very easily put you away. Which, principled or not, is where you belong. But we're not going to do that because, Tully, you're nothing. You're a piece of filler on page thirty. Those other guys are headlines. And we're after headlines."

"You really know how to make a guy feel wanted."

Loncraine laughed. "Don't worry. After word gets out of what you're going to do, they'll make you feel very wanted."

Tully tried not to shudder. "I go along, you get your headlines. What do I get?"

"Something more like what Renzo's got."

Tully had this picture of Renzo he just couldn't shake. He saw him lying back in a beach chair on some sun drenched stretch of white Polynesian sand that started at the edge of a turquoise sea and ran straight back past Renzo's chair to a line of distant palm trees waving in the breeze like one-armed cheerleaders. Renzo's face was pink beneath a broad straw hat and his grin was wide and crooked. And all the time dark skinned girls wearing nothing but sarongs and carob oil brought him rum punch and kisses.

Tully said, "Where do I sign?"

After that it was quick.

"You realize, of course, the size of the risk you're taking."

Tully shrugged. "I've been to prison before. But I've never been to Fiji."

"Okay. We'll get you out of here as soon as we can. Then we'll make sure you get safely to the trial and, once the trial is completed and the verdicts are in, we handle your relocation. Then you're on your own. Any questions?"

"Two. First, after this is over, I'd like to thank Renzo for giving me your name."

Loncraine shook his head. "No, Tully. We don't release any information about people in our program to anyone. We wouldn't tell Renzo's mother where he is. What's the second question?"

"I was just hoping you'd move me oughta here right away." Tully hoped his nervousness didn't show.

Loncraine shook his head again. "You'll be fine for the time being. It won't be long." He pointed at one of the cops, who had been standing silently the whole time. The cop slipped from the room and returned with Tully's guards.

"You guys always do this on Sunday morning?" Tully asked as he stood up.

Loncraine stood too. "We have a trial in less than two weeks. We want to nail these bastards. We don't have time to waste." He shook the wrinkles out of his suit, tucked the file under his arm and left with his two escorts in tow.

Tully went back to his cell. Larue was still in bed. He lifted his head when Tully came back in. "You don't look any less damned than you did before," he said.

Tully stared at him, irritated by the delay and Larue's smirk. "All things come to him who waits," Tully said as the most Biblical thing that came to mind.

"Christ almighty," Larue said and turned to face the wall.

*   *   *   *   *

The next morning it was Larue's turn. They came and told him he had a visitor. This surprised him and he spent a long time sitting on the edge of his bunk scratching his head until the guards got impatient and dragged him from the cell.

Larue had spent seventeen of his thirty-eight years behind bars of one kind or another. Either as a convict or, in one of his few attempts at going straight, as a bartender until he was caught pouring short shots with one hand and shortchanging the till with the other. In all that time, no one had come to visit him except court appointed lawyers and his mother, twice when he was still a juvenile. But after he got out from his second stint he learned that she'd moved and left no forwarding address. The thought of a visitor both puzzled and scared him.

It didn't surprise Tully. He set about making his bed, tucking the corners in loose instead of in the tight military fashion he preferred. He was working at the head when he heard footsteps behind him and a rough voice whispered his name.

Tully spun around ripping the coarse prison issue blanket from the bed and swinging it in front of him. The blade tore into it and Tully pushed the blanket forward and grabbed a thick forearm as it sliced up past his face and twisted it away from him, seeing the blade dimly in the weak light.

The attacker shoved Tully back, knocking him onto the bunk and fighting to pull his arm free. His other hand threw wild punches at Tully's head and gouged at his eyes. Tully tried frantically to squirm to his feet but fell off the bunk and the assassin landed on top of him, pinning Tully to the floor.

Desperately, Tully bent his head forward and sank his teeth into the arm. He tasted salt and sweat and sank his teeth deeper until he felt the hot spurt of blood that gagged him. He drew back, choking and spitting, and only then did he hear the screams. The shank lay on the floor beside him and the arm was yanked away. Tully spun onto his stomach, picked up the knife and turned on his attacker who was doubled over across the cell with his left hand clutching his bitten arm. Tully jumped on his back and buried the knife in his side, holding onto it like a handle on a mechanical bull as the man bellowed and shook and tried to knock Tully loose by slamming him against the wall. Tully pulled the shank out and plunged it in again and again, each time driving out a cry of higher pitch and greater intensity. By the time he heard footsteps running across the bullpen, the man lay on the floor, the blade sticking from his throat.

Tully looked down at him and recognized him as a con named Baker who'd come in the day before. The shank, he noticed then, was not made from the sharpened handle of a spoon or some other utensil. It was a hunting knife. And not a cheap one, either

Two guards, bristling with shotguns, burst into the cell. Tully looked at them angrily. "Put those go damn things away and get me the hell outa here," he said. "I want solitary and I want it now."

As they took him out to one of the jail's three isolation cells, Tully couldn't stop wondering just who the hell Luciani had sent to see Larue.

* * * * *

Tully was only in solitary a few days. Even that was too long. The walls were starting to close in on him so tight he woke up sweating thinking he was in a casket. And he found himself pacing in tight fast circles, his eyes staring hypnotized at the eyelets where the laces should have been. As he made each tiny circuit it was like he was twisting the knot in his stomach tighter and tighter until, when he heard the big key rasp into the keyhole, he jumped a foot in the air and spun around low with his fists bunched tightly at his sides, thumbs tucked in and knuckles point out.

The first thing into the cell was a gun barrel and Tully thought, "Jesus, they're everywhere." But when no shots came he knew it wasn't anybody fulfilling a contract. Then a guard came in, unarmed, brushing past the gun barrel. His riot stick swung from his belt. Two men came in behind the guard and suddenly there was no room to turn around. Tully's immediate impulse was to run at them and shove them out, there wasn't enough oxygen for all of them. He felt the terror rise in his body, starting from his knees and racing upward to settle behind his eyes in a kind of seething burning mass. He was sweating and his heart raced and he wanted to scream but didn't. He knew it would use up too much precious air. Instead he glared at the intruders.

Both men with the guard were big federal types. One was a dark man with black hair that lay in thick bands across the backs of his hands and fingers and with a single eyebrow that ran across his forehead above both eyes. Combined with the bald spot at the back of his head and his receding hair-line he made Tully think of a bear that had been prepped for the electric chair. The guy holding the gun was just as tall but thicker and fairhaired with a raccoon mask of freckles spread across his face. He grinned. He looked like some kid from a cartoon who'd grown up and taken steroids.

The dark one spoke first. "I'm Walker," he said. He jerked his thumb towards his partner. "This is Levine." The grin spread wider. "We're going to babysit you till the trial's over."

They took Tully out of the cell and the guard locked it behind them, and Tully wondered if he was afraid some agoraphobic might try to break in. They walked along the damp corridor, past other cells and a guard propped up next to a coffee vending machine. Walker had a gun too, now, a semi-automatic pistol of large calibre that Tully didn't want to be anywhere near if he started firing.

In the wide open spaces of the corridor, Tully gulped down the stale air. "Where are we going?" he asked once he'd had his fill.

"The hell outa here," Levine said. "This environment isn't healthy for you."

"Tell me something I don't know. They got a contact out on me?"

Walker looked over at him and his eyes were as emotionless as buttons. "I thought you wanted us to tell you something you didn't know?"

They stopped walking at a steel door which, Tully could see through the small wire-reinforced window, opened onto a small checkpoint and waiting area. On the other side of that was the door to the outside.

Levine's grin was gone. "We're going out now," he said. "Keep you mouth shut. Move fast, but not any faster than us. Don't run. Keep your head down. Hit the outside doors and through. Don't look around. There's a limo out there. Tinted windows and the back door will be open. Just climb in and we'll be right with you. Got it?"

Tully swallowed and nodded and the uniformed guard opened the door. They went through it one at a time and crossed the waiting area in a fast moving knot. The guard stayed well behind. Tully was vaguely aware of a blur of faces as they passed. Then they were gone. Tully wasn't even sure how the door ahead of them opened but it did and they were through and Tully dove into the embrace of the waiting limo with Levine and Walker right behind him and the car door shut before Tully realized he hadn't drawn a breath since they left the corridor. He looked up at Levine and saw that he was grinning again.

They took Tully to a mid-town hotel he'd never been in before but he knew was expensive. He figured the feds weren't paying rack rate. Their room was on the fifteenth floor with a view south over the city that would have been spectacular except they kept the blinds closed and wouldn't let Tully go near the windows.

Four days after they arrived someone came to the door who Walker and Levine must have been expecting because when they opened it only one of them had his gun out. It was a uniformed city cop and he came in carrying a dark blue suit and a new shirt, still in the wrapper, and a burgundy tie. There were also new black leather shoes that looked like they'd been spit shined and a pair of black cotton socks and two pairs of underwear. Tully guessed that was in case his nerves got the better of him. And finally there was a new electric razor. Tully figured the beard was going.

The next morning they got up early and told Tully to shower and shave and get dressed.

"You're on," Walker said.

Tully put the clothes on and his body told him how much they cost but that didn't make his stomach feel any better. He was just finishing his half-Windsor when there was a knock on the door and Loncraine came in. "Are you ready?" he asked.

Tully nodded. "Oh, yeah."

"Just don't get rattled. Do everything Walker and Levine tell you. And don't pay any attention to anybody else once the trial starts. I may see you again after it's over."

"You mean if they don't whack me."

Loncraine looked at Tully flatly. "Good luck," he said and left. Five minutes later, so did Tully.

The trip to the courthouse was uneventful but Tully couldn't sit still. He was looking all over and his legs were pumping up and down like pistons.

At the courthouse the car rolled to a stop and they were off before it halted dead. Up the stairs and through the big glass doors without incident and then down the long corridor to the main courtroom behind the high oak doors.

They walked the length of the corridor, Tully sandwiched between Walker and Levine. They walked in step, their arms brushing, the syncopated clocking of their footsteps sounding determined and dangerous. But Tully knew it was a lie. Underneath it he was sick with fear. The closer they got to the courtroom the thicker it got with cops. Uniforms with open holsters mingled with plain clothes with microphones in their ears and Uzis under their coats. They were everywhere. Forming a cordon to hold back the curious and scanning constantly on the lookout for anything that might spell trouble.

At first Tully thought it was a lot of fuss for him, but then he realized they were more likely there to protect the defendants than one Crown Witness. It amazed him that a group of men who did the things these guys had done could inspire the forces of law and order to go to such great lengths to ensure due process. If things were reversed, the accused would just be blown away in an alley and that would be the end of it.

While the cops were watching the crowd, Tully was watching the cops. Any one of them could be on the take. Only there to splash his brains on the wall. And anyone could burst out of the crowd like Jack Ruby and gun him down before anyone else could react. If that happened, Tully hoped at least somebody'd take a good picture of it. Each step closer to the courtroom doors didn't relax him, it just made him feel closer to the time they'd take him out. He didn't think for a minute they'd let him get onto the stand without another attempt. So when the doors swung open he expected to see a shotgun levelled at his belly on the other side. Instead there was a bedlam of more cops, lawyers, reporters and Luciani and Benedetto and the other defendants, all of whom glared at Tully with looks that would've killed anybody with a heart condition.

Then the judge came in and the trial started. Tully sat and fidgeted through it and what happened went past him until they called his name.

In the end, Tully spent four days on the stand, returning each night to the hotel and going through the same agony every morning. But as each day passed and there were no attempts made on his life he felt closer and closer to freedom.

By the time he was through, he'd given a phone book's worth of names and addresses and he'd supplied a list of cause and effect that made the Begats look like an average family with two kids, two cars and a cat.

He climbed off the stand, weary after his last long day, and he left as he had before except this time knowing he wouldn't be forced back. He was on the last leg and he settled in to the hotel to wait it out.

The trial wrapped up in two more weeks. Tully read the headlines and chuckled. He was on his way.

They'd brought him some casual clothes. A pair of jeans and a plaid shirt, a bomber jacket and Kodiak boots, a pair of aviator Ray-Bans and a baseball cap from a farm implement manufacturer. He slipped into them and he felt more free right away. "How soon till we leave?" he asked.

Walker looked at his watch. "Twenty minutes. They're just giving the car a final check."

Tully figured it wasn't for wiper fluid and tire pressure.

While they were waiting, Loncraine came again. He was dressed like he'd stepped off the pages of the kind of catalogue you don't find in backwoods outhouses. "You're off, Tully," he said.

"Yeah, and I can't say I'm sorry to go."

Loncraine nodded. He'd heard that song before. "I just didn't want you to go thinking we don't appreciate all the risks you've taken. And everyone, right up to the Attorney General, is very pleased with the results."

Tully shrugged. "It was a way out."

The phone in the room rang softly. Walker picked up the receiver but said nothing into it before hanging up. "They're ready for us," he told Levine.

"Let's go."

Tully waved at Loncraine and they slipped out the door and down the hall to the waiting service elevator. It rattled its way down much too slowly for Tully who twitched and fidgeted and watched the floor numbers descending like in a nightmare. Finally they shook to a stop and the door opened and Walker and Levine went out first. The car was there waiting and they got inside. Walker climbed behind the wheel, Tully slipped into the passenger seat and Levine sat in the back. By the time the door shut solidly and locked behind them the car was already away from the curb and rolling.

"Where to?" Tully asked, excitement rising in him despite the tension.

"Nowhere special just yet," Walker said.

"Let's just see who's following us," Levine explained.

"If anybody." Walker said it as though he never doubted for a second that someone would.

They threaded through downtown traffic for several blocks, crossing on more than one red so no one could pull up beside them at an intersection.

After half an hour, Tully said, "Jesus it's hot in here."

"It won't kill you," Walker told him.

"Can't we roll down a window or something?"

Levine reached forward and rapped the window beside Tully's head with a knuckle. "Bulletproof," he said.

"Bullet resistant," Walker corrected without taking his eyes off the road.

Tully tugged at his collar. "I'm sweating like a pig."

Levine stared at Tully and Walker stared at the road. "Then shut up," Levine said. "Talking raises the body temperature."

Tully shut up and Levine settled back into the shadows of the back seat.

Ten minutes later, Walker said, "You got 'em?"

"Yeah," Levine said.

"What're you taking about?" Tully asked.

"We're being followed," Levine told him.

"Wine Mustang. Three cars back," Walker added.

"You sure?" Tully asked.

Walker and Levine didn't say anything and Tully pressed his back hard against the seat and he could feel his heart pounding.

The car was heading south now on a stretch of road which wound through a valley beside a brown and sluggish river. At its very bottom it lead into an urban wasteland of unused spur lines and scrap metal yards populated more by idle freight cars and rusting automobiles than people.

"This is perfect for us," Levine said.

"Christ, this is perfect for them," Tully screamed.

"Stay calm," Levine said as he took a shotgun from under the seat and pumped a shell into the chamber.

"Stay down," Walker said.

Tully slipped off the seat and crouched below the level of the padded dash. He looked over at Walker who was driving faster now, but looking almost continually back in the rearview mirror.

"No cars," he said quietly. "Now." And Tully watched as he reached over and lowered the power window to Levine's right. Tully's heart beat even faster.

Then Walker's foot jerked off the gas like it had been burned and it hammered down on the brake and the car shuddered and squealed and skidded as Walker wrenched the wheel around in a hard arc and Tully pitched forward against the dash as the tail of the car swung around wildly and then he was tossed back against the seat again as Walker's foot jumped back on the gas and the car fired forward, rushing towards the oncoming Mustang. Tully couldn't see the other car but he could imagine the confusion. Then the violent roar of the shotgun buried his thoughts. In the confined space the sound hammered its way into his brain and he threw his hands over his ears but each succeeding crash only seemed louder and louder until his head grew numb. Looking back he saw Levine, gun barrel out the open window, firing and pumping and firing and pumping, spent shell casings popping into the air and spinning through the smoke to disappear behind the car. In the brief instants between the firing, Tully heard the whine of car engines and the shattering of glass and once, he thought, the sound of a man screaming. Then, above his head, the window cracked and he looked up to see it flare into a spider-web pattern but it didn't break. A moment later, Levine drew the gun back inside the car and Walker shut the window again.

"They won't bother us anymore," Levine said.

Tully climbed back up on the seat and looked back to see the Mustang sitting askew in the middle of the road, crippled, smoking and leaking fluids like blood.

Walker reached out to touch the windshield, running a finger along the cracks. "Bulletproof," he said.

As they drove onto a highway which ran west from the city following the line of the lake, Tully started to laugh. "Whatever they're paying you," he said, "it ain't enough."

"We're just doing our job," Levine said.

They drove further and further into farming country. As they climbed the skyway which took them over to the south side of the lake, Walker asked, "How's it look?"

"All clear," Levine answered.

Tully clapped his hands and rubbed them together. "Sand and sunshine here I come," he chuckled.

Walker laughed. The only time Tully ever heard him do that. "You guys are all the same," he said.

Tully grinned as images of palm trees and native girls danced in his head. Until he felt the cold muzzle of Levine's pistol press against the base of his skull and, in that instant, he realized exactly where Renzo was.

Murder In The Green
TED WOOD

Ted shares the distinction, along with William Bankier, of appearing in every volume of the Cold Blood *series. In fact, in* Cold BloodII, *Ted had two stories: one under his own name and one under his pseudonym Jack Barnao - making him the winner for those who keep score. A former member of the RAF, a policeman in London and Toronto, and an advertising copywriter, Ted is one to the key figures in the renaissance of Canadian crime fiction. His hard edged Reid Bennett novels, beginning with the award winning* Dead in the Water *in 1983, proved that Canadians can be as tough as anyone, and that Muskoka can be as dangerous as any back alley on the planet. Writing as Jack Barnao, Ted has also published three novels about former SAS agent turned bodyguard John Locke. This story, from* Cold Blood V, *demonstrates Ted's facility with plot, character and dialogue.*

The soggy lawn squelched under their feet and Cassidy looked down distastefully. "Why'd anybody bother to murder the guy? He'd've caught his death of cold in a couple more days camped out here, dumb bastard."

Wall sniffed. "Show some respect for his civil liberties. He was making a statement, picketing Queen's Park. Ask any of these other cold, wet dimwits."

They reached the tent where the uniformed officer was standing. A gaggle of protesters, the men all with beards, the women all without make-up, had formed around the tent. They were hectoring the officer who was enduring them, as he was enduring the thin November rain.

One of the bearded men shoved his "Stop raping the planet," placard in front of the detectives. "We demand justice," he shouted.

"Right on, brother," Cassidy said. "Let me through and the process starts."

"Let them through," a woman shouted. "They have to start burying the truth."

"Thank you for your cooperation, madam," Wall said.

"I'm not a madam. I'm Ms," she snarled.

"Whatever." Wall nodded to the uniformed officer. "In here is it?"

"It?" the same woman screeched. "He referred to Jonathon as 'it'."

The young policeman said, "The body's inside, detective, but the scene's messy. Before they called the Parliament security guy down off of the steps, half this crowd had gone in to take a peek. I've secured the scene since I've been here but it'd already been disturbed."

"Great," Cassidy said disgustedly and ducked to enter the tent. It was dim inside, what light there was in the November morning filtered even further by the canvas of the tent. Wall pulled a little penlight out of his raincoat pocket and checked the still figure in the sleeping bag which lay on top of a piece of foam rubber.

The dead man had been in his forties, Cassidy judged. He had a beard, of course, the nifty Che Guevera model. His eyes were open and there was a black thread of dried blood from the corner of his mouth down to his ear. His sleeping bag had a crusted dark stain around the heart.

"Somebody snuck in while he was sawing it off and stuck a knife in his heart," Wall said.

"Pity," Cassidy said.

Wall glanced at him oddly. "I didn't know you were a treehugger."

"No more'n anybody else," Cassidy said. "But I've got Leaf tickets tonight. They're playing the L.A. Gretzkys."

"Scratch that one," Wall told him.

Cassidy didn't answer. He was looking around the tent. "I figure the best way to preserve the scene is to slash the canvas let the M.E. take his looksee without tramping in here any more. That way we'll be able to make a better examination of the scene after."

"Wrecking the tent. That's gonna go over big with the locals," Wall said. "Who's gonna break it to them."

"You, of course." Cassidy ducked to leave the tent. "You're a touchy-feely nineties kind of guy. Me, I'm the old-fashioned storm trooper type, they'd riot if I told them."

They wriggled out and stood up. Two more police cars had arrived and uniformed officers were quietly trying to ease the protesters back from the tent. Naturally they were protesting.

"You want to go call the coroner while I get on with this?" Cassidy asked.

"Sure. And I'll get a wagon. We can strike the tent and take it downtown for a closer look."

"Indoors, out of the rain? Not just a pretty face, are you?" Cassidy said.

Wall walked off and Cassidy turned his attention to the protesters.

"Why are we being excluded? What's your agenda?" A young woman was shouting into the face of an equally young policeman. She'd be pretty if she gave herself the chance, Cassidy thought. He took out his little rosewood snuff box, stooping slightly to keep the precious tobacco shielded from the rain and took a pinch.

The same young woman shouted. "This pig's doing drugs."

"Snuff," Cassidy said, and sneezed on cue. "Want some?"

She recoiled in horror.

Cassidy sneezed again, happily, blew his nose and asked the woman, "Who's in charge here?" He shut the lid of his snuffbox with a satisfying little click and slipped it back into his pocket. His ploy had worked. She had stopped shouting and was staring at him like an entomologist with a new kind of bug.

By now, the protesters had all fallen silent, not sure what kind of reaction was called for. Most of them had lowered their placards, inverting them and resting the message on their feet to keep the cards off the wet ground, like soldiers at a cenotaph, reversing arms. "Well?" Cassidy asked again. "Is anybody in charge."

A short man with a grey, bushy beard stepped forward, trailing his placard in one hand. He spoke in a booming voice. "We don't subscribe to conventions such as being in charge. I am, however, the secretary of Greenworld."

"And your name is?" Cassidy smiled with scrupulous politeness.

"George Steiner," the man boomed. He probably practiced booming in the shower, Cassidy thought. Not that he spent a lot of time in showers.

"Well Mr. Steiner, can you tell me what the sequence of events was last night?"

"It's Dr. Steiner," the little man corrected. "If you mean what time did we go to bed, I can't answer for everybody but I retired at midnight."

"And was the gentleman in this tent, Jonathon Mallory, is it? Was he already in his tent?"

"I think so. Just the watchperson stayed up after that, tending the fire."

"And who was that?"

"Sister Estelle." Steiner turned and nodded at the woman who had done all the screeching earlier.

"Thank you, sir. I'll have to speak to you at greater length later on. Will you still be here?"

"Not even murder can keep us from our mission," he said grimly.

"Good for you," Cassidy said. "But in case you change your mind, can I have your name and address, please?" He expected an argument, remembering the horror stories older men had told him of the sixties when protesters had been trained to refuse to give names and to exchange clothes with one another in the paddy wagon. Steiner was not so difficult. He gave an address and Cassidy wrote it down, along with the notation, '5 ft. 4. 160, beard' in case the good doctor was playing games.

Cassidy excused himself and spoke to the young woman who had lowered her placard and was weeping softly. "I'm sorry to have to ask you questions, but it's essential," he said.

She looked up at him, rain and tears mixed on her bleak face. "Go on." Most of the other people in the group had gathered around, listening warily.

"First off, could I have your name, please? Dr. Steiner called you Sister Estelle but I can't be that familiar."

He thought she would argue but her grief was genuine.

"Stella Lenchak," she said. "What's your question."

One of the men said, "You don't have to tell him anything. Estelle. You've got rights."

Cassidy looked at him mildly. "So did your fearless leader. Now I'd like to help find out who cancelled his. Could we have a little space here, please?"

The woman turned to the other people. "I'm okay. This is important."

The same man repeated, "You don't have to," but she just nodded and turned back to Cassidy.

He said, "Thank you, Ms. Lenchak. I'm told you stayed up after the others had retired for the night. Is that right?"

"I had the first watch," she said.

"You were a sentry, what?"

"We had no need of sentries, or so we thought. I tended the fire."

"I see. Kinda like a vestal virgin," Cassidy said easily.

"Are you being funny?" she snapped.

"I didn't think so," Cassidy said mildly. He craved a pinch of his comforting snuff but didn't want to send her off on a tangent. "You what? Stood, sat, watching the fire?"

"I sat. On a groundsheet with another over my head and shoulders."

"Where? Could you show me, please?" He tilted his hand, like an usher towards the circle of ash where the remains of the campfire stood. A few logs lay there, steaming in the rain.

She walked with him to the side of the circle and pointed to the ground. "I was sitting there."

"Facing the fire?" She nodded. Her back had been to the murder scene, he saw. "Was it raining hard at the time?"

"Poured down, the whole four hours," she said. "But I kept the fire going. Not like this." She dismissed the steaming mess with a flick of her hand.

"Was anybody else moving around?"

"Everyone had retired," she said.

"Yes, in your own group. But were there any other people around?" He found the correct cueword. "Any homeless persons, for example."

"I saw nobody," she said.

She had nothing more for him and he wrote down her name and address and went back to the group. Most of them volunteered names and addresses, although they insisted it was not necessary, they would be camped in front of Queen's Park until the government promised to stop all logging in Algonquin Park. One man refused to give his name. "I don't have to tell you a thing," he said proudly.

"No sir, you don't. If you want to obstruct the quest for justice for your leader, that's your democratic right," Cassidy told him loudly. "If you think trees are more important than the life of a man, go to it. But if you had any respect for him, you'd help. You decide. I'll be back."

He turned away, leaving them to chew that over as he watched Wall returning with the coroner in tow.

The coroner was an aging dandy. Today he was wearing a trenchcoat along with his usual homburg hat and cigarette. He shook hands with Cassidy. "Couldn't you have found a nice warm indoor murder, Jack?"

"We don't pick 'em Doc. Just pick 'em up." He led the way to the tent where Dr. Steiner was talking to the uniformed man. Cassidy introduced the coroner and then Wall sprang his request on Steiner. "We're going to have to impound the tent and its contents, anyway, Dr. It would help our investigation if we cut the tent up along one side. Is that all right with you?"

"I don't own this tent. I'll have to ask the others," Steiner said fussily.

"Be a leader," Wall told him. "We've got to do it anyway, why not give us permission?"

Steiner thought about that for a second then nodded his head. "Right. Do what you have to, officers."

Wall brought out his Swiss Army knife and dug it into the rain-tightened canvas of the tent wall. It went through with a satisfying little pop and he ran it down the height of the wall, then went back to the top and cut horizontally, opening a gaping inverted L.

"Thank you, I hate tents." The coroner tossed his cigarette aside and stooped to look in. He reached for the throat and then straightened up and checked his own watch. "Can't be certain but I'd think he's been dead since around two a.m.."

"Great. All this crowd was curled in their own tents, they say," Cassidy told him.

"Well somebody was moving. Somebody with a knife. Stuck it right in his heart by the look of it. I'll know better when I get him to the morgue."

Wall took out a piece of chalk and ran it around the body, making an outline on the foam rubber. "Okay then, I'll get the guys to move him to the morgue," he said. "Then we'll pull the tent down and send it in for the crime scene guys."

"He's about number six on my hit parade," the coroner said. "I won't get to him until late today at the earliest."

"That's okay. We've got a bunch of things to do first," Wall said gloomily. "Thanks for turning out."

"No choice," the coroner said. He brought out an old silver cigarette case and offered it to them. They shook their heads and he lit up and stomped away, waving over his shoulder.

Steiner was standing a little way off, nervously. He came back now. "What did he say?"

"Said your man was stabbed in the heart." Cassidy dumped the news on him roughly, checking his reactions. The short man put his right hand over his own heart defensively. "Poor Jonathon."

Wall said, "Tell me about him, sir. What was he like?"

Steiner took a deep breath, gathering himself like a singer, then he started speaking in a low, deliberate voice. "A wonderful, caring man. Concerned for the planet, for the human race, for world peace."

"What did he do?" Cassidy asked. "Like for a living, when he wasn't saving the world."

"Don't you dare mock him," Steiner breathed. "You weren't fit to tie his laces."

"Pardon me," Cassidy said. "I'm not being flippant. It's just we don't come across good guys much in our line of work. It's a shock to my system."

Steiner looked at him sternly but went on. "He is, or rather was, a publisher. He published Greenworld ."

"Must admit I've never seen a copy," Wall said. "Was it a subscription only kinda magazine?"

"An alternative publication," Steiner agreed. "Not in large circulation."

"Where would we get a copy?" Wall asked.

Steiner frowned. "Is that important?"

"I don't know until I've seen it. Could be useful," Wall said.

"What was his full name and address, do you know, sir?" Cassidy asked. He took that down and then asked the big question. "Who were his enemies?"

Steiner shook his head. "Until this happened, I didn't think he had any."

"He must have made enemies," Wall said softly. "All this picketing. He must've teed people off, company owners, like that."

"Multinationals," Steiner said and his eyes widened. "Of course. That's where to start looking, officers. The environmental criminals he confronted. One of them took their revenge on him."

"It's been my experience that those guys use lawyers, not violence," Cassidy said. "Fate worse than death, whole flock o' lawyers after you. Like being pecked to death by parrots."

Steiner looked at him suspiciously. "Do you always conduct yourselves with such levity?"

Wall pulled a sober face. "Death is a fact of life, doctor. We work with it all the time. We have to ventilate."

Steiner frowned. "I don't like it."

"I don't like murder," Wall said. "But we deal with it every goddamn' day, doctor. And we deal with it our way."

"Right," Cassidy said. "Our uniformed officer tells us that a number of the people here went into the tent to view the deceased before security was called. Can we find out which of them did?"

"Of course, if it will help." Steiner gave them a last quick look to check if they were grinning and then led them back to the gaggle of protesters who had gathered around the remains of the fire. As they walked over Cassidy looked at Wall and mouthed "ventilated?"

"Right," Wall mouthed back. "You'd know the word if you read anything outside the sports pages."

Steiner was talking earnestly to his troops. All of them were listening carefully except for one lean man who was trying to breathe life into the fire, using a pile of tiny wood shavings he had cut from the edge of the pole that held his "spare our forests" placard. He had piled them on top of one dull red spot on a wet log and was crouching to blow on it, ignoring the rest of them as smoke rose from his pile of chips.

"It's important to the job of finding out who killed Jonathon that these men know who went into his tent this morning," Steiner said. "It does not jeopardize our agenda to help them. I trust everyone will do what they ask."

"Who found him, and when?" Wall asked.

"I did." It was another woman, young and plain. With her hair and cheeks soaked with rain she looked forlorn.

"And you are Ms...?" Cassidy asked.

"Hunter. Debbie Hunter. I had made a pot of coffee and I took a mug in to him."

"That happened at what time?"

"Seven-thirty." She stifled a sob. "He hated getting up early."

"Who else was up at that time, besides you?"

"Just Douglas." She nodded at one of the beards. "We were making coffee together."

"And you went in and found him. Then what?"

"I screamed," she said. "I just screamed and Douglas came running up and I told him and he went in."

"Was the tent flap sealed when you went in?" Wall asked her. She nodded and he short-circuited her story. "And then everybody got up and came over to see what was going on, right?"

"Most of us did," she nodded.

"Could I have the names, please, of everyone who went into the tent?" Cassidy asked and then wrote as a dozen or so of the people volunteered their names and addresses.

"I'm not being personal here," Wall began, "But if this were a hotel, instead of an encampment, we would need to know who was in which room. Can you tell us please, who was in which tent?"

Like Noah's Ark, Cassidy thought as he sketched the scene and wrote down the details. Here they were saving the world while they shacked up in couples, two to a tent. Male-female in most of them, male-male in one, female-female in another. The two men sharing the tent were standing close together, intimately. The two women, Stella Lenchak and Debbie Hunter, the vestal virgins, did not seem to have anything going between them.

The man at the fire had finally coaxed a small blaze from his chips and was busily splitting another placard pole into kindling with a heavy clasp knife.

Cassidy looked at it and the strength the man was using to split his wood. No sweat for him to go through a man's chest, he thought. "I see this gentleman has a very practical knife here," he said. "Are all of you carrying camping gear like this?"

It seemed all the men were. They sneered at him for sneaking around to the question of who had a knife, but they all produced knives on cue, plus matches. Always matches, Cassidy noticed. This bunch would have fried in hell rather than carry an ecologically unfriendly lighter.

"We hear that Jonathon was stabbed," One of the men said as he showed his knife.

"Looks that way. The M.E. has to check," Wall said.

"Lots of weapons here," the same man said grimly. "How will you ever know who did it."

"We'll find out," Cassidy told him. "That's a cop's way of making the world a better place."

A blue paddy wagon pulled up at the edge of the park and then a car. Two plainclothesmen got out of the car and walked toward them. "Who's the wagon for?" one of the men asked roughly. "Are you arresting us?"

The detectives ignored the question, walking over to meet the crime-scene men. "I like the sound of this job," one of them said in greeting. "Wrap the crime-scene up and take it back to the office. It should happen more often."

"Listen, I want it checked real clean," Cassidy told them. "As soon as the ambulance has taken the body, strike the tent and lay it out as flat as possible in the wagon. Then go through that thing like you were chasing microbes."

"Plenty of 'em in there if that hairy bunch has been in it," one of the crime scene men said. "The ambulance on its way?"

On cue the ambulance pulled in at the curb, behind the police car. "There. All modern conveniences," Wall said.

The two detectives watched while the body was removed. The protesters all came over to watch as well, standing back, behind the orange crime-scene tape silently as the body was lifted out. Then the crime-scene men struck the tent, leaving all the pegs and poles attached, folding it flat and getting two uniformed men to help them carry it by the corners and place in the wagon. It lay inside almost flat.

"Nice work," Cassidy said. "Give it a good going over. We'll be back later. We've got to go check out the deceased's pad."

"Don't get any on you," the plainclothesman warned.

The dead man's apartment was a surprise. Instead of the squalid basement they had expected, they found a penthouse in a forty-year old apartment block in a treed section of the city. It was spacious and well-furnished, with a mixture of antiques and comfortable modern items. There were landscape paintings on the wall and one lacquered screen with mountains and cranes flying.

"Looks Japanese," Wall said.

"Looks like money," Cassidy said. " Judy dragged me out to the antique show in Yorkdale last spring. They had a screen like that there. Price was nine thousand bucks. I've bought cars for less."

"This guy didn't own a car. Cars pollute. Screens don't," Wall reminded him.

They went further into the apartment, to the bedroom with a queen-sized bed, covered with a beautiful handworked quilt. "This guy, Jonathon Mallory, he was divorced, right?" Cassidy queried.

"For years," Wall said. "So how come he's got all the good furniture and the lady-like linen, right?"

"Girlfriend?" Cassidy said. "Somebody must've thought he was cute, nifty little beard an' all."

"But nobody at the rally, love-in, whatever the hell it was, was anxious to own up to sleeping with him."

"Maybe he didn't screw disciples," Cassidy said. "Anyway, he must've had money. Let's see if we can find where it came from."

The next room they went into was Mallory's office. It had a big computer setup, a large worktable covered with files, and a pile of magazines with the title "Greenworld" on the cover.

Wall picked a copy up and flicked through it. "It's got ads in it. I didn't expect that. Figured with his politics he'd stay away from the running dogs of capitalism."

Cassidy took a copy and checked. "Yeah. I figured that too, all this holier than thou crap and yet he's taken somebody's bucks for a page."

"Dull ad," Wall said. "Look at this one. "Hackman's Paints, colouring your world, safely" and some crap about not polluting."

"No big companies in here," Cassidy said. "No Esso, or Ford or Dupont or anybody big. All small places."

"Maybe that was how he kept his conscience clear," Wall said. "The little guys don't pollute, whatever."

"Or maybe the big guys wouldn't touch a book like this," Cassidy frowned. "I don't know who would've read it anyway, but look around. This thing was most likely printed right here, on his computer. So he wasn't paying big printing bills. Must've brought it out for pretty much the cost of the paper it was printed on."

"Too small for the big advertisers? That what you're saying?" Wall wondered.

"I don't know. Anyway, Let's check, see what all he's got here."

Their search uncovered Mallory's personal papers, including his bank-book and a set of books for his magazine, printouts from the computer. Wall frowned over these. "Advertising revenue. Would you believe it, these Mickey Mouse outfits were paying as much as two grand for one of his ads." He pointed out an entry. "This is last month. Hackman's Paints. Two thousand."

"Ads are expensive, aren't they?" Cassidy shrugged. "Hell, it costs a fortune to get an ad on the Superbowl."

"I don't think this guy Hackman sells enough paint to advertise on the Superbowl," Wall said. "I've never heard of Hackman's Paints. Have you?"

"No," Cassidy said carefully. "Let's go talk to them."

They made a list of companies who had advertised in Greenworld and checked the addresses. Four were in Calgary, three in Montreal, one in Vancouver, but the others were all in southern Ontario, largely Toronto. They started their inquiries at Hackman's Paints.

They found themselves at a low, shabby factory building in the east end of the city. There was a heavy smell of oil in the air and the place had a grubby, Victorian feel. They flashed their ID to the receptionist and a wor-ried-looking young man came out to meet them. "I'm Rod Hackman. What can I do for you gentlemen?" He seemed nervous.

"I'm Detective Sergeant Cassidy, this is Detective Wall, Homicide Squad. We'd like a word, in private, please Mr. Hackman."

Cassidy saw the receptionist's eyebrows go clear up to her hairline as Hackman led them back through the big, open manufacturing floor.

It was hot and noisy and the workers were wearing paint-smeared coveralls. Hackman led the way to his office. It was small and cramped and had not been painted in a long time. There was a low window overlooking the floor and Hackman's desk was against it, where he could keep his eye on the work.

He sat down heavily. His face was the colour of lead. "You said you were from the homicide squad? How does that affect me?"

"Maybe it doesn't," Wall said easily. "We're making inquiries into the death of one Jonathon Mallory. He's an environmental activist, published a magazine called Greenworld."

The news did not make Hackman any calmer. "How can I help your inquiries?" he asked.

"Well, we notice that you're a regular advertiser in his book, magazine, whatever. We wondered if you could tell us anything about him," Cassidy said. "Like you must have met him, on business and so on."

"I have met him," Hackman said slowly. He cleared his throat and Wall and Cassidy exchanged glances. He was guilty as hell. But of what?

"When was that, sir?" Wall asked.

"Every month. He would come around to discuss our advertisement."

"Don't companies usually have an agency to do that kind of thing for them?" Cassidy asked. "Like, my wife's cousin is in the business."

It was the first time Wall had ever heard that but he said nothing, just looked at Hackman, his face radiating interest.

"The big companies, yes," Hackman said. "We're not in that league."

"Don't do much advertising, sir? That what you mean?"

Hackman cleared his throat again. "Not much, no. A little in the trade publications, you know, Canadian Paints and Finishes, Colourworld, things that go out to the wholesale buyers."

"How much would a business need to spend, to have an agency working for them?" Cassidy asked.

Hackman frowned. "Look, officer, I'm trying to run a business here. You come in and tell me that some guy I do business with is dead. Okay. I'm sorry to hear that. If I can help, I will. But where the hell is this leading, all this advertising talk?"

The phone rang before Cassidy could answer and Hackman swept it up. At once his face changed, taking on a soft, salesman's expression, friendly, relaxed. "Rog. Nice to hear from you. How's everything?" He swung his chair so he was facing out of his window and waited before saying. "Ten thousand? Hey, no problem. I can get it to you by the fifteenth, no sweat. But come on, I give it you at that price, I'm nothing but a busy fool."

It took five minutes to complete the call, then he hung up and turned back to the detectives, his face set like stone again. "This business about advertising. I don't have time to instruct you in the science of marketing, officers. With all respect. If you've got some questions that make sense, please ask them. Otherwise, I'm too busy for this."

"Fine. How about this one?" Wall asked. "How come you never even asked how or when he died?" He paused. "Like did you know already, sir?"

"If you must know, it was on the radio news at noon. I was out at the coffee truck when it came on and I heard it then."

Hackman said, "I felt sorry for the guy, for anybody who gets him-self killed, but I've got eighty-seven people depending on me to keep this place running, to keep them working, keep their families fed. Mallory's not around, too bad for him."

"How many magazines, outside of, what did you call them, trade publications? do you advertise in?" Cassidy asked. "And don't waste time looking in file folders for answers because you know the answer, don't you?" He paused and added "Sir" after the fact.

Hackman looked at him and worked his mouth nervously. "You can't come in here shouting at me," he whispered.

"Who's shouting?" Wall asked. "I was here, I didn't hear my partner shout. He asked you politely for an answer. What is it, Mr. Hackman?"

Hackman's mouth worked again and the word that came out was barely audible. "None," he said.

"There." Cassidy beamed. "Didn't hurt a bit, did it?"

"What are you getting at?" Hackman asked, in a raspy voice.

"I'm asking why a man who's stretched to the limit for a buck would blow around twenty-five grand in a year to run ads in a magazine nobody but a bunch of hairy activists and maybe some left-wing politicians ever reads," Cassidy said.

"Right," Wall nodded agreeably. "Like it seems to a couple of police-men that perhaps the late lamented Jonathon Mallory had found out some-thing bad about Hackman's Paints. Like maybe you dump solvents down the public sewer system, whatever. And he gave you a choice. Like what's it to be? A regular ad for x number of months, or a bunch of picketers outside your front door killing off any goodwill you have left in this business."

Hackman reached into his desk drawer and came out with a pill bottle. He shook out a couple into his hand and swallowed them. "I didn't kill the sonofabitch," he said. "But I'm sure glad he's dead." He picked up a coffee mug and drank down whatever was in it, pulling a face as he did so. "And that's all I'm going to say."

Cassidy stood up. "Thank you for your help, Mr. Hackman. We'll be in touch." He and Wall nodded and left the office. Hackman watched them through the window as they crossed the paint-splattered factory floor and then picked up the telephone and dialled an internal number.

When the other person answered Hackman said, "This is Rod. Stop payment on the cheque to Greenworld and don't write any more." He listened, nodding impatiently and then said, "That's right. We're not advertising there any more."

The detectives made two more calls on Greenworld advertisers before returning to headquarters. The executives at both companies were better poker players than Hackman would have been but from both they came away with the same certainty that they were right.

"Great," Wall said as they walked into their office. "So we've got, what, twenty-some people with a motive but we're no closer to finding out who stuck a knife in the bastard. They're all glad, that's all."

"So let's talk to the crime scene guys. Maybe the guy who did it dropped his business card," Cassidy said. "We're due a little luck."

They stopped off at the eighth floor and went into the crime scene office. A clerk was working on a computer on a desk pushed so close to the door that it would hardly open. Beyond her the crime-scene tent was standing with one side slashed completely out.

"You here for the jamboree?" the clerk asked sourly.

"Cheer up. We'll have a campfire later, roast weinies," Wall promised.

She looked at him and rolled her eyes. "Doug. It's the brains," she called over her shoulder.

Douglas Findlay, the senior crime scene man was kneeling in the tent. His partner was standing beside him, taking notes. They both turned to the detectives and the senior man stood up, brushing at his knees.

"So," Cassidy said. "What news of fresh disasters?"

"Lots of staining," Findlay said.

"What kind?" Wall had his own notebook out.

"What would you expect from a heart wound?"

"Blood," Wall said. "Any sense to it?'

"Not a whole lot. Couple of smears, like handprints."

"They must have been made at the time of the stabbing. The blood looked pretty crusted when we got there," Cassidy said.

"The prints are unreadable," Findlay said. "Just smears. I'd say you're right. Someone made them at the time of the killing. That means it's the perp. We'll do our best to read them. Think you can get palm prints from all the people there?"

"I can try," Cassidy said. "But the natives are not friendly. They'll probably tell me to crap in my hat."

"The knife had been wiped on the sleeping bag," Findlay went on. "Hard to say how long the blade was but it looks like a broad blade, a sheath knife, hunting knife."

"The coroner will have an idea on that," Wall said. "But they're all carrying jeezly great camping knives. We'll never get a match."

"Found something else," Findlay said lightly. "Saved the best for last. Look at this." He turned and picked up a plastic evidence bag off the desk. It contained a little plastic applicator with a piece of paper in it.

"Okay. I give in," Cassidy said. "What is it?"

Findlay grinned. "It's a pregnancy test. And yes, I've checked it out with my friendly neighbourhood drugstore and it's from the Instachek company. It turns green like this when it's positive."

"So the rabbit died first," Cassidy said. "Thanks Doug. Can we borrow that?"

"For sure," Findlay said. "Got a femme to cherchez, have you?"

"Got a couple," Cassidy said. "But before we go, let me have a look at the tent, can I?"

"Oh ye of little faith," Findlay said. He was peeved but trying not to let it show. He stood back while Cassidy lifted the flap of the tent and peered in.

Cassidy nodded. "Thanks Doug. You done good, like always. Now there's one other thing I'd like you to arrange for me."

"Shoot," Findlay said.

"Can you get somebody to take a look down all the drains in the roadway around Queen's Park. Start at the crime scene but head each way. I think you'll find a knife down one of them within a hundred yards."

"Will do. You go get 'em," Findlay said and the two detectives picked their way out of the tight door.

"Back to the scene?" Wall asked as they got into the car.

"Not yet. I'd like a minute at the morgue first," Cassidy said.

"You're the boss," Wall said. "But what the hell for? Like it's one of the broads, right? One of them must've been playing kissy-face with fearless leader. It got serious when she got pregnant. She shows him the evidence. He talks about the importance of his work and how he can't be tied down with a wife and kid, she cancels his check. Right?"

"Right," Cassidy said. "No argument. Only which woman was it?"

"You're gonna find out at the morgue?" Wall asked. "I think so." Cassidy said. He dug out his snuffbox and took a mammoth pinch, sighing with pleasure. "Don't disturb my train of thought. I'm making like Sherlock Holmes here." He blew his nose and Wall sighed and drove.

They were still too early at the morgue. The coroner was sorting out the human debris from a multi-car pileup on the 401 and his assistant told them that he would not be examining Mallory's body until the following morning.

"That's okay," Cassidy said cheerfully. "Can I take a quick layman's look at the dear departed?"

"Of course." The assistant led them down to the storage room and rolled out the drawer with Mallory's name on it. The body was as it had been in the tent, still wrapped in its light blue sleeping bag.

Cassidy looked at it for about a minute, not touching anything then said, "Thank you. That's fine. Let's go."

Wall said nothing as they drove on up to Queen's Park. By now there was a crowd of curious onlookers gathered around the fringe of the campsite. The demonstrators were huddled together, talking among themselves. Their placards were stuck in the ground around their camp like flags around a fort, but the heart had gone out of the protest.

The two detectives walked over to the encampment and nodded to the uniformed sergeant in charge of the scene. He nodded back and kept out of the way.

Steiner was in the middle of a group discussion and he looked up angrily when he saw the detectives.

"We've been told we have to strike camp. It's not fair. We won't do it."

"I'm not here about that, Dr. Steiner," Cassidy said.

Steiner ignored him. "It's the ultimate insult. We've had one of our number murdered and now the cause he gave his life for is being spurned."

"Yeah," Cassidy said. "I'd like to speak to Ms. Lenchak and Ms. Hunter please."

The two women were on opposite sides of the ring of people around Steiner. They both looked anxious.

One of the men said, "What's this about?"

"It's private, sir. If you're an attorney and the group has retained you, you're free to accompany the women. Otherwise, I would ask you to stay out of it."

"I'm a friend. We've got to stick together," he said angrily.

The two women had come forward, nervously, not speaking. Cassidy gave them a big smile. "Thank you, ladies. Can we have a little privacy, please?"

One of the other women shrilled, "Chauvinist. The word is women, not ladies."

"I stand corrected," Cassidy said with the same huge smile. "Ms. Lenchak, Ms. Hunter. If you please."

He led them away from the crowd, out under the shelter of a bare tree. From the steps of the parliament buildings a photographer with an enormous lens was taking their picture. Cassidy turned his back to him. So did Wall. Without making an issue of it they had sheltered both women from the camera.

Cassidy said, "The investigators who went through the tent made a couple of discoveries. One positive, if you'll excuse the pun, one negative."

He paused but neither woman spoke and he continued, "The positive find was this." He produced the plastic bag and held it up. Both of them peered at it, neither one spoke.

"This is a pregnancy tester, tradename Instachek." He waved the bag. "When it goes this shade of green it means that the person using it is pregnant."

He lowered the bag. "Now, all of the other women in your group seem to be teamed up with men. You two aren't."

"Stereotyping," Stella Lenchak said bitterly. "Everyone has to be in pairs. My mother thinks so, you think so. The whole bigoted world thinks so."

Cassidy said, "I submit to the pair of you that, whichever one of you is pregnant felt the same way. You went into Mr. Mallory's tent with the news. He refused to take it seriously. No agreement to marriage or to a," he paused and used the words as if they were in italics, serious commitment. "So, you stabbed him through his cold hard heart."

"This is ridiculous." Debbie Hunter snapped. "We're women, not monsters. We're not capable of such a thing."

"Heaven has no rage like love to hatred turned," Wall said. "Nor hell a fury like a woman scorned."

The women stared at him in astonishment and Cassidy said, "You have to excuse my partner. He read a book once."

"Congreve," Wall said happily. "The Mourning Bride."

"Yeah. Well," Cassidy said. "This little bag narrows it down to one of you two. You both had the opportunity, while you were on watch and the rest of the campers were asleep. The question was, which one?"

Wall took over now, with the practiced ease of a longtime partner. "We could have asked you to take a pregnancy test, but you'd have refused, which is your right. And we could have watched you until you had an abortion. But that would have been a shabby way of doing things.

The women were looking at one another. Both had the same expression of horror on their faces and Cassidy realised that both of them had been sleeping with Mallory, but that the other had not realised.

"So." He slipped the bag back into his pocket. "All of that watching and fussing was out of the question. But, like I said, the crime scene lads found something else. Something negative."

"What was that?" Stella Lenchak asked, through tight lips.

"That was the absence of stains," Cassidy said. He saw a man walking towards them and recognized Findlay, dangling something in a plastic bag. He'd found the knife, obviously. Good, that would have fingerprints and blood on it, probably.

"Ms. Hunter," he said softly. "You told me you took Mr. Mallory a cup of coffee at seven thirty. He was dead. You were beside yourself with horror. People came running. But you never spilled a drop in the tent, did you?"

Suddenly both women burst into tears. Stella Lenchak put her arms around Ms. Hunter and held her, rocking her gently. "No jury will convict you," she said. "He was a lousy chauvinist sonofabitch. He deserved what he got."

Hephaestus
ERIC WRIGHT

Eric is one of the giant figures in Canadian crime fiction. He's also one of the most honoured. In 1984, Eric won the first Arthur Ellis Award ever for his debut Charlie Salter novel, The Night The Gods Smiled. *In 1988, Eric won the first Arthur Ellis Award for Best Short Story for his "Looking for an Honest Man" from* Cold Blood: Murder in Canada. *Since then, he's won each award a second time, making him the winningest author in Arthur history. After 10 Salter novels, Eric's recent books have been departures.* Buried in Stone *brings Sergeant Mel Pickett, a former Toronto cop who appeared in the Salter stories, to centre stage.* Death of a Sunday Writer *introduces female private eye Lucy Brenner. And* Moodie's Tale *is a hilarious and autobiographical non-crime novel. It's a picaresque tale about a young Englishman's adventures in his adopted Canada. This story from* Cold Blood II *reveals Eric's darker side.*

On the fourth day, Clayton was sitting with Jensen at the bar by the pool. They were watching the video of the day's picnic, an amateurish, incoherent production which was being received with huge enjoyment by the crowd at the bar, most of whom had been on the picnic, an excursion to an island round the bay, complete with barbecue, free wine and games. Everybody on the screen looked slightly drunk, and the games involved a lot of "mooning" as the celebrants competed to expose their bottoms to the camera. Occasionally the scene switched abruptly, and the audience at the bar howled with glee as they remembered what the camera could not show. The film ended amid applause and comments like, "Good thing that camera didn't come around our side of the island."

Jensen said, "You should have gone, Fred. I wonder if they set up a shrine to Dionysius?" He was a man in his early forties with a round, moon-like face and very large horn-rimmed glasses, who smiled constantly. Clayton had met him and his wife on the first day and stayed with them ever since because, like him, the Jensens had come for the peripheral activities, not to join in the organised fun. When Clayton first arrived at the vacation club and was greeted by the combination of summer camp and college pep rally with which the management made everyone feel at home -- group she-nanigans which involved learning the club song, with gestures, and singing it every night to the setting sun -- he made a huge effort to keep his distance, refusing to wear a coloured ribbon to show which "team" he was on for the week, taking no part in Olympics day, and so on. The effort worked, for by the second day the Jolly Organisers, as the camp staff were known, began to leave him alone. Jensen made no effort at all. One look at the amusement on his balloon of a face, one remark -- "Ask the Leader if I may be excused the compulsory games if I attend the torch-light rally later, will you?" -- and they never bothered him again. Thereafter the three of them watched the highjinks on the beach, did not participate in the show put on by the Jolly Guests (the name the management gave the holidaying patrons), and avoided the disco altogether. By the third day there was an imaginary circle around the three of them, carved out by Jensen's stream of commentary, very vicious and very funny, on the activities of the other people. Occasionally Clayton experienced a twinge of discomfort when one of Jensen's remarks had an extra cutting edge. The Jolly Organisers who tried to involve them in the fun were trained to be cheery, and they would shrug at his response to them, smile and walk off, but they weren't either stupid or inhuman. Occasionally Clayton caught a glance from one of them that showed clearly enough that whatever their public face, they were very much aware of Jensen's contempt for them and their club. Once incident in particular made Clayton nearly want to apologise for Jensen, distance himself from him. One of the Jolly Organisers was a man who called himself Kiki. Most of his duties consisted of clowning around, wearing outlandish costumes and pretending to "flash" the girls on the beach. One day Clayton and the Jensens were helping themselves to lunch, buffet-style. Part of the display was a label, "Lobster Salad". Beside it, an assistant chef invited the guests to help themselves, but when they lifted the lid of the pot, there was Kiki's head, grinning at them like a decapitated lunatic. It was quite a shock -- Kiki had a very powerful grin -- and it caused a lot of hilarity. Jensen saw the joke from another part of the dining-room before he could get caught by it. Clayton watched him fill up his plate with macaroni salad, and approach the pot, looking innocent. When he lifted the lid and saw Kiki, he reacted in mock dismay and dumped his salad all over Kiki's head. Everyone else thought his was a wonderful, accidental reaction, the best yet, but Clayton was watching Kiki as the chef cleaned off his head, and his eyes were on Jensen. Then he looked at Clayton, very briefly, but for long enough to make Clayton wish he wasn't such a well-known Jensenite. But in the end, Clayton laughed with Jensen, preferring to be in the circle with Jensen and his wife rather than outside on his own.

Why had they come? For the tennis, Jensen told Clayton. The club's major daytime activity was tennis, and Cynthia was an avid player, like Clayton. And like Clayton, the Jensens were curious about what these places were really like. Tennis was both the reason and an excuse.

Cynthia Jensen was at least ten years younger than her husband, an attractive blonde made slightly too thin by the amount of exercise she took and by her devotion to fruit-juice instead of food. While she played tennis, Jensen went for walks with his camera -- he had several of them including a movie camera -- and sometimes he swam in the pool, though he was self-conscious about exposing himself because he never sun-bathed and when he took his clothes off, all the golden bodies got some revenge for the contempt he had for them when he was dressed.

Clayton joined them for brunch after the morning's tennis, and they idled the day away together until it was time for the five-o'clock session. They stuck together for meals because it was the only defence against the club practice of mixing up the guests for different tables at every meal, a custom which meant that on the first night Clayton ate with seven French people who ignored him, and the Jensens ate with a group of weight-lifters from Chicago who, Jensen said, could have earned their living in English movies as stock American boors. The three of them spent their time on the beach. Jensen assumed Clayton was of their party from the start and spoke as if the three of them were on Mars, trying to make sense of the native inhabitants. The other guests were not entirely homogeneous. The superb tennis facilities attracted a fair number who came for that alone, and on one occasion Clayton fell in with four psychologists from New York who were very good company after hours. But Jensen wanted no part of any larger group. He needed Clayton as someone to enjoy his misanthropy, and a larger audience would have recoiled from him, and perhaps even defanged him. Jensen was like the kind of father who can create attitudes within a house, tyrannise it with his world view, but when the family takes an excursion the children realise that strangers are impervious to their father's influence, that there are other ways of seeing and dealing with the world. So the father tries to keep the children prisoners at home rather than risk any diminution of his influence. Jensen was like that. Once Clayton was accepted, he was assumed to share Jensen's every attitude. Clayton understood this and let it happen. Jensen's was very funny; he suited Clayton for a week, as did his wife. All of them were getting what they came for.

Cynthia was not in Clayton's tennis group. The players were graded from one to six, according to ability, and Cynthia was a three, whereas Clayton was a four. They played at the same time, learning the same skills but at different levels. On the first night Clayton went to the disco, but once he had met the Jensens he never bothered again. (Jensen said, "I only go the discos to exercise my wife"). Cynthia said very little. She played tennis, read best-sellers, and smiled at the stream of entertaining malice that emanated from her husband. Clayton hadn't spent many hours in their company before he was speculating about them, but he gained no clue to their relationship. Jensen discouraged chat about private matters. It suited him to treat Clayton as a mutual observer of the mating games that were being played around them, but he never introduced a personal note.

Inevitably they talked about the reputation of the club and whether it was living up to it. Cynthia and Clayton were up early, and they could confirm that at dawn not a few souls were criss-crossing the grounds on their way home. Jensen was a very close observer of the way partnerships shifted between one day and the next. He was particularly interested in one couple from the Mid-West whom he overheard telling others that this was the eleventh club they had stayed at. This couple prowled along the shore, hand in hand, scanning the beach as though looking for a lost child. On the third day they found another couple and were hardly seen again.

And then, on the fourth day, the world changed. Clayton hadn't played tennis that afternoon, and he and Jensen were awaiting the arrival of Cynthia after her game. Jensen looked at Clayton after the video of the picnic ended and said, "Cynthia is having an affair, if that is the word for it."

Clayton waited for the joke, but none came. "When?" he asked, eventually, after he had got his breath back. "She's either playing tennis or with us."

"When she is supposed to be playing tennis," Jensen said, "she's fornicating."

"Who with?"

"One of the tennis pros, I think."

"The tennis pros spend all their time on the court," Clayton said. "There is no way."

Jensen shook his head. "They get time off," he said. "Perhaps she is fornicating with all of them, one at a time." His demeanour, like his tone of voice, was unchanged. He might have been discussing any of the guests. "Haven't you noticed? When she is supposed to be playing tennis, she's not always there."

"She isn't in my group," Clayton reminded him.

"Right. So you wouldn't notice. This morning I followed her down to the court where she was supposed to be playing. She wasn't there. The pro, rat faced boy with yellow hair, said he hadn't seen her since the first day. She is fornicating with someone. Playing the two-backed beast."

"How do you know?"

"What possible other reason could there be?"

Cynthia appeared on the other side of the pool and waved to them.

"What are you going to do?" Clayton asked.

"I don't know yet. This picnic has given me an idea though."

His wife approached and he stopped talking. When she arrived, sweaty, with a small blister on her thumb, Clayton looked at Jensen to see if he doubted that at least on this occasion she had been playing tennis.

"Have a good game, dear?" Jensen asked.

"The best since I arrived." She plopped down into a chair at the side of him.

"Why don't you give Fred here a game?"

"We're not in the same group." Cynthia stood up. "I need a drink," she said and walked over to the bar.

Clayton had no need to think. Under the circumstances, he had to act, to warn her about her husband. He followed her to the bar on the pretext of needing another drink himself. There was no time to introduce the subject gently. "You husband thinks you are having an affair," he said.

She looked at him as if he had made a joke. "Does he, indeed? Who with?"

"A tennis pro, maybe."

That was all they had time for, but it was enough. He had done his duty, and now it was up to her. They walked back to Jensen, and she sat down and reached to push back a bit of hair that was sticking out over one of Jensen's ears. That was it, for then, and the evening passed like all the others. When Cynthia had changed, they ate dinner, watched a series of sketches put on by the Jolly Organisers, and went to bed.

The next morning Clayton got up a little earlier than usual and stood among the trees, watching the Jensens' door. Cynthia appeared, in tennis clothes, and started off towards the courts. Shortly afterwards Jensen came out with a camera hung from his shoulder, but instead of following his wife, he struck off along a path that led over the hill to a village around the other

side of the cliffs. He seemed uninterested in Cynthia, or where she was going, and Clayton wondered as he followed her towards the courts, if he was
getting a glimpse of a very strange marriage.

After lunch the three of them were sitting by the pool, drinking coffee, watching an advertisement for a sailing excursion that was being shown
on the video screen. Cynthia picked up her beach bag and Clayton got
ready to join them in a walk down to the beach. Jensen put a hand on his
arm. "You go ahead, Cynthia," he said. "I want to tell Fred a dirty joke I
heard this morning."

She wrinkled her nose in mock disgust as she walked away. Jensen
turned to Clayton. "I've thought of a way to get my revenge on Cynthia,"
he said. The sun sparkled on his glasses. "The video we were watching
yesterday gave me an idea. Do you know the story of Hephaestus?

Jensen was a broker of some kind, but he had had a good education,
and he enjoyed playing the role of the scholar, stuffing his conversation with
literary and classical allusions. One day as they were watching the parachute skiers climb the sky, he compared them to Icarus, wondering which
one would get too near the sun, hoping he would be there when it happened.

"No," Clayton said. "Who was Hephaestus?"

"You may know him as Vulcan."

"The god of rubber tires?"

For a moment, all of Jensen's contempt was focussed on Clayton.
"No," he said. "The smith-god. He made fabulous armour for the other
gods, that sort of thing. He was married to Aphrodite. Now Aphrodite was
unfaithful with Aries, the god of war -- a lecher and a braggart, by the way
-- and Helios the sun-god saw them at it and told Hephaestus. Hephaestus
then fashioned a very strong, very thin net, which he hung over his bed. The
next time that Aphrodite and Aries came together Hephaestus dropped the
net, catching them in the middle of the act and making it impossible for
them to move. Then Hephaestus invited all the gods over to look. How the
gods laughed."

"What has all this to do with Cynthia?"

"Let's go for a little walk. I'll show you."

He took them along the path that Clayton had seen him take that
morning, away from the tennis courts, over the hill, and then through some
scrub until they reached the cliff edge. They had walked through two hundred and seventy degrees and were now on the other side of the tennis courts,
looking down at the beach. About fifty yards along the cliff path he stopped.
"Look down there," he said.

Clayton looked and saw an indentation in the cliff-face like a huge mine-shaft with a deep crack down the side. The eye was led down the shaft to a patch of sand that was nearly enclosed by the cliff. As they watched, a couple came along and climbed over the rocks, through the gap in the cliff face to the patch of sand inside. The shadows at the bottom were too deep to see who they were but what they were doing was obvious enough. It was a perfect love-nest.

"What has all this to do with Cynthia?" Clayton asked.

"I overheard some people talking about this place. I put two and two together and it seemed possible that Cynthia knew about it."

"So?"

"Hephaestus." Jensen tapped his camera. "Instead of a net I have this."

"You intend to take pictures of Cynthia making love? Have you seen her?"

"Oh, yes. I've seen her all right. Look through this." He handed Clayton his camera.

Through the view-finder, the same scene was visible, perfectly framed by the circle of rock.

"You can't see who it is," Clayton said. "It's too dark."

"Not in the morning. The sun comes up there..." Jensen pointed out to sea, "...and it sendsa powerful shaft of light into the cave about eight o'clock. When my Aphrodite and Ares were locked in each other's arms, Helios himself is on his way south."

Clayton realized then the monstrous plan that Jensen had devised. "You are going to photograph them, and show it on the camp video?"

"I'm not going to. I have." He pointed to the camera that Clayton was still holding, and reached for it.

Clayton snatched the camera back and Jensen lunged for it and stumbled. He fell forward and Clayton twisted to keep the camera out of his reach, then stiff-armed him to keep him from grabbing at Clayton's trousers as he fell. Jensen disappeared over the edge, falling like Icarus, not to the sea, but to the rocks below.

Clayton stood staring at Jensen's descent, and two Jolly Organisers came out of the bushes, Kiki and the rat-faced tennis pro with the yellow hair.

"I'll take the camera," Kiki said. "Now tell us what happened."

Clayton told them: Jensen and he were taking a walk and Jensen had fallen over the edge as Clayton got ready to take his picture with his own camera. "It was an accident," he said.

The Jolly Organisers looked at each other. "This could get compli-
cated," Kiki said. "Okay, you were up here taking pictures, and he took an
extra step backwards. Okay?" Kiki looked at Clayton, and continued to
speak slowly. "That's what happened. Okay? Danny and I were walking
along here. We saw it all. You were twenty feet away from him. Right,
Danny?"

Danny nodded and turned away.

Kiki walked to the edge of the cliff. "He was here and you were
there. Okay?"

Clayton stared at him gratefully. "It wasn't my fault," he started to
say, but Kiki cut him off.

"How could it be? You were twenty feet apart." He waited until he
was sure that Clayton understood.

"What were you doing here?" Clayton asked.

"That's easy. See that guy?" Kiki pointed to a figure floating high
above the sea, dangling from a parachute. "Danny was up there this morning and he thought he saw a Peeping Tom, taking pictures down the tunnel
of love. That's the local name for it. So when we noticed you two heading
this way with a camera, we decided to take a look."

Down below the beach was full of people; faces were turned up looking at them.

"You were *there* and he was *here*," Kiki said. "Okay?"

"You know what he was doing?" Clayton said. "He was spying on
his wife, taking pictures of her."

"Let's go down now," Kiki said, cutting him off. "And shut up."

It stayed that simple. There was a routine investigation and a verdict
of accidental death. Someone fell off a cliff while he was taking pictures.

Clayton never saw Cynthia again because she left with her husband's
body, but he stayed around and played tennis all he could for the last two
days. On the last night, as he was thinking about going to bed, Kiki came
up to him at the bar. "Some of the Organisers are having a party tonight,"
he said. "In Danny's room. Why don't you join us?"

Clayton was astonished and very pleased. About an hour later he
made his way to the staff quarters where seven or eight of the Organisers
were drinking beer and listening to music. If seemed to be a stag party,
which surprised Clayton. He took a beer from Danny and made himself at
home. Soon the reason for the absence of any girls was made clear as someone switched on the television screen and the pornographic movies began.

The Organisers cheered and derided the performances in a couple of small films, then Kiki said, "The next one is special."

It was an amateur effort jumpy and awkwardly filmed, like the picnic video, but eh images were clear enough. It began with a shot of Cynthia walking along the beach in her tennis shorts and then disappearing into the cave in the cliff. The next shot was straight down the shaft, focussing on the patch of white sand now brilliantly lit, where Cynthia's lover was waiting. Soon they were naked and the camera zoomed down on the wriggling pair. His face was obscured at first, but in the natural course of things the camera caught a frontal view as he lay back with his hands behind his head. Even Clayton's appendectomy scar was clearly visible.

He made for the door but Kiki was already in the doorway. "We always have a party on Friday nights for a few of the guests," he said. "Have a good trip home."

That was two years ago. They move those organisers around a lot so that now, whenever he hears of anyone who has spent a week at one of the clubs, Clayton always wonders, was Kiki there, and was there a party on the last night, and how long does a videotape last? Forever?

Current Events
VIVIENNE GORNALL

Vivienne Gornall is a freelance writer who lives on a small farm north of Toronto where she raises sheep, chickens, trees and children. Her work has appeared in Harrowsmith and Cottage Life magazines. This is her first published mystery story. One of the greatest achievements of Cold Blood *is the number of new authors who got their start through publication in the series. Vivienne is one. "Current Events" was written for a crime fiction writing class and was published in* Cold Blood V. *It's insightful and moving and rings disturbingly true. It's also one of the two first stories to be included in this collection.*

I heard the deep growl of a tractor's diesel at the end of the gravel driveway.

"Damn." I raced into my bedroom and quickly zippered up a track suit over my lycra riding outfit. I shoved my leather gloves inside my bicycle helmet and put it back on a shelf in the clothes closet. Damn, I wasn't going to get to ride my bike this afternoon.

The tractor eased round the long curve and through the wide band of evergreens that sheltered the house from the road. It was my brother-in-law on his John Deere, a plow attached to the three-point hitch. The blades were raised high above the damp gravel, lifted like a woman's long skirt to avoid mud puddles.

Ross threw back the tractor door and lowered himself to the ground. His left hand removed a sweat stained CO-OP cap, his right hand smoothed back his thinning hair. It gave me a jolt every time I saw him. He was so much like Ted.

I watched his stiff-legged gait to the kitchen door. He reminded me of a billy goat I had once owned whose knees creaked like a rusty gate when he walked. I opened the door, a smile on my face. Ross's forehead was the colour of mashed potatoes in contrast to his windburned cheeks.

His eyes were shy and refused to meet mine. They scoured the stoop, like a hen searching for bugs. "Found somethin' in my turnip field, Margie," he said.

"What is it?"

"Somethin' I think ya oughta see." His lips, cracked from years in the sun, pressed shut. Ross still worked all the land surrounding my bungalow.

I pulled on an old green duffel coat. We walked out to the back forty in silence. The long undulating curves of the furrows resembled velvet-black caterpillars crawling over the rolling fields. His fall plowing was almost finished.

"I's just plowin' under the stubble when ol' Jip seen it," he said as we approached a shallow valley between two curving hills. I could see a splash of colour in the depression, like a pendant nestled in a woman's cleavage.

Jip ran forward to greet us, his quivering nose thrust into the air. "Guess I dug up somethin' that was meant to lie fallow," Ross said.

I approached the thing pulled loose from the ground by the plow. The sweet heavy smell of putrefaction hung on the fall air. Blue-bottle flies rose in a hum as I walked closer.

It was the remains of a man lying face down on the ground. A bare arm, its rotted muscle grey and fibrous, poked through the remnants of a dirty yellow tee-shirt. The blackened, decomposing fingers had contracted into hooks and grasped a lump of earth. Strands of pant fabric lay splayed on the soft caterpillar ridges. The leg muscles were tunnelled with worms. A knob of bone, the colour of old Jip's eye teeth was visible at the hip through the wasted flesh.

I fell to my knees and dug the head loose from the shallow grave, the taste of bile rising in my throat. A shot of adrenalin hit my heart with the kick of a plow mule. It was my husband, Ted.

Ross pulled me away and put his arms around me. I could feel his body shivering against mine.

I crossed myself. Ashes to ashes, popped into my mind. Dust to dust.

Ross helped me home across the fields and into the house. He sat me at the kitchen table and slipped off my muddy boots then put a log in the stove to chase the cold from the room. I saw how the seams of his green work pants strained over his ample bottom as he wrestled the log into place.

The kitchen was heavy with the smell of chores that clung to Ross's clothes. He rubbed his callused hands over yesterday's whiskers, the knuckles thick and malformed from years of hard work and cold.

"Often wondered why Teddy never sent word after he left. Didn't sit well with me. We bin tuned to watch out fer each other. Twins are like that. Two peas in a pod."

He scratched his cheeks with nails as hard as horns. "I told the police Teddy had the gypsy blood. So I just figured he'd left again like he did twenty years ago. Course he comes home with you ten years later. Who'd a thought," he mused.

"I remember building this house when youse was just married, Teddy supervising, me doin' the work. We didn't ever talk much. Twins don't seem to need to."

I'll never forget when Ted disappeared, seven months ago. It was April. The air was full of the smell of dark earth and fresh spread manure. He travelled around Western Ontario stocking the stores with wrapping paper, greeting cards, stuffed animals, perfumed soaps.

Ted never said when he was coming home. He liked to surprise me by returning when I least expected it. His route usually took about five days.

I didn't have a car of my own so he made sure I had enough milk and bread and staples from Stouffville, the little town nearby. He wouldn't want me to run short and have to phone one of the neighbours scattered along the concession road. Ted wasn't one for having anyone involved in his affairs.

He had been away eight days when I phoned his Head Office to ask if they had heard from him. The receptionist said he hadn't called in but not to be concerned. She brightly reminded me that Ted was placing Mother's Day stock in the stores and since he was their best salesman "no news was good news" as far as she was concerned. "And won't his commission cheque be big next month?" she enthused.

I waited until the following weekend and when Ted still hadn't returned, I called Ross. He contacted the police.

The officer asked me if Ted was having an affair. I had to laugh at the suggestion. Ted would never do that. I was the most important thing in his life. He adored me. Didn't the cashiers at the A&P tell me and any customers willing to listen that I was lucky to have a man like Ted? He was always helping with the shopping, pushing the cart, picking items off the shelves, paying the bill. He wasn't like most men. Stepping inside a food store with their wives to shop for groceries was beneath most of them. The cashiers liked to point that out.

The police found his car at Yorkdale Centre in Toronto, thirty miles away, a few days later. There were no signs of foul play.

They checked his bank account and found he had withdrawn one thousand dollars the day he disappeared. Eventually he was listed as another runaway husband. I knew inside me they were wrong.

A few neighbours brought over tuna-noodle casseroles for my freezer and Ted's employer set up a trust fund for me. I got a job in town at a wholesale electrical supply outlet and life returned to normal.

But each morning before I left for work, I liked to sit at the kitchen table and scan the fields, looking, watching. Spring ripened into summer and the freshly tilled fields turned green with turnip leaves. Fall came and I watched the harvesting of the turnips, their skin the purple colour of a bad bruise.

The kettle whistled on the back burner. I buried my face in my hands. I heard Ross lift the boiling kettle off the element, then shuffle around the kitchen making tea. He put the pot under a quilted cozy to steep, warmed my cup and carefully poured the tea out for me. I was touched by his kindness.

All I could grasp was that Ted had been found in Ross's turnip field. I wiped my eyes and stared at my fingers, stained and rough from the gardening and housecleaning. Ted would have taken hold of them and teasingly called them housewife's hands. His had been well manicured. They looked like the paper napkins he sold, so soft and pretty.

The tea was good and stopped my shaking. I picked up the quilt I was working on and started to do a little hand stitching. Ross didn't say a word. He just stared into space.

My mind reviewed the circumstances leading up to Ted's disappearance in the spring. It was just a year ago when it all started.

Ted had always liked me at home but I found my days long. He never wanted children so for years quilting had been my passion. Last fall I asked him if I could try to convert the attic into a small studio.

When he wondered why, I fumbled for an answer. "I need a place to lay out my fabric. I've so many ideas for quilts and I need space. I'd like to start selling them." Mainly I yearned for a room to call my own. It was hard to put into words.

The next morning Ted took me to the local lumberyard and told me to buy anything I needed. I bought 'Do it Yourself Wiring' and 'Renovating the Attic'. Ted joked and winked at the staff as he struggled to the car with my tools and supplies.

I gave myself a nasty shock when I installed power on the landing at the top of the stairs. That was a day to remember. I had inserted a screwdriver between a mounting screw attached to the outlet on the front of the junction box and the live wires coming into the box. The metal screwdriver must have completed the circuit between the wires and the screw. An electrical charge shot through my body. It gave me a scare and new respect for electricity. I re-read that wiring book from cover to cover until I understood it thoroughly. Later, Ted bought a floor lamp from Sears and plugged it in. It worked.

I managed to hit my fingers several times with the hammer. My aim was terrible. I went back to the books for help, adjusted my grip and changed the angle of the nail. Eventually I could sink a nail in three blows. My aim was deadly.

"What did my princess do today?" Ted would ask as soon as he walked in the door. The attic was the first thing he wanted to see. He was not a handyman and I could tell he was impressed with my carpentry skills, despite my battered fingers.

I spent the whole winter building my studio. I painted the ceiling and walls a creamy white and installed pine shelves. I covered the floor with a bright rag rug I had made years ago. Fat quilted cushions were scattered around the room.

Ted and I wrestled an old table up the open stairwell to the attic. I was glad the narrow stairs had no railing on the right side or we would never have got the table into the room but I scared myself when we did it. The stairs were steep and treacherous so I installed a wrought iron handrail into the wall a few days later.

I may as well admit it right now. I had one secret from Ted. I knew how important it was to him to have a wife with traditional values. He hated the feminist movement and declared it was the cause of family breakdown. But I still wondered what it would be like to have him help make the meals and clean the house. What would it be like to have a job in town? I actually envied the cashiers who were on their feet for hours at the A&P. At least they knew they were alive.

My secret was that I had bought myself a bicycle. Not one of those three-speed steel framed bikes from Canadian Tire, but a twenty-one speed, microshift, TIG welded, alloy frame racer.

Ted would have been terribly upset if he had known. He'd have worried about me on the road and ranted about the chance I took of being abducted or worse. He would have forbidden it.

He would also have quickly figured out that I stole the money. Bit by bit I took it from his wallet. One glorious day I hitchhiked to a town named Aurora, ten miles west and bought the bike and the riding clothes.

When I knew he would be away for several days I pulled the bike out of the root cellar, put on my stretch suit, gloves, sunglasses and helmet and rode with the wind. I liked to go out early in the morning when the neighbours were in their barns milking and return in the late afternoon when they had already started evening chores. No one ever guessed.

Every marriage has its secrets.

"This's bin a terrible blow, Margie." Ross stared out the window at the plowed fields, the darkening sky. "First snow's comin'."

I put down the quilt and finished my tea. I had been lost in thought.

Ross hesitated then walked to the phone. "Best I call the police," he said, sweating from the heat of the stove. "Sure as hens lay eggs, Teddy didn't bury hisself out there. It's a wonder I found him. Once'd I got this year's crop off I's goin' to bed 'er down in alfalfa. Wouldn't of bin plowed fer 'nother five years at least."

I dropped the needle. I couldn't stand the thought of anyone seeing Ted's decomposing body. "If you phone the police there'll be an autopsy. They'll probably cut Ted's body apart and take out pieces to probe and poke. You mustn't let them. He'd hate it."

Ross spoke softly from across the room. His eyes were impossible to read. "Teddy looked after you like a prize pig. What happened to my brother, Margie?"

I shrugged, my heart breaking.

"You can tell me," he said. "Haven't I always been here for youse? When Teddy disappeared, you didn't have nobody to turn to. Didn't I check on you? Didn't I say you should of come and lived with me? Family takes care of family. I told you that."

It was the kindness of his words that convinced me to tell. I had carried the burden of Ted's disappearance since spring. Could I possibly make Ross understand? There was so much he didn't know about his brother.

"Would you like to see this quilt I'm working on?" I said.

He cocked his head like a robin looking for worms, then nodded.

How I loved my quilts. I poured my heart into those pieces of fabric. My latest creation was almost finished. It was the size of a single bed cover. All that was left was some hand stitching and the border.

The centre was dominated by an enormous cross, a symbol of my Catholic upbringing. Rays of coloured fabric cascaded in all directions like heavenly light. They were everywhere. I had worked the upper right in an old pattern called double wedding rings. The two bands were linked together in an unending design. The upper left was another traditional pattern called log cabin. It symbolized our home together. The lower half was filled with farm scenes.

I laid it on the table in front of Ross. He gently touched the surface of the quilt with his great gnarled hands. "Looks real good," he said.

"It's about me," I said. "See the cross in the middle? That's the church. Those long beams of colour show how the church touched all parts of my life."

Ross looked closely. The rays spread over the surface, connecting with everything. It was extremely intricate.

"There's my childhood at the Catholic school, there's my marriage, there's my father giving me away to Ted. I was just a girl."

I could see Ross puzzling through the designs, trying to keep up with my story. He would look at me, then look at the quilt. All his life he had worked with animals and crops and weather, trying to figure them out. He had had his successes and failures over the years.

But women were a mystery to him and he had never married. He once told Ted that if you wrapped all your worries together with a stout piece of binder twine, they didn't come near a woman for trouble. He said that trying to understand a female was like trying to guess when a cow would freshen. She'd sneak that calf by you the one time you weren't looking and then bawl at you for not being there.

"I like that one the best," Ross said. He pointed to the farm on the lower half of the quilt, its rolling fields passing from one season to the other in shades of brown, green, gold then white. "It looks so peaceful under the snow."

I started to stitch again. My needle rose and fell, creating a long curving pattern on top of the quilt, like a line of fencing. "Ten stitches to the inch," I said proudly.

What a strange time to be discussing my quilt. My husband lay dead in a turnip field.

"Yer tellin' me 'bout Teddy."

I nodded. "The attic had been finished for less than a week and I had it nicely organized. Ted had been drinking all evening. I was upstairs quilting. He walked into the attic and started to stuff my squares and bolts of fabric and patterns into garbage bags. He didn't say a word. I didn't either. It was best to keep quiet when he was drinking. He threw the bags down the stairs and told me to take them out to the garbage. Then he moved all his things in. It was as if I didn't exist."

I stopped talking.

Ross's eyes burned into me. "Don't slack in the traces, Margie."

I didn't want to go on, but I did. "Ted forced me up to the attic and said it was his study now. I was to get undressed because the first thing he wanted to do was 'study' me. Thought he'd made a big joke."

I rubbed my hands together. "Do you understand what I'm telling you?" I was cold again.

Ross's eyes never left my face. He didn't answer.

"Ted went back downstairs. I heard him bumping around in the kitchen, pouring himself another beer. I got undressed. When I saw him stumble on the stairs I became concerned. I knew he was very drunk. I called to him, "Ted, be careful. Grab the railing.

"You know how steep and narrow those open stairs are, Ross. He reached for the lamp on the landing to turn on the light. He stumbled and his beer spilled. He slid to his knees, lost his balance and fell back down the stairs. He hollered at me but there wasn't anything I could do. He was dead by the time I got to him. I couldn't save him."

I looked at Ross. "So if you go to the police, they'll probably say I pushed him down the stairs or that we had a fight." I stopped for a breath. "I swear, Ross, I never touched him, except to bury him."

I began to cry.

"Stop bawlin' like a cow with milk fever," Ross said. "Everythin's goin' to be all right. Yer like me, Margie. If it wasn't me savin' his hide I guess it was you doin' it. And Ted would want his passin' to be private-like. But I can't leave him lyin' out there on the ground, like an old seed bag. It's not fittin'. He needs proper buryin'. Family takes care of family."

Ross nodded as he spoke. "Course I can't think of a better place for him to be than in my turnip field. It's class one soil and it's got new tile drainage. Come home to his roots, didn't he?"

He smoothed his hair once more. "This'll just be between you and me, Margie. Don't you worry 'bout nothin'. I'll get out my backhoe and bury him proper. It's not the first time I've cleaned up after him."

He left the kitchen a few minutes later.

I sat by the fire and quilted. It calmed me. I knew that Ted could be truly laid to rest. I hand-stitched a cross on the quilt, in the farm's brown spring earth and put his name and the year of his death underneath.

I heard the sound of Ross's backhoe in the driveway a few hours later. The kitchen door banged opened and he walked in. He shuffled his feet a little on the mat, his eyes meeting mine.

"It's gettin' dark in here, Margie. Where'd mother's old fringe lamp get to?"

"I put it upstairs months ago."

A piece of hay clung to his bottom lip. He scraped his top teeth over the lip and pulled it into his mouth.

"I done the chores then buried Teddy." There was a long pause. "The way I see it, you an' me got a lot in common, Margie. We don't mind gettin' a little shit under our nails. So I thought we could help each other out now and then, know what I mean?" He knelt down and undid his work boots. The smell of fresh manure and sweat was overpowering.

"I always took care of Teddy. I left school and worked the farm so he could stay in school. He tol' me he needed a house after he came back with you and I severed off five acres fer him. I even built it for him. I saved his hide lotsa times when he got drunk and picked fights. I've hauled his ass out of more messes than I care to remember."

He smiled at me. "Course there's many the time he did the same fer me. Two peas in a pod my daddy used to say."

Ross sat heavily in the kitchen chair. "Get me a tea, would ya' Margie?" He shuffled uneasily. "Ted told me you was pregnant when youse got married."

I could barely hear his voice it was so low. I smiled to myself. One thing about farmers, they knew everything about everybody. They didn't always let on, but they knew. Except Ross didn't really know his own brother, his twin.

"Did he tell you when I lost the baby?" I said.

Ross nodded. "He was broken up about it."

I put the tea on to steep then settled into a chair across the table from him. He scratched the top of his head with his broken nails.

"Did he tell you how?"

He gave no answer, just a shake of his head.

"I didn't have his dinner ready when he came home from one of his long trips. He'd never tell me when he'd be back. I was sick and I hated the smell of food so I found it difficult to be in the kitchen. When he saw I didn't have the meal ready, he hit me."

The silence in the kitchen was terrible. I started sewing my quilt again. "He said he'd make sure the baby knew who was the boss in this house, too."

My hand went to my abdomen as if once again protecting the child from the blows. "I lost the baby that night."

Ross' face was filled with pain. "He beat you?"

"Lots of times."

"So why did ya stay?"

"Where was I going to go? I didn't finish high school. I didn't have any money. Where was I going to go?"

"He was a hard man, Margie. I admit that. He had a mean streak. I hauled his ass outa manys a mess."

Ross looked at me like he was sizing up an open heifer at a cattle auction. "Now I'm haulin' yers out," he said. "I took the backhoe out to the turnip field and dug a grave any man would be proud of. Teddy is down so deep even ol' Jip can't smell 'im. I'll seed it down to alfalfa and a nurse crop, come spring."

The heat from the stove made his forehead shine like paste.   "I'll have it now, Margie."

I sat still, not comprehending.

His big hand flashed across the table and caught me square on the cheek. "My tea, Margie, I'll have it now."

I jumped out of the chair, my face seared by the pain of the blow. I could feel my cheek flushing crimson.

"My daddy used to keep mother straight just like that. He'd say, 'That's fer nothin', wait'll you do somethin.' It made her mind him, fer sure."

I quickly poured Ross a cup of tea and placed it in front of him.

"You pour yerself one and come sit 'side me," he said.

I shook my head.

"I ast you nice, Margie. After all, family takes care of family. You'll do well by me. Now pour yerself some tea and sit here." He stood up and pulled out a chair.

I sat down on the seat, poised close to the edge. Ross stood behind me. He lowered his massive hands to my hair and then onto my shoulders. I jumped and tried to rise but he pushed me back down.

"Now you said you got nowheres to go so just settle yerself."

His hands roamed down to my breasts. "Guess we'll keep what happened to Teddy 'tween us, right Margie? Jist you and me." His voice was a croon.

His thick fingers undid the zipper on the front of my track suit. His heavy body pushed rhythmically into the back of the chair. I could feel his mouth, sour and wet in my hair, the stench of fermented haylage on his clothes, suffocating me.

"Now get yourself up to the attic 'cause I want a turn studyin' you. I'll be along soon's my tea's cooled."

It was happening all over again. I climbed to the attic and lay against the cushions hugging them close, waiting, my body so weary. I soon heard the soft squish of Ross' damp wool work socks as he approached the stairs. I watched his head and torso come into view. He had removed his workshirt. The arms and neck of his undershirt were banded with old sweat, like tree rings. His hands were feverishly undoing the belt buckle.

"Ross," I called. "Be careful. Grab the railing."

He grasped the wrought iron bar with his left hand pulling his heavy body upwards. "You like the light on or off, Margie?"

"On," I whispered. I watched his tongue wet his lips. His left hand slid farther along the railing, his right hand reached for the lamp on the landing.

His thumb pushed the switch and the lamp exploded. Ross' body lifted and arced backwards then crashed to the floor below.

I rushed down the stairs and stood near his bulk, my legs shaking. His socks smoked. The air was acrid with the smell of burning wire, flesh and wool. The Lord giveth and the Lord taketh away.

Today is memorable. I feel like going to confession. Forgive me, Father for I have sinned. Old habits die hard. Later, I'll hand-stitch the border onto the quilt - a tedious job. That would be my penance.

Earlier today I cleaned up the shattered glass on the landing. I found a small piece of scorched fringe in the attic. It must have blown into the room during the explosion last night. Luckily I found it. It could have been discovered by the wrong person. I can't afford mistakes like that. Goodness knows I made enough of them in my life. Ted was one of them.

My thoughts rushed out like water at spring break-up. He was never my husband, he was my keeper.

Ted enjoyed hurting me. Bending my fingers, hitting me very carefully so no one could see a mark. Of course he was always sorry afterward. He'd treat me so well for awhile that I'd think my mind was tricking me or I was going crazy.

I know why he didn't tell me when he was coming home, why he did all the shopping, why he chose everything in the house. Control. All I loved was the attic and he took that from me too.

Ted used to say that I was dumber than a dog. Well, I learned a few tricks. One of them was wiring. I learned that electricity followed the path of least resistance. That Saturday night last spring, after Ted tossed my quilts out of the attic and moved his things in, I knew it was time. There was no place for me to go. I had lost more than the attic.

I quickly re-wired the lamp he had bought for the landing while he was in the kitchen getting another beer. He grounded himself by grasping the wrought iron railing. The electricity passed right through his heart because he offered less resistance than the lamp. Ted made his electrocution more effective by spilling beer over his hands.

Afterwards, I manoeuvered his body into the little garden wagon attached to the lawn tractor. I drove him out the back to Ross' turnip field. It had been disced a few days before and was ready for the transplants. It was easy to dig in the soft earth. I buried Ted's business clothes, briefcase, wallet and the remains of that ugly Sears lamp in a deep hole, not far from his body. I had heard Ross tell Ted he would seed it down with alfalfa next spring.

Monday morning, I opened Ted's banking drawer. He didn't bank in Stouffville. He knew everyone there and didn't want them involved in his financial affairs. He had chosen the town of Aurora, where I bought my bike.

I filled in a withdrawal form for one thousand dollars, forged his signature and put the form in my fanny pack. I wore gloves in case the police fingerprinted the slip of paper, but I don't think they bothered.

I put the fanny pack and a track suit inside my backpack, along with my helmet and gloves, then lifted my bike into the back of Ted's car and drove to Yorkdale Centre. I didn't have a licence but over the years, fear had taught me ingenuity and given me the will to survive. I could have driven a Sherman tank if it had been necessary. I wore gloves the whole time.

There were hundreds of people pulling into the parking lot. I was invisible in the crowd. I slung my knapsack on, took my bike out of the car and rode north.

The bike ride to Aurora was one of the happiest and most carefree in my life. Outside the bank I locked my bike to a post, slipped into my track suit then stood in line trying to look as bored and depressed as the rest of the customers. It was difficult.

I made it home slightly ahead of the hard spring rain that obliterated my tracks out to the turnip field.

Ross' body was the devil to get out of the house last night. He was heavier than Ted. I rolled him out the door and into the backhoe's scoop and buried him in the valley with Ted. Two peas in a pod.

I returned the backhoe to Ross' farm and walked home as it began to snow, covering my tracks.

It stopped snowing during the night. Good. The fields are white but the roads are bare. More snow is forecast for tomorrow. I'm going riding as soon as I finish sewing on the border.

My story is right here in the quilt. The double wedding rings go on and on forever, like a Greek motif. Look closely. There's a break in the rings marked with my baby's tiny cross.

The log cabin design is intricately mismatched. It could never be a home where children laugh and play.

Throughout the quilt the great shafts of colour from the cross grasp at the images, coiling around everything like the tentacles of an octopus.

I stitched a cross for Ross in the white fields of the family farm, the place he said looked so peaceful under the snow. I put his name and the year of his death underneath. Family takes care of family.

An Eye for an Eye
NANCY KILPATRICK

Noted as one of Canada's leading writers of horror fiction, Nancy's work includes the novels Near Death, As One Dead *and* Child of the Night, *as well as almost 100 short stories. A 3-time nominee for the prestigious Bram Stoker Award, and also for Canada's Aurora Award, Nancy is also a regular contributor to the acclaimed* Northern Frights *series of dark fantasy anthologies published by Mosaic Press. Nancy's first foray into short crime fiction, "Mantrap", won an Arthur Ellis Award in 1993. This story from* Cold Blood V, *Nancy's second in the crime field, incorporates elements of the horrific and raises disturbing questions about the nature of justice.*

Alexander Mifflin was stabbing my mother as my brother Bill and I walked in the back door. I dropped the Eaton's shopping bags I carried and screamed. Last-minute gifts tumbled into the pools of bloody mince meat. Mifflin turned. He and Bill fought. Bill outweighed him; he had wrestled at college. I rushed to my mother's blood-soaked body. The knife was lodged in her eye and, desperate, I yanked it out. Mother died in my arms seconds before Bill brought her killer to the ground. Before I could dial 911. Before she could say goodbye.

I know what you're thinking, the same thing the media is saying— I'm a psychopath. What makes me believe I have the right to be judge, jury and executioner? Your silly questions have nothing to do with me. I have that right by virtue of the fact that I have fought to stay alive in the face of shattering despair. You know yourself, it's survival of the fittest. You've thought that, even if you can't bring yourself to admit such a politically incorrect idea. I was a woman with a mission. Mission accomplished. If you'll hear me out, I know you'll understand.

Four years after my mother's death I came to the conclusion that murder is not so terrible. We all die anyway so what's it matter when or how. That might seem a jaded statement, but you know in your heart you've thought the same thing. We all have. It follows then that if one murderer can get off virtually scot free, why not another? Why not me?

I used to believe in divine justice. Then I grew up. For a while I had faith in our man-made justice system. When that failed, when jurisprudence let a guilty man walk away with his freedom and my mother's blood on his hands, I grew up some more.

Who would avenge my mother? Who would stop that madman from repeating his crime against humanity? No one. No one but me.

Let me start closer to the beginning, the easiest place to try to make sense of me and my 'crime', although there's no sense to his senseless crime.

The evidence was tangible, not circumstantial: Alexander Mifflin, a thirty-five-year-old Caucasian male broke into our North Vancouver home on Christmas Eve, ostensibly to steal anything of value. My mother was preparing mince meat pies for the holiday dinner the next day. The lights were out in the rest of the house—apparently she had been working in the kitchen and when the sun set turned on only one light. He surprised her there. She fought him—she was a large, strongly built woman of Scandinavian ancestry who did not give herself over easily to being intimidated. No one would have ever called her a coward. Neither is her daughter.

It was apparent they struggled. Chairs were overturned, the floor was a sea of mince meat. A paring knife lay on the table, to trim crusts, but he reached to the white ash knife rack and pulled out a Henckel with a six inch blade. Mother always loved good knives and had the blades honed by the man with the knife-sharpening cart who came by weekly. The coroner commented on the sharpness of the blade, because the twenty-eight stab wounds were, for the most part, clean. There were seven in her chest, two in her stomach, one in her left leg. The knife penetrated her diaphragm. She was left-handed and that side received the worst treatment. But the majority of the stab wounds were to her back, puncturing both lungs, one kidney, and, because the blade was so long, her heart. The most gruesome sight was to her left eye, where I found the knife lodged. The blade had pierced her brain. As I withdrew it, pale matter seeped from the wound. I can still see the tissue, like wood pulp.

I lived in a state of numbed grief. At the funeral I couldn't cry. Later, when we sold the house, before I left for college, as Bill and I sorted through my mother's belongings and I asked for her knives, he stopped and advised me, "Connie, try to forget what happened and get on with your life." But how could I forget?

No fourteen year old should have to experience what I did. Unless you've seen death close up, you cannot know how shocking it is. When the body seems to sigh. When the light fades blue lace crystal eyes to flat dull agates. When a kind of gas—maybe it was her spirit—wafts from the open mouth and ascends, rippling the air. My mother was gone. Her murderer would pay.

But he did not pay. Four years passed before Alexander Mifflin came to trial. I waited patiently through the delays, the motions and counter motions. He opted for judge only, no jury, knowing that ordinary people would find his acts against my mother incomprehensible. Still, through my frozen grief, I had faith.

But he'd had a bad childhood, a therapist testified, and had paid in advance. A minister assured the court that Mifflin attended church, helped out in the community, would be missed. He was a father, out of work, with a lovely wife and children to support. Not a crazed dope fiend, but a decent man, just desperate, said his brother. A police officer reported he'd been a suspect in several crimes and charged with burglary once before, but those charges had been dropped for lack of evidence. The court ruled that information inadmissible. Mifflin testified he did not recall reaching for the knife. He did not realize he stabbed my mother. Twenty-eight times. When I pulled the knife from my mother's brain, effectively I destroyed his fingerprints.

All throughout the trial I felt nothing, just stared at Mifflin, memorizing how he looked, his mannerisms, and finally his cursory testimony. The entire process had been like mining a vein that turned out to be corrupted. And the further along we traveled, the worse it got. The delays only helped his case. And the deals. Not murder one for Mr. Mifflin, who pleaded guilty, but manslaughter. Twenty years. He had already served four, he would be eligible for parole after another six.

The system failed me. But I vowed not to fail my mother.

How do you kill a murderer? It's not as easy as one might think. It takes a lot of planning. Alexander Mifflin was paranoid—he assumed everyone had an intent as evil as his own. I understand paranoia. I've lived with it since that Christmas Eve. I have not felt safe since because there are other Alexander Mifflins in the world and you never know when they will invade the privacy of your home and take control of your life and stab you or a loved one to death. You understand that, I know. You read the news. You have the same fears.

During those years of growing up without her, when I needed my mother most, I developed a plan. The day he entered that penitentiary as a convicted prisoner, legally I changed my name. I earned a BA, and then a master's in Social Work. All the while I was doing time too, waiting for Mifflin.

In anticipation of his release, I changed my hair color, even the color of my eyes—I needed contact lenses anyway, and blue to green was not much of a stretch. The business suit and crisp haircut that had become my disguise were a far cry from the sweater and skirt and shoulder length hair he would remember.

With my excellent grades at university, I could have taken a job anywhere, but I wanted to work for the province, in correctional services. Normally the so-called easy cases—like Mifflin—are the plums and newbes are assigned the junk no one else wants. I told my supervisor I needed extra work and begged for Mifflin's case—I wanted to research a case with a good prospect for rehab. She was happy to get rid of an extra file folder.

That Thursday morning of his release—Thor's Day—I phoned his wife and told her not to bother taking the six hundred kilometer bus ride to the prison. "I'll get him," I assured her. I left a message with the warden's office with instructions for Mifflin to meet me at the gate; I would drive him home. It was partially true—I did meet him at the gate.

The day was overcast, I remember, with steely clouds hanging low over the British Columbia mountains, determined to imprison the sun. The day suited my mood. It's inappropriate to feel jolly when a life is about to be extinguished. Even I know that.

I watched him walk out of the prison a free man. Mifflin reeked of guilt. But his guilt would not bring back my mother, and I wasn't about to forgive him. He would not make it home to his lovely wife and three children. He would not resume his good works in the community. He wouldn't make it past the parking lot.

Mifflin hadn't seen me in six years—since the case finally came to trial. My testimony had been brief. Over that week as the travesty of justice unfolded, he faced front and didn't look at me, although my eyes were drawn to him like iron filings to a magnet. I will never forget his left profile.

He looked the same, although his muscles were more developed—presumably from working out in the prison gym—and his cheeks more gaunt.

"Mr. Mifflin," I said, removing my glove and extending a hand. I wanted to feel the skin of this killer, the flesh that held the knife that had ended my mother's life. Is the flesh of a killer different from normal flesh?

Would I feel the slippery blood of my mother that had seeped into his pores ten years before, blood that could never be washed away?

He shook my hand. His grip was not as firm nor as cool as I'd anticipated, but mine made up for it. He looked at me skeptically. "Shelagh McNeil," I said, "your new case worker."

Mifflin ran a hand through his greying hair; his brown eyes reflected confusion—he didn't know what to do with me. Maybe it was hard for him to be in the presence of a woman without a weapon of destruction.

"I have a car," I said. "This way."

I slid behind the wheel of the tan Nissan and he got in on the passenger side. I sat without turning the key, staring at his left profile.

He fidgeted, punched his thigh in nervousness, looked out the window. "Mind if I smoke?" he asked, pulling out a pack of Rothmans.

"Yes I do," I said.

He slid the pack back inside his jacket submissively. The silence was getting to him.

Finally he turned. "Do you need my address?"

"I know your address."

He scratched his head. "Can we get going? My wife's waiting. Christmas, you know. The kids and all."

"I know everything I need to know about you, Mr. Mifflin. All but one thing."

He waited, expectant.

"How did you feel as you murdered Mrs. Brautigam."

"How did I feel?" Now he was really uncomfortable. "Look, I talked to a shrink about all this, inside." He shifted and turned away from me. "Can't we talk about this later?"

"That's not possible, Mr. Mifflin."

He turned back. His eyes narrowed. He struggled to make a connection but there wasn't enough left of the girl who had watched her mother die. And it wasn't just the physical changes. I was no longer vulnerable, but he was.

He put his hand on the door handle. "Look, I'll catch the bus."

"The last bus is gone," I told him, "and I believe your parole stipulates that you are required to meet certain conditions, including working with your social worker. I simply want to know how you felt, that's all. When you stabbed Mrs. Brautigam twenty-eight times, and her blood gushed out, splattering you with red gore, and her screams filled your ears. And her son and daughter watched their mother die. How did you feel?"

He turned away. In a small voice he said, "I don't remember."

"I need to know how it feels," I said, slipping a hand into my briefcase, "because I don't remember feelings either." I hit the automatic door lock.

His head snapped back.

I used both hands to plunge the knife into his left eye. I had sharpened the Henckel daily after the police returned it. Most of the six inches slid in as easily as if it were pie dough I was cutting. I felt the finely-honed steel pass the eyeball and enter the pale brain tissue.

His hands had clamped around my wrists; I couldn't tell if he was trying to pull the blade out or helping me push it in as far as it would go, but I held tight.

Mifflin went rigid. He stared at me for a moment, his face creased with uncomprehending horror, his pierced brain struggled to make the awful connection. His hand clutched the handle and he yanked the blade out. Blood spurted into my face, across the windshield, over his brand new prison-release shirt. He was shocked. Before he could react, I grabbed the knife and stabbed him twenty-seven more times, counting aloud. He didn't struggle, like my mother. He did not possess her character. The same character her daughter possesses.

The media would be surprised to know how passionate I felt as I stabbed him. My feelings, the first after so many years, were surely different from whatever Mifflin must have felt as he murdered my mother, although I'll never be certain. Pressure lifted from my heart when I pierced his. My mind cleared of thoughts as blood and brain tissue gushed from his mutilated left eye. His body cooled and I defrosted. I watched his life dwindle much as I had watched my mother's life fade, and now I feel released. Finally I've reached the end of the corrupted vein and moved beyond that constricting tunnel into a world of complete and utter freedom. I have arrived back where I began, into a state of innocence. Justice has been accomplished. Don't you agree?

Many questions have been asked about me, but I have questions of my own and I hope you'll consider them calmly and rationally now that you've heard how it was. Do I deserve a worse fate than Mr. Mifflin's? Is my crime more heinous than his? I'm charged with murder one. The papers say I'll get life in prison unless I plead insanity, but I can't do that. He killed my mother. I killed him. What act could be more rational? An eye for an eye. Isn't that the purest form of justice? You decide.

The Year of the Dragon
TONY ASPLER

*A founding member of the Crime Writers of Canada and the organization's
first chairman, Tony has two distinct writing careers. He's Canada's most
widely read wine writer. He's also a prominent writer of crime fiction, often combining both areas of expertise. He wrote the excellent novel* Titanic
in 1988. *Unrelated to the recent movie, it's about a wine steward involved
in murder on the doomed liner. He is also the creator of wine writer/
detective Ezra Brand in the recent novels* Blood is Thicker than Beaujolais,
Death on the Douro *and* The Beast of Barbaresco. *There is no wine in this
story from* Cold Blood II, *however. But there is just a vivid evocation of
place and character, and a palpable sense of dread.*

Sailors usually won't admit it, but we get tattooed when we're lonely in a
foreign port.

And a little bit drunk. You have to be a little bit drunk to stand the
pain.

Tattoos are accidents like wounds, something that happens to you
when there are no women around. I know because I have a dragon on my
back. It was done by a man in Toronto's Chinatown after a woman had
walked out on me.

One sticky summer in 1976 our ship was forced to tie up on the
lakeshore because of a stevedores' strike in New York. The owners said we
had to wait it out in Canada instead of returning with an empty hold to our
home port of Amsterdam.

A bunch of us went into town the first night to tour the bars. When I
got talking to a woman they left me behind. I was fascinated by her ears.
Instead of earrings she had tiny blue butterflies tattooed to her lobes. They

looked so real with their iridescent wings you'd think they would fly away if you touched them.

I asked her where she had them done. She told me about a Chinese tattooist who worked above a restaurant on Gerrard Street. She said his name was Mr. Wha and she showed me the back of her left lobe where he had signed his name. A true artist proud of his work.

I bought her a few drinks and then she told me she had to get home to her husband. I had nothing else to do so I went looking for this man who could paint butterflies on a woman's flesh that made you want to reach out and touch them.

I found the restaurant she mentioned in a rash of old brick buildings. There was a sign in the doorway next to it written in Chinese. Underneath it said in English: "Tattoo Upstairs".

The stairwell was dark and smelled of grease and garlic. I hesitated and was about to turn around and walk out into the street when a light came on above me.

"Come up, please," said a voice that sounded like a flute.

I climbed the stairs and saw a man kneeling on a carpet in the centre of a darkened room. He was dressed in a white shirt, baggy trousers and leather sandals. By his side was a block of wood bristling with bamboo canes. Next to it were egg cups set on a plastic tray. Each was filled with a different colour. A bright light hung above his head throwing the rest of the room into deep shadow.

"I am Mr. Wha. You have come to have your body painted."

He made it sound more like a statement than a question. The ageless face, the colour of putty, looked up at me and smiled.

"Please take off your shirt."

He rose to his feet and began examining my skin. He ran his fingers over my shoulders. His touch was as gentle as a woman's but his wrists were thick and muscular like a weightlifter's.

"What does your skin feel it needs?" he asked.

I shrugged, not knowing what design I wanted.

"Haven't you got any pictures I could choose from?"

I felt myself swaying. The effects of the whiskey I had drunk and the overpowering smell of garlic made the room spin.

"You are not ready," he said. "Come back when you feel your body is a canvas."

From the shadows another voice called out something in Chinese, harsh and threatening. I peered into the darkness and dimly made out the figure of another man seated quite still in the corner.

Mr. Wha sighed.

"This is The Year of the Dragon and that is what you will have. The Dragon is the King of the Seas."

The other man said something else in Chinese and Mr. Wha clicked his tongue.

"It will cost $100, please. In advance."

He held out his hand. I reached into my pocket and felt for five $20 bills. I handed them to him but before he could take the money the other man snatched it and moved to another room. In the light I caught sight of his eyes. They were black and menacing, the blackest eyes I had ever seen.

Mr. What motioned me to lie down on the floor. The carpet smelled dusty and I turned my head towards the kneeling artist so that I could watch him work.

He opened a straight razor and began to strop it expertly on a leather. He drew the blade over my back, explaining that he had to remove the hair. Then he reached for a rag, dipped it into a colourless liquid and began to rub it all over my back.

"Alcohol," he said. "Everything will be clean. You will heal quickly."

He selected a bamboo cane and inspected the long needle sticking out of the end. First he dipped it into the alcohol and then into the tiny pool of red paint. With his left thumb and forefinger he spread the skin on my shoulder tight and held the needle poised over it. He shut his eyes and his lips moved without sound. He remained in this position for a full minute before he opened his eyes again and brought the needle down, piercing my skin.

His wrist worked as quickly as a sewing machine, each tiny point of pain becoming a dot of colour which spread into a line.

For two hours I lay there wondering what he was doing and when he rose I asked for a mirror.

"I have not finished," he said. "You must come back every day until it is captured."

"But my ship could sail any day," I protested. "I want it finished now."

Mr. Wha shook his head.

"You cannot rush a dragon. I am coaxing it out of your flesh. Out of your muscles and sinews. It will appear when it is ready. You must let me finish. Come to me tomorrow," he said.

He showed me to the door and bowed.

I returned the next day as soon as I got off duty. Mr. Wha was waiting for me, kneeling on the carpet as I had first seen him. He smiled when I came in.

"It looks great," I said, as I took off my shirt and lay down on the floor.

"You should not look at it until it is finished," he chided me.

For five days I returned to Mr. Wha and each day I learned a little more about him. He was an artist in Hong Kong and had come to Canada with his wife and young son to join his older brother who owned the restaurant downstairs. He helped to support his family by his tattooing. His wife worked in the kitchen. "Long hours," he said, with distaste, and I got the feeling that life in Toronto was hard for him.

Once his son came upstairs to watch his father at work, admiring the way he manipulated the needles. The boy said nothing to me but I saw in his eyes the respect and love he had for his father.

Mr. Wha's brother put his head around the door from time to time, to see how the work was progressing. He ignored me completely as if I were a wall on which his brother was painting a mural.

My shipmates began to wonder where I went each day. They joked that I was with the butterfly woman. I didn't want to show them my dragon until Mr. Wha said he was satisfied. I felt that somehow I would be betraying the artist to take my shirt off in front of my bunk-mates just yet.

I was glad that the stevedore strike allowed me to visit Mr. Wha each day. I would lie on the floor for two hours while he breathed fire into the dragon on my back. He could only work for two hours, he said, because his wrist tired after that.

In spite of the pain of the needles, I felt at peace in his presence. He explained to me how he applied the colours and how he used the contours of my back in his design. Occasionally, he would ask me to flex my muscles.

When he finished he had me stand up with my back to a full-length mirror. He handed me a small looking glass so that I could see the reflection without having to contort my body.

The left side of my back, from the waist up to the shoulder, was filled with a whirling red and yellow five-clawed dragon. Its terrible black eyes were the eyes of Mr. Wha's brother. The dragon breathed with me. When I moved it moved, its scales shimmering in the light. When I flexed my muscles its jaws opened, its belly swelled and it really looked as if it breathed fire.

"Now you are a dragon," he said, "and every dragon has a story."

"It's wonderful, Mr. Wha. It's alive."

Mr. Wha looked frightened and he handed me my shirt.

"You must go now," he said.

There were tears running down his face.

When I returned to the ship I was summoned before the Captain. He had received orders to sail home immediately. All hands had been called back on board and I was not at my post. I explained why I was late and took off my shirt to show him.

The Captain studied my back in amazement. He said he had never seen anything like it in all his years at sea. He was so intrigued he forgot to discipline me.

"The guy even signed it," he said, "like a real artist."

And sure enough, there were Chinese characters under the dragon's tail that coiled around above my kidneys.

Mr. Wha had told me that the colours would remain as bright and vivid as they were now until the next Year of the Dragon came round.

I made a vow that twelve years later I would return to Toronto to show him the dragon he had "coaxed" from my flesh. Perhaps he could do another picture for me on my right side.

*   *   *   *   *

The Gerrard Street restaurant was still there and so was the doorway leading up to the room above. But there was a new sign now. "Tattoo Parlour -- Expert body painting," it read.

I walked up the stairs. Twelve years had not dissipated the smell of grease and garlic which seemed to ooze from the newly painted walls. I knocked on the door. A young Chinese opened it and I recognized the face of Mr. Wha's son, now grown to manhood.

The room was brightly painted and the walls were hung with various designs of fish and birds and serpents. In the centre was a chair that resembled something you'd see in a dentist's office. Next to it was a table with electrical tools and wires running into a switch box.

"I'm looking for Mr. Wha," I said.

The young man's face remained expressionless.

"I am Mr. Wha."

"No, your father."

"My father has been dead for many years," he said.

"I'm sorry to hear that. He made me a beautiful tattoo. I wanted to show him how well it's lasted."

"May I see it?"

I removed my jacket and shirt and hung them on the back of the door. Then I stood with my back to the mirror. As soon as he saw the red and yellow dragon, the young man nodded his head.

"I remember."

He moved closer to me to study the design. I glanced at his face in the mirror and could see his expression soften. It was the same look he wore while he had watched his father creating the design.

He put his fingertips on the head of the dragon and traced its curving line down my back.

Suddenly, he pulled away as if my body had given him an electric shock. He started shaking and hurried into the next room. No sooner had he disappeared than he was back again, dragging a middle-aged woman behind him.

She wiped her hands on her apron, protesting in Chinese as she came.

The young man turned me around and pointed to my back. She leaned in for a closer look. Then she too drew back in horror and fled into the room from which she had just been dragged.

"What the hell's going on?" I demanded.

The young man regained his composure and asked me to lie face down in the chair.

"Why?" I asked.

"The tattoo needs refreshing. It is my father's work but it is very old. I will do it for nothing. In memory of my father."

Puzzled, I sat down and the young man began to apply oil to my back.

"What are you doing?" I asked.

"First," he said, "I must remove my father's name."

"No," I said. "I don't want it taken off."

"But the moment I work on it it is no longer his."

"It's a work of art," I replied. "You don't take Van Gogh's name off a painting just because you're getting it restored."

"But you do not understand. In our culture a man who paints another man's body must not leave his name there."

I rose from the chair and pushed him aside, grabbing my shirt and jacket as I made for the door.

"I'm proud to have your father's name on my back." I shouted. "And if you had any respect for his memory you'd leave it there."

The young man stood in the middle of the room shaking as I slammed the door on my way downstairs.

I walked the Toronto streets thinking about Mr. Wha and his son who had followed in his footsteps but had abandoned the old methods. Why did he want to erase his father's name? And why had the woman, who was obviously Mr. Wha's widow, reacted the way she did?

At times like this, when you're alone in a foreign city, you return to familiar places. I sought out the bar where I had met the woman with butterfly ears twelve years ago. It had changed little but I was not interested in the surroundings. I just sat in a booth, drinking whiskey after whiskey, remembering the feel of the needles in my back and Mr. Wha's soothing, flute-like voice.

It was dark when I called for the check. I reached for the wallet in my inside pocket but it was not there. Surely Mr. Wha's son would not have stolen it. It must have dropped out when I snatched my jacket from the hook.

I explained the situation to the bored waiter who accepted my watch by way of payment. A Rolex I had bought in Singapore. I told him I would redeem it as soon as I picked up my wallet from the tattoo parlour.

I raced back to Gerrard Street to find that the sidewalk outside the restaurant had been cordoned off with fluorescent yellow tape. A policeman stood in the doorway to the upstairs rooms.

"I'm sorry, sir," he said, "No one's allowed up there."

"What happened?" I asked.

"Police business, sir."

"But I was just here, a few hours ago."

The policeman suddenly became interested in me.

"Is that so? If you wouldn't mind coming upstairs with me, sir."

He held my elbow as he ushered me up the stairs.

The room was swarming with men. Some were in uniforms; others in civilian dress, dusting surfaces for fingerprints. The dentist's chair was draped with a sheet. In the adjoining room I could hear the sound of a woman sobbing.

"This gentleman says he was here earlier today, Inspector Chou."

He was addressing a Chinese man in a blue lounge suit. At first I was surprised to see a Chinese detective heading an investigation but it made perfect sense. A crime committed in Chinatown. Who better to understand the workings of a tight-knit community that keeps itself to itself.

"Ah, you must be the owner of this."

He held up a plastic bag which contained my black leather wallet. I put out my hand but he drew it away from me.

"You have saved me a great deal of trouble by returning for it."

He beckoned me closer to the chair and pulled back the sheet. Lying there was Mr. Wha's brother, his staring black eyes as menacing in death as they had been in life.

A bamboo cane protruded from his right ear. A trickle of blood had dried on his neck.

"Do you know this man?"

"I saw him twelve years ago when I had my tattoo done."

The detective frowned.

"I must warn you that anything you say will be taken down and may be used in evidence against you."

For one moment I thought he was joking. How many times had I heard the same words in cheap movie houses?

"But I don't know anything about this," I protested. "I just came back for my wallet."

Inspector Chou continued to watch me. I could feel the dragon on my back. Its scales twitched and shivered; they seemed to slide over each other beneath the sheen of my perspiration. The police thought I had killed him.

"Look, you can check with the bar down the street. I was there all afternoon. I had to leave my watch because I couldn't pay. You have my money in my wallet there."

I could hear the desperation in my voice. Yet I felt compelled to keep talking.

"I didn't kill him, I tell you."

"Who did you see here?"

"I saw Mr. Wha's son and a woman who looked like his mother."

"And why did you come this afternoon?"

"I came to show Mr. Wha the tattoo he did twelve years ago. I had no idea he had died."

"Why did you leave your wallet behind?"

"Because I left in a hurry."

"Why?"

"The man, Mr. Wha's son, wanted to change the tattoo his father had done. I got angry so I left. But I never touched anyone."

The detective replaced the sheet over the corpse's face.

"Before we fingerprint you, may I see the tattoo, please?"

I felt awkward taking off my shirt in front of a room full of policemen.

"Please be so kind as to step to the window," said Inspector Chou.

His voice seemed to purr with suspicion.

The red and yellow dragon reared in the glow of the streetlights outside. I could see the inspector's eyes open in admiration. He called one of his associates over and together they scrutinised my back, talking softly in

Chinese. Then he called to the photographer and directed him to take pictures of my tattoo.

"When did you say you had this done?" asked the Inspector.

"I told you. Twelve years ago," I replied. "Mr. Wha signed it but I don't know if he put the date. I don't read Chinese."

The two men conferred again and the Inspector asked me to accompany him to the police station to make a statement.

In the car, he questioned me about the dead man, Mr. Wha, his wife and his son. I told him the little I remembered of my conversations with the artist.

When we arrived at Police Headquarters he showed me into a room and asked me to wait. Eventually, he returned with another photographer.

"We would like to take some more pictures. If you would kindly remove your shirt again."

"I would like to contact a lawyer," I said, although I knew no one in Toronto, let alone a lawyer.

Inspector Chou rubbed the tips of his fingers together and looked sad.

"All in good time."

"But why am I here? I had nothing to do with this," I protested again.

Inspector Chou whispered something to his associate and then turned back to me.

"I'm prepared to believe that," he said.

"Then you have no right to hold me."

"I'm sorry, sir. We know who killed the man you identified. What we didn't know was why. Until you came. You are -- how shall I put this? You are the link."

"What you are talking about?"

"The artist who drew that remarkable dragon on your back created more than a work of art. He also made a diary. Where each scale connects he drew world pictures."

"What did he say?"

"Turn around and I will read it to you."

"It says: 'My wife works hard. She resists my brother Chi's advances. I know he will kill me tonight. I see it in his eyes."

The words Mr. Wha spoke twelve years ago suddenly came back to me. "Now you are a dragon and every dragon has a story."

AGMV
MARQUIS
Québec, Canada
1998